A Trip
With
Trouble

A Trip With Trouble

Diane Kelly

St. Martin's Paperbacks

First published in the United States by St. Martin's Paperbacks, an imprint of St. Martin's Publishing Group.

A TRIP WITH TROUBLE

Copyright © 2022 by Diane Kelly.

For information, address St. Martin's Publishing Group, 120 Broadway, New York, NY 10271.

www.stmartins.com

ISBN: 978-1-250-81599-6

Our books may be purchased in bulk for promotional, educational, or business use. Please contact your local bookseller or the Macmillan Corporate and Premium Sales Department at 1-800-221-7945, ext. 5442, or by email at MacmillanSpecialMarkets@macmillan.com.

Printed in the United States of America

St. Martin's Paperbacks edition / November 2022

10 9 8 7 6 5 4 3 2 1

To Tracy Xander Hartman, who plays to the beat of her own drum and makes the world all the more interesting because of it.

ACKNOWLEDGMENTS

I am so grateful for the talented team at St. Martin's Press who take my stories from draft to publication. Thanks to my editor, Nettie Finn, whose insights and suggestions are always spot-on. Working with you is easy and enjoyable! Thanks also to Executive Managing Editor John Rounds for all you to do to facilitate the publication process. Oodles of appreciation go out to Sara Beth Haring, Sarah Haeckel, and Allison Ziegler for all your hard work on marketing and publicity. Thanks, too, to Danielle Christopher and Mary Anne Lasher for the perfectly designed cover for this book.

My ongoing gratitude to my agent, Helen Breitwieser, for all you do to keep me under contract and doing what I love.

Props to Colene Drace, who schooled me in all things biker chick. Big thanks also to the Beech Mountain folks who provided tips on riding in the area, including Beverly Brinkman, Bradley Blackwell, Melissa Whipple, and Jeff Melando.

And last but certainly not least, thanks to you readers who chose this book. Enjoy your time in the Blue Ridge Mountains, and hang on for a wild ride!

CHAPTER 1

Misty Murphy

Shadows chased each other across the grounds of the Mountaintop Lodge as dappled sunlight streamed through the beautiful orange, red, and golden leaves. Autumn had arrived in Beech Mountain, North Carolina, spreading its glorious colors across the peaks and valleys. With the season came the so-called leaf peepers, tourists from the low country who ventured to the higher elevations to enjoy the fall foliage where it arrived first. My lodge would be hosting a group of these peepers, who were scheduled to arrive at any moment. The Dangerous Curves, a female motorcycle club from Raleigh, had booked all of the guest rooms with plans to take rides in the area and enjoy the autumn splendor. They'd been smart to plan their arrival on a Monday. The area wasn't as crowded midweek, and they'd have less traffic to contend with.

My assistant, Brynn O'Reilly, and I wrangled with a couple of scarecrows in front of the lodge. I'd bought the traditional log-cabin inn only a few weeks earlier, on the same day I'd turned fifty, signed divorce papers, and sent my youngest son off to college. I suppose that makes me a multitasker. It might also make me as nutty as the acorns scattered about. But living in the mountains had been my dream as long as I could remember. Hitting the half-century mark had made me realize that the time to live my dreams was dwindling. I didn't want to look back at the end of my life and have regrets. It was now or never. I chose now.

Fortunately, my split from my husband Jack had been amicable, our relationship having long since settled into more of a routine than a romance. My ex and I remained friendly, and still considered ourselves and our sons to be a family. In fact, the three of them would be coming up to the lodge next month so we could spend Thanksgiving together. I could hardly wait to catch up with my boys. Like most college kids, they communicated via terse texts. Each of my inquiries—*How's dorm life? How's the cafeteria food? How are your classes?*—earned the same single word response—*Fine*. Though I'd love to know more, I took their short replies as a sign they were busy studying and having fun. I'd press them for details when I saw them in person. And as much curiosity as I had about their lives, I was quite busy with my own—especially since the scarecrow I was currently wrestling refused to sit up straight.

I looked up from my labors to see Patty Williamson, owner of the Greasy Griddle Diner across the parking lot, walking toward us. Patty was a pretty black woman with lively curls held back from her face by a pumpkin-print headband. She wore a ruffled apron over her clothing and held a steaming mug in each hand. With it being a Monday afternoon, her diner wasn't busy. Our little tourist town came to life on weekends, when vacationers ascended the two-lane road up the mountain, driving bumper to bumper, seeking a temporary escape in our wonderful corner of the world.

As Patty stopped before us, she offered a smile as warm as the sweet drink in the mugs she held out. "I bought an apple press and drove down to the Orchard at Altapass to get three bushels of apples yesterday. I'm trying out cider recipes. Thought y'all might enjoy a hot cup."

"You thought right. Thanks." Poppy's Coffee Shop had the town's coffee market covered, but cider would make a unique addition to the diner's drink menu. I took a mug and returned Patty's smile.

As Brynn echoed my sentiment, the late-afternoon sun reflected off her long, wavy hair. Her tresses bore an autumn-like auburn hue much like the golden orange of the steaming apple cider. Brynn was willowy, with a penchant for colorful bohemian dresses, giving her the look of an Irish fairy. My hair, on the other hand, was more similar to the ground coffee I poured into the urn each morning. I wore what had essentially become my lodgekeeper uniform—a pair of jeans, a red and black buffalo plaid shirt, and hiking boots. Being up here in the mountains, I could get away with the casual, outdoorsy look.

Though we three women each had our own personal style, we also had a lot in common. We were all hardworking, savvy businesswomen. Patty had run her diner successfully for years, not an easy feat in a town where weather could be fickle and significantly impact tourist traffic. I, of course, owned the lodge, which had been in the red when I'd bought it. It was yet to be seen whether I could turn things around, but business had been going well and I remained optimistic. Until recently, Brynn had operated her own residential cleaning business, preparing rental properties for vacationers. Desiring less paperwork and more stability, she'd applied for the job as my assistant manager at the lodge. I felt fortunate to have her. She'd proven to be a reliable, if somewhat eccentric, employee.

Brynn took a sip of the drink and moaned in bliss. "Delicious."

Patty continued to talk cider. "The press I bought is an old-fashioned manual model." She flexed her bicep. "My arms have gotten quite a workout. They haven't looked this good since my thirties."

Though there were many great things about being this age, the loss of muscle mass was not one of them. I poked her arm. Her flesh was nice and firm. "Wow. Maybe I should help you out, spend some time cranking the press."

Brynn took things a step further. "You two could arm wrestle at the diner. I'll take bets."

"Great idea!" Patty said, playing along. "You in, Misty?"

"Absolutely not. Last time I arm wrestled was with my youngest son and I ended up with bruised knuckles." *You'd think a kid would go easy on their mother.* After downing a generous chug of the warm drink, I set my mug down on the rolling cart that held a push broom, rake, and long-handled tree pruners. Turning back to the task at hand, I tried to seat the smiling scarecrow on the hay bale. Despite my best efforts, he flopped forward like an inflatable air dancer.

Brynn snorted. "That scarecrow could use some Viagra."

Patty had a more realistic solution. "A wooden stake ought to keep him upright."

"I'll see what we've got in the shed." Pulling my key ring from my pocket, I strode across the grounds to the storage shed and unlocked it. My fluffy white cat watched me from the window of our room where she lay on the sill, absorbing the sunshine. I'd named the cat Baroness Blizzard, but my sons had dubbed her Yeti and the nickname stuck. Apparently, she found my activities boring. Her mouth opened in a wide yawn, revealing her sharp fangs and pink tongue. She settled her head on her paws and closed her eyes.

As the shed door swung open, a musty, earthy scent emanated, the smell of seasons past. The shed housed a variety of implements ranging from a leaf blower to a wheelbarrow, as well as snow shovels, hand tools, and assorted pieces of lumber and trim. I gathered two wooden stakes, a spool of twine, and a mallet, and carried the items back to the hay bale. After hammering the stakes into the back of the bale, Brynn and I affixed the scarecrows to them with the twine and stepped back to assess our handiwork. The scarecrows sat firmly upright now. Patty declared the decorations "festive."

Brynn and I finished our cider. Rather than taking the mugs back to her diner, Patty rinsed them at the outdoor faucet and positioned the mugs in the scarecrows' hands so that it appeared they were enjoying drinks from the Greasy Griddle. *Cute.* Turning to me, she cocked her head. "Got a head count for the morning?"

When I'd bought the lodge, Patty had graciously agreed to cater a daily breakfast on site. It was a convenient perk for my guests, and it kept the diner's tables open for other hungry patrons, allowing her staff to serve everyone more expeditiously. She charged me a reasonable price, too, allowing me to offer the amenity without busting my budget. "We'll have twenty-two guests tonight," I said, "plus Rocky and me."

Brynn lifted her chin to indicate the parking lot. "Speak of the devil."

A blue king-cab pickup eased from the asphalt onto the lawn. A shiny metal toolbox was mounted in the truck's bed behind the rear window. A stack of firewood secured with netting filled the remainder of the bed. The flatbed trailer was piled high with firewood, too. The driver's door sported a sign that read High Country Handyman Service. Behind the wheel sat the devil to which Brynn had referred, and what a handsome devil he was. Rocky's sandy brown hair bore hints of gray, like a cougar's, and his closely trimmed beard accentuated the chiseled angles of his jawline. He sported a cotton shirt that stretched across his broad shoulders. The charming and capable Mister Fixit had come to my rescue when the back of the lodge had collapsed due to soil erosion. The two of us shared a simmering attraction, but with my divorce being so recent I was in no hurry to rush into another relationship. Besides, Rocky and I were both mature adults with grown children. There was no ticktock of a biological clock spurring us to action. We could take our time.

Standing in the back seat and hanging his head out of the open window was Molasses, Rocky's enormous Bernese mountain dog. The sweet beast weighed in at over a hundred pounds and bore a coat of beautiful black fur with the breed's distinctive white stripe down the nose, the light swath trimmed in rusty brown. Rocky acknowledged us ladies with a lift of his chin and an "afternoon" before sliding out of his truck and letting Molasses out of the back seat. While I retrieved the wheelbarrow from the shed for Rocky, Molasses moseyed over to Brynn and Patty, flopped onto his back, and received the belly rubs he'd come for.

Rocky donned a pair of worn canvas work gloves, loosened the netting from the firewood, and began to move the split logs from the bed of his truck into the wheelbarrow. I snagged a spare pair of gloves from the shed to help him. As we worked, the crisp, clean scent of aromatic pine awakened my senses. "Some of this wood is balsam, isn't it?" I knew the smell well, having hiked the Balsam Trail at the summit of Mount Mitchell many times. The mountain was the highest in the Appalachian Range and sat less than two hours' drive to the southwest, one of the primary points of interest along the Blue Ridge Parkway.

"Balsam," Rocky confirmed with an affirmative dip of his head. "Some spruce pine, too. Makes a great-smelling fire."

When I'd bought the lodge, he'd built a beautiful deck behind it. The guests enjoyed the lodge's outdoor space, so he'd later expanded it, adding steps that led down from the deck to a stone terrace surrounding a fire pit. The stone was a beautiful addition, held the soil underneath in place, and blended well with the natural scenery. What's more, stone was easy to sweep and wouldn't catch fire if a stray ember landed on it. No doubt the lady bikers would enjoy sitting outside around a fire during their evenings here, after their invigorating daily rides.

Patty gave Molasses a final scratch, stood, and was about to return to the diner when a low rumble met our ears, echoing off the nearby peaks as if the mountains themselves were growling. The ground beneath our feet vibrated, too. It felt like the earth was coming alive. Patty's brown eyes went wide. "Is this another earthquake?"

In August of 2020, a 5.1 magnitude quake had hit the area, centered in the town of Sparta seventy miles to the northeast. The quake was the largest to hit the state in over a century and had damaged hundreds of buildings near the epicenter, rattling windows and nerves as far away as Charlotte. Since the quake, there'd been hundreds of minor aftershocks. Still, I knew the noise and vibration didn't come from Mother Earth. It came from my arriving guests.

CHAPTER 2

Yeti

Instinct pricked Yeti's ears, yanking her out of her lovely stupor. Blinking, she lifted her head from her paws. A rumbling noise came from outside and the windowsill began to vibrate under her, as if the earth was purring.

She cocked her head to listen more intently. The sound escalated into a full-out roar, and her heart raced in response. She had no idea what was making the racket, but whatever it was seemed to be heading right for the lodge. *I've got to hide!*

Yeti leaped from the sill, scrambling to gain purchase on the wood floor of the hotel room she shared with Misty. After a few seconds of slipping and sliding, she managed to skitter under the bed. She cowered in the darkest reaches as the roar overtook the lodge, shaking the windowpanes. Yeti's body shook, too. *What's out there?!*

CHAPTER 3

Misty

Rocky, Patty, Brynn and I turned in unison to look at the two-lane road that brought people up the mountain. We could see nothing yet but a trio of terrified deer dashing across the pavement and disappearing into the woods. The roar intensified, echoing off the nearby ridges before reaching a teeth-rattling crescendo. On hearing the noise, Patty's patrons in the Greasy Griddle turned their heads and craned their necks to look out through the front glass.

Around the bend came the first of the motorcycles, leading the train like a mighty steam engine. The rider slowed to turn into the parking lot of the lodge. The four of us on the lawn raised our hands in greeting, and the lead biker returned the gesture. The red Honda sported a low seat, perfect for the petite female rider. The word "Shadow" stretched down the side of its gas tank, along with simulated flames. The rider's red helmet matched the bike, the tinted faceplate obscuring her features. Affixed to the top of her helmet was a small gold crown. She wore black studded boots with jeans, a fringed black leather jacket, and fingerless black gloves—classic biker chick gear. I wondered what I'd look like dressed in her outfit. Ridiculous, probably. I didn't have the props to pull it off. *But it could be fun to pretend . . .*

As she pulled her motorcycle into a spot in front of the lodge, the parade of bikes and bikers continued. A golden yellow bike emblazoned with Ducati Monster. A lime green Ninja, its tall, long-legged rider sporting a green and white jumpsuit along with a lime green helmet. What appeared to be a racing bike ridden by a woman in black gear with a pink stripe down the side. A blue motorcycle with a windshield, saddlebags, and a pillion seat ridden by two curvy strawberry blondes. A stocky woman in a classic helmet and goggles pulled up in what appeared to be an old-school black motorcycle with a sidecar. The black and gray terrier mix riding in the sidecar sported a black helmet and goggles, too, his coarse beard blowing back in the breeze.

Patty's brows rose. "A dog in a sidecar? Now I've seen everything."

Though I loved my cat, I had to admit that having a pet who could go along on adventures held a definite appeal.

Rocky ran his gaze over the leather-clad women rolling past us. "These ladies are wearing more cowhide than a herd of Holsteins."

Though the riders had approached in single file, leaving some space between their bikes, a silver Suzuki eased out of its place in line as it neared the lodge. The rider revved the engine, sped past several other cyclists, and careened into the parking lot, leaning precariously to the side as she banked. She righted her bike and revved the engine again— *VROOM!*—popping a wheelie. She rode on the back tire to the end of the lot, nearly running over a dawdling ground-hog, before lowering the front tire back to the asphalt. She whipped her bike around and, with another loud rev of the engine, sped back toward the incoming line of motorcy-cles. She turned sharply in front of the Ninja, cutting off the procession and forcing the Ninja's rider to brake hard to avoid colliding with the reckless rider. The others behind the Ninja veered to the right or left, the orderly line of rid-ers now randomly kinked. Fortunately, none of the motor-cycles crashed into each other, a minor miracle.

Taking up the rear was a white GMC Yukon. The enor-mous SUV pulled a black trailer emblazoned with the Harley-Davidson logo. The SUV pulled into the lot, circled past the diner, and pulled sideways across the parking spots in front of the lodge's east wing, stopping a few feet short of Brynn's old Prius. The door opened and a lithe, long-limbed older woman slid down from the driver's seat, ap-pearing elegant in her knee-high black lace-up boots, black jeans, and fitted light gray sweater. Her shoulder-length sil-ver hair shimmered in the sunlight, as sleek and shiny as the chrome on the motorcycles. But while the glint off the chrome was bright, the glint in her eyes was furious. "Er-ika!" she snapped, storming toward the young woman on the silver Suzuki. "Don't you ever pull a stupid stunt like that again! You could've hurt somebody!"

Erika removed her helmet, shook out her bushy purple-hued hair, and rolled her eyes. "Chill, Gerri. Everyone's fine. No need to get your granny panties in a bunch."

The short-haired Latina who'd ridden the lead bike hustled over. Though not as old as the woman from the SUV, she was at least my age, in her fifties or maybe early sixties. She pointed a finger in Erika's face. "Nobody talks to Gerri like that!"

Rocky, Brynn, Patty, and I exchanged looks. We'd expected a group of female bikers to be a spirited bunch, but we hadn't expected them to bring strife along with them.

By this time, Gerri had reached Erika. She took the younger woman by the shoulders. Though her grasp was gentle, her voice was firm. "C'mon, Erika. We've talked about this. We've got to stay single file for safety."

Though I knew little about motorcycles, riding single file made sense. In my driver's education class decades ago, the instructor had told us to leave open space around our cars so that we'd have a way out in case we needed to swerve. If two motorcycles rode side by side, they'd have fewer options should they need to evade an obstacle or oncoming vehicle.

Erika's shoulders remained rigid and she turned her head away. The older woman released Erika's shoulders and sighed. "I have half a mind to make you sit out tomorrow's ride."

Erika's fists clenched and her head spun as she wheeled on Gerri. My heart skipped a beat in fear she'd strike the group's matriarch. "I'd like to see you try, boomer!" she bellowed. "I came up here to have fun. You can't keep me off a public road, Gerri-*atric*."

Reyna raised her finger again. "Apologize! Now!"

Murmuring in agreement, several of the other bikers closed in, their expressions tight as they stared their reckless member down. Patty quirked her lip as she cut me a look that said *She's too old to be acting like a spoiled brat.* I gave my friend a discreet nod in agreement.

Erika glanced around, realizing she was surrounded and outnumbered. "Jeez! All right! I'm sorry. Are all of you happy now?" Her sarcasm nullified her apology but the group backed off anyway, as if realizing this was as good as it would get.

Gerri's chest rose as she heaved a heavy sigh. "That was your last warning, Erika," she said with resignation. "And just so you know, calling me old isn't the insult you think it is. You'll end up with a few wrinkles, too, one day—if you don't get yourself killed first." Gerri turned to Patty, my staff, and me and offered a contrite cringe. "Sorry about this first impression, folks. I promise we'll all be on our best behavior while we're at the lodge."

"Darn," Brynn said. "Misty and I were hoping you biker chicks would liven things up."

The ladies laughed—all but Erika, anyway—and I gave Brynn a grateful smile for breaking the tension.

Rocky gestured to the bike with the sidecar. "What kind of bike you got here?"

The dog-toting black woman who'd been riding in it pulled off her helmet, tucked it under her arm, and slid her goggles up over her lively curls. "It's a Ural Gear Up," she said. "They're Russian built." She went on to tell us that the bikes were originally built for use on the battlefield in World War II. "They're one of the best bikes for off-roading." She reached down and unclipped the harness holding her dog safely in place. The terrier turned his head up, and the woman took off the dog's helmet and goggles before motioning for him to get out of the sidecar. The cute little beast put his paws over the edge and slid down to the sidewalk.

I bent down and looked the dog in the face while rubbing his ears. "Did you have a nice ride?" His wagging tail told me he'd enjoyed feeling the rush of air in his face, while the tag hanging from his collar identified his owner as Bessie. Before I could read his name he wiggled, and the tag disappeared under a tuft of gray fur. I looked up at Bessie. "What's his name?"

"Shotgun." She pointed to her sidecar. "Because he rides shotgun."

It was a perfect name for him, not only because he rode next to her but because, with his shaggy hair and scraggly gray beard, he resembled a grizzled cowboy from the Old West.

Reyna put two fingers in her mouth and issued a shrill whistle. When the ladies turned to her, she waved them over. "Let's get a group photo for our Facebook page." She pointed to the sign on the lawn that read Mountaintop Lodge. "There's a good spot."

The women formed a semicircle around the sign. The group included riders of all shapes, sizes, and races, bonded by their shared love of the open road. Reyna stood in front of the sign and called out instructions, making sure everyone could be seen. The tall young woman who'd been riding the green Ninja held back, standing a few feet away from the others.

Reyna motioned again with her hand. "Get in there with the others, Katie."

Katie frowned and took a step backward. "I don't like getting my picture taken. I'm not photogenic and I'll tower over everyone like an awkward giraffe."

The young woman was selling herself short, figuratively that is. She stood nearly six feet tall, and while she didn't quite have the ultrathin physique of a supermodel, nonetheless appeared quite fit. She was attractive, too, with large blue eyes trimmed in thick, dark lashes and lush black hair that hung down to her ribcage.

Reyna issued a *pshaw*. "If you're so awkward, why'd you get hit on by every man in that biker bar on Fontana Lake? Get over here. Everyone should be in the picture."

Katie didn't move. "It won't be everyone. Lexi hasn't arrived yet."

Undeterred, Reyna said, "We'll get one with her later. I'm not taking 'no' for an answer."

Erika made a show of cracking her knuckles. "You heard our queen! Get your butt behind this sign right now or I'll drag you over here!"

Katie exhaled sharply, but headed toward the group. Reyna held out her phone and called to me. "Would you mind taking the picture?"

"Not at all." I stepped over and took the phone from Reyna. Katie circled around the back of the women and hunkered down between two of them until only her face and a sliver of her green collar showed. Crouching like that, she appeared to be only average sized. Reyna stood at one end of the group, while Gerri stood at the other, the two of them forming bookends of sorts. I carefully centered the image, making sure to get the lodge and the distant ridge in the background. I counted down so they could put on their best smiles. "Three, two, one." As I tapped the button to snap the photo, Katie turned her head slightly, looking off into the distance to my left. "Let's try one more." I counted down again, and again Katie turned her head. *Wow. She really is camera shy.*

As the group disbanded, Reyna collected her phone from me. The women strode over to their bikes and secured them in various ways. Some used a chain and padlock. Others attached some type of metal device to the wheel. Curious, I gestured to one of the devices. "What is that?"

"Wheel lock," said Bessie. "It prevents the tire from spinning so the bike can't be rolled away. Motorcycle theft is pretty common. Bikes are easier to steal than cars. Two people can lift one up and carry it off. Some thieves just roll them away."

A white woman with copper-colored curls scowled. "My bike was boosted six weeks ago. I got my insurance check, but it wasn't much. I replaced it with a new model, but now I've got a monthly payment I didn't plan for." She patted the seat of her new Triumph Tiger. "I've put every security device there is on this baby. Wheel lock. Alarm. Tracker. Chains. I always make sure the steering is locked now too."

A black woman with a bandana over her hair said, "I took my husband's BMW out on one of our rides two weekends back. The next day it was gone. It was probably just coincidence, but my husband thinks someone might have followed me home. They took it right from our driveway." She shook her head. "The nerve!"

While the other women left their bikes uncovered for now, Katie covered her lime green Kawasaki Ninja with a black cover. If I hadn't seen her ride in on the neon green bike, I'd have no idea what type of motorcycle stood under the cover. As she stepped away, I noticed that the cover bore the Indian Motorcycle logo, complete with the image of a Native American man wearing a headdress. She might have borrowed the cover, or maybe it went with another motorcycle she'd owned. Maybe she got it secondhand. At any rate, it didn't match the brand of the bike that sat underneath but it served its purpose.

Rocky pointed to the SUV and addressed Gerri. "Looks like you've got a full cargo bay. I'll round up a cart and load your luggage."

"Thanks." Gerri tossed him her keys.

While Rocky went to collect the ladies' baggage, I bade goodbye to Patty and motioned for the bikers to follow me and Brynn inside. "Let's get you all checked in."

With Gerri and Reyna appearing to be the leaders of the group, I figured they deserved the two rooms at the far end of either hall. In addition to a window looking out to the front or back of the lodge, the end rooms featured an additional window with a view to the side, offering the occupant a chance to privately take in a beautiful Blue Ridge sunrise or sunset. Of course, all guests could enjoy a great view of the mountain sky from the back deck and grounds. Put off by what I'd witnessed on their arrival, I gave Erika Hursey our least desirable guestroom, the one next to the guest laundry room, which also housed the noisy vending and ice machines. She'd serve an unwitting penance. Brynn slid me a knowing glance when I handed Erika her key.

Rocky rolled the fully loaded luggage cart into the lobby. Most of the women had packed light in small, soft-sided bags and backpacks made for carrying on motorcycles, but a large designer suitcase sat on the cart, too. Those who'd already checked in walked over to retrieve their bags from the stack. As Gerri waited for them to round up their things, Rocky said, "Your Yukon looks big enough to live in."

She chuckled. "The cargo space is a bonus. We bought it to pull our camper. It's a thirty-eight-footer."

"Wow," Rocky said. "That's a big sucker."

"Largest model we offered," Gerri said. "My husband ran an RV dealership in Raleigh."

"Aha!" I raised a finger and spoke to her over the counter, where I was checking in another rider. "That's why your last name sounded familiar." The last name on her reservation was Burnham. "I drove by Burnham Camper Country hundreds of times when I lived in Raleigh." The place sold RVs, campers, and pop-up trailers, as well as four-wheel all-terrain vehicles. With its sky-sweeping spotlights and enormous inflatable sasquatch, you couldn't miss the place. I noticed she'd used the past tense when she spoke of her husband's involvement with the business, saying he "ran" it rather than "runs" it. "Has your husband retired?"

The woman's wince made me instantly wish I could take my question back. "No," she said. "We were both intending to retire at the end of the year, but God had other plans for Norman. He was diagnosed with cancer a year ago. He didn't suffer long, luckily. He passed in late April."

I bit my lip. "I'm so sorry, Gerri."

"It's been hard," she said, exhaling in resignation. "But Norman made it to seventy. A lot of people don't live that long, and we had ten good years together before he passed."

Only ten years? The birth date on Gerri's license was 1950. I'd been curious and had looked when checking her in, inspired to see a woman her age still taking motorcycle trips. In light of her age, I would've expected her and her husband to have been close to their golden anniversary. If they'd only had ten years together, they must have married much later in life.

She straightened, as if to force the weight of grief off her shoulders, and her face brightened. "The girls and I have been looking forward to this week. We come up to the mountains every fall to enjoy the leaves."

"We're happy to have you," I said. "If you need anything, don't hesitate to call the desk."

"Will do." As Gerri stepped away from the counter, a ringtone sounded from inside her purse. She reached inside and retrieved her phone, frowning when she read the screen. Nonetheless, she tapped it to accept the call, put the phone to one ear and her index finger to the other to muffle the ambient noise. I didn't intend to eavesdrop, but with her standing only a few feet away it wasn't hard to overhear her conversation—her end of it, anyway.

"I'm on a ride in the mountains," she said matter-of-factly. "I'll address your request when I return home next week." She tapped the screen again, ending the call without saying goodbye. She slid the phone back into her purse and closed her eyes for a moment, pinching the bridge of her nose. Although she'd maintained an even tone on the call, she was clearly annoyed. I hoped her time in the mountains would allow her to set her cares aside for a while and relax.

Gerri opened her eyes and glanced at the cart. Now that most of the other bags had been removed, she was able to get to her large suitcase. Though Rocky offered to take Gerri's bag to her room, she declined his assistance, seeming to be the type of woman who prided herself on her independence. She extended the handle on her suitcase and rolled off down the east wing to her room, directly across from mine.

The next to step up to the counter were the strawberry blondes who'd rode up on the motorcycle together. The two turned out to be sisters, Dahlia and Daisy Blume, born just over eleven months apart according to the birth dates on their licenses. A pair of eyeglasses with thick lenses perched on Dahlia's nose, and a hearing aid curved over the top of her ear. "How's your Wi-Fi?" she asked.

"Fast and reliable." I'd contacted the provider and upgraded the inn's service shortly after buying the place. No sense leaving guests frustrated by slow internet speeds when the rate increase was reasonable.

"Good," she said. "I've got papers to grade and scores to enter."

"Ah. You're a teacher, then?"

"American literature," she said. "I teach at Wake Tech."

I was familiar with the school. Wake Technical Community College had several branches spread throughout the city of Raleigh and surrounding suburbs. A friend and I had taken a non-credit cake decorating class at the Beltline branch years ago, when I'd still been married and living in Raleigh. The class had been fun, though I'd gained three pounds eating my homework.

Daisy gave her sister a sour look before turning to me. "I took Dahlia's class when I decided to go back to school last year. She only gave me a C plus."

"Nuh-uh-uh." Dahlia wagged her index finger. "*You* only

earned a C plus. If you wanted an A, you should've done more than just regurgitate the Cliff notes on *The Great Gatsby.*"

Daisy groaned. "Maybe sharing a room was a bad idea." The grin that tugged at her lips said she was only teasing her sister. Dahlia's head toss said she knew it.

I noticed Dahlia held a short metal cane angled in front of her. It had a strap at the top so it could be hung from a wrist or hook. The cane was white with a red tip, similar to the canes that blind people used to maneuver about. But this device was much too short to be used for navigation. Both of my boys had been in the high school marching band, and the length reminded me of the batons that the drum majors used to lead them. I'd been in charge of fundraising for the band boosters, a thankless but nevertheless rewarding task.

Daisy saw me eyeing the cane and nudged her sister. "Tell her about your cane, Dahl."

Dahlia raised it up a few inches to give me a better look. "This is what's known as an 'ID cane.' It's not so much for me as for everyone else. It lets people know I'm visually impaired. This model is made of graphite. It's lighter and stronger than the aluminum models." She tapped it gently against the edge of the counter as if to demonstrate.

Daisy grinned. "The cane comes in handy for keeping her students in line."

Dahlia snorted a laugh. "I haven't hit one yet. Been tempted many times, though." She showed me how the cane came apart in three pieces held together by an elastic cord inside the hollow sections of metal tubing that formed it. Now that she'd pulled it apart, I could see that each section had silver connectors at the ends. "The cane fits in my handy hip holster." She slid the disassembled cane into a small black sleeve clipped to her belt and raised her palms. "Voilà."

"I just learned something new," I said. "Thanks."

As the sisters headed off to their room, the dark-haired woman in the black and pink leathers stepped up to the counter. When I greeted her by the full name on her license, she said, "Call me Kris."

I completed her registration and handed her keys over the counter. "Just let us know if you need anything. Enjoy your stay, Kris."

Katie was the next rider up to the counter. "Hi," she said. "My reservation is under the name Katie Martin."

I got a better look at her up close now. While she was the tallest of the bunch, she also appeared to be the youngest, in her early twenties, not much older than my sons. I could only guess at her exact age, because when I asked for a driver's license and credit card, she grimaced.

"My wallet was stolen," she said, "so I don't have my license or a credit card. But you take cash, right? I can pay in full up front."

Though it was standard procedure to require identification, there was actually no legal requirement that I verify someone's identity before providing them with lodging. ID was merely an internal security protocol. But with the motorcycle club occupying every room and the group implicitly vouching for this young woman, there seemed to be no risk in allowing her to stay. I'd put her in Room Three, the one next to mine.

"No worries," I told her. "Cash is fine." I told her the total for the week and she unzipped her fanny pack. She pulled out her keys and lay them on the counter before counting out bills from a white envelope that seemed to be serving as her temporary wallet. I noticed her keychain featured a bulldog. I pointed to it. "Is that Uga?"

Katie's face clouded in confusion. "Uga?"

"The University of Georgia mascot." A friend back in Raleigh had attended the school. She told me every bulldog mascot since 1956 had been named Uga, an acronym for the school.

"No," Katie said, a bit shortly. "The keychain has nothing to do with a school. I just like bulldogs. My family had one when I was a kid."

She slid her keychain and change into her fanny pack, and proceeded to fill out the lodging contract, including the part that asked for her vehicle's license plate number. Hikers occasionally parked in the lodge's lot to access the trailhead, but my lot was big enough that an extra car or two wasn't a problem. But even though I had yet to encounter problems with unauthorized vehicles clogging my lot, it was best to know whose vehicles were on site.

Katie bent over to pick up her backpack, revealing a thin strip of golden-blonde roots at her part. I was a little surprised. Seemed lots of women lightened their hair, going from brown to blonde, but few went in the other direction and dyed their hair darker. Still, hair color was fun to play around with, and rich colors could add warmth to a woman's look. I'd varied my own hair color over the years, adding highlights and lowlights and hiding my graying roots so that I didn't look like the Bride of Frankenstein. Of course, many women changed their hair color and style after a bad breakup, as if by changing their look they'd no longer be the woman who'd been dumped, cheated on, or mistreated. If nothing else, a new look provided an emotional reboot, a fresh start. I handed her the key to Room Six, which faced the front of the lodge. "Enjoy your stay, Katie."

CHAPTER 4

Misty

A half hour later, the ladies had finished unpacking and freshening up, and reconvened in the lobby to make dinner plans. Brynn and I suggested several local restaurants, and the women divided into smaller groups depending on their palates. They were smart to head out early. With it being October, sunset would come soon. The curvy mountain roads could be dangerous in the dark, especially this time of year when both bear and deer were more active than usual. The bears were busy eating and drinking to fatten themselves up for winter. Bucks, meanwhile, were looking for mates. Time for every Bambi to search for his Faline.

Not one to waste time when there was work to do, Brynn stood from the desk. "I'll round up the clean towels and fold them before I go." With that, she headed off to the laundry room.

Molasses lay splayed in front of the fireplace, his chin to the floor, looking like a bearskin rug with his black fur.

Meanwhile, Rocky was out back, stacking the firewood in a neat pile at the edge of the woods, far enough away that it shouldn't draw termites to the lodge. I stepped to the plate glass windows at the back of the great room and surreptitiously watched him work. The man might be pushing fifty, but he was still strong and in darn good shape. He knew how to handle all sorts of tools, and could fix virtually any type of appliance and repair any sort of structural damage. He could build things from scratch, too. His skills appealed to something fundamental and primitive inside me, the part that said this man could keep me safe and sheltered. My ex-husband had been a good provider, but he was useless with hand tools. He'd hired skilled contractors to handle even the most basic of tasks at our home.

Rocky turned around, caught me watching him, and sent a wink my way. I held one hand out beside me and put the back of the other to my forehead, miming a swoon. Though we'd yet to act on our mutual attraction, we'd openly acknowledged it. I hadn't felt ready to jump into a new relationship, but I was starting to wonder what I was waiting for. Some romance could be fun. Still, what if things didn't work out? It would be awkward and I might lose my handyman.

Before I could give the idea of dating Rocky much more thought, the desk phone rang. I could tell from the phone's display that the call had come from an outside line. I picked up the receiver. "It's a beautiful Blue Ridge evening at the Mountaintop Lodge. How may I help you?"

A male voice came over the line. "Is Sadie Hardin staying there?"

Sadie Hardin? My mind did a double take. He had said *Sadie Hardin*, right? Not *Katie Martin*? The names rhymed. I enunciated distinctly as I spoke. "Did you say 'Sadie Hardin'?"

"Yeah."

"No," I said. "There's no guest here by that name."

The man paused for a moment. I heard a rustling noise as he put his hand over the receiver, and the murmur of a whispered conversation. He returned to the line. "Are you sure?"

"I'm certain," I said. "I verify my guest's ID when they check in." Well, I hadn't verified Katie's ID since her wallet had been stolen, but she was part of a group. That had been good enough for me to trust that she was who she said she was.

The guy hung up without saying goodbye. I hung up, too, and mulled things over. In these days of cell phones, it was rare for a guest to get a call on the lodge's landline. Add in the fact that the caller had asked for a person whose name— first *and* last—rhymed with a current guest's, and things got even more strange. Maybe my earlier thought about old boyfriends and new hairstyles had been on the nose. Maybe Katie had recently come out of a bad relationship and was reinventing herself. If so, I hoped she'd find her time in the mountains to be therapeutic. Nothing like being immersed in nature to restore one's soul.

The roar of a motorcycle engine put an end to my mulling and drew my eyes to the front windows. A rider rolled up on a pearly white and turquoise Kawasaki. She climbed off her bike, removed her helmet, and came inside. She was Asian American, with a heart-shaped face and dark hair styled in a carefree, helmet-friendly pixie cut. She carried only a large backpack, clearly a light packer, too.

I welcomed her with a smile. "You must be Lexi."

"That's me." She swung her backpack up onto the counter. "Better late than never, huh?" As she retrieved her wallet from her pack and handed me her license and credit card, Brynn returned with a heaping basket of clean towels, filling the air with the scent of fresh linens.

I swiped Lexi's card and waited for the machine to respond. "Your friends will be glad you've arrived. They took a group photo earlier and mentioned it was incomplete without you."

"Aw, that's sweet." She smiled for an instant before her mouth turned down in a frown. "I wish I could have ridden up from Raleigh with them, but I had to be in court this afternoon."

Court? Uh-oh. Had this woman gotten herself in trouble? I'd heard of outlaw biker gangs, but the ladies who'd arrived earlier hadn't seemed like the criminal type—other than the rebellious Erika, perhaps.

My concern must have been written on my face, because Lexi raised a palm. "It's not what it sounds like. I was in family court. Finally got my divorce." She threw her hands up in the air and waved them in jubilation. "Hallelujah! I'm free!"

"Congratulations." I handed Lexi's license and credit card back over the counter.

Brynn angled her head to indicate me. "Misty recently got divorced, too."

"Oh, yeah?" Lexi looked from Brynn to me. "Was your husband worthless like mine?"

Looks like Katie isn't the only one with a bad ex. "Actually," I said, "my ex-husband was a nice guy. Responsible and hardworking."

"I've got two questions, then. One, why'd you leave him? And two, what's his phone number?"

The three of us shared a chuckle before I said, "My ex and I wanted different things out of life, and we realized we couldn't have them if we stayed together." It really was as simple as that. I'd always yearned to live in the mountains, but Jack had no interest in relocating to a higher elevation. If I'd forced him to move here with me, I'd have felt guilty and he'd have felt resentful. If I'd remained in Raleigh with him, the feelings would have been reversed.

Lexi's lips pursed. "My husband got a case of the seven-year itch."

Brynn stopped in the middle of folding a washcloth. "Crabs, you mean?"

"Brynn!" I cried, hoping our guest wasn't insulted.

I needn't have worried. Lexi snorted, but in humor. "Would've served him right if he'd been infested. When I discovered he had a side piece, I moved out. I didn't leave a note or tell him where I was going, either. Just grabbed my things, tossed them in a friend's car, and left. Haven't been back to our place or seen the loser since. He didn't bother showing up to court."

"He's still in your old place?" Brynn finished folding the washcloth and plucked another from the laundry basket. "So, he got to keep all the furniture? The TV? The dishes?"

"Eh." Lexi lifted a shoulder in a half shrug. "None of it was worth much. Besides, I wanted a clean break and didn't want to keep anything from my former life—other than my

Vulcan, that is." She hiked a thumb over her shoulder to indicate her motorcycle outside. "Todd gave it to me for my thirtieth birthday two years ago. Of course, he bought himself a bike a few weeks later. A more expensive model, too. Wasn't even his birthday, either."

"He sounds like a real peach," Brynn said wryly as she stacked the folded washcloth on top of another and wrangled a towel from the basket.

I gave Lexi her room key and my standard spiel. "Call if you need anything. Enjoy your stay."

Once Lexi had gone, Brynn finished folding the towels, went to the closet to load them onto our housekeeping carts, and rounded up her purse. "See you tomorrow!" she called as she headed out the door.

With everyone gone, the lodge was quiet, and I took advantage of the lull to get online. I found the Facebook page for the ladies' motorcycle club and scrolled down until I found the photo I'd snapped outside earlier. Reyna had posted it already. I shared the post on the lodge's page, adding a note that read *Thrilled to be hosting these fun-loving ladies! We'd love to host your group, too.* It couldn't hurt to publicize the fact that the lodge was the perfect place for small groups to gather and was also motorcycle friendly.

As long as I was online, I figured I might as well take a look at my sons' social media accounts. While they might not give their mother the details of their lives without a bit of cajoling, they'd happily provide information and pics to the general public via Instagram. If I wanted to know what they were up to, I could find out with a little snooping on the internet. Jack Jr., or J.J.'s, account showed a video clip of him playing Frisbee with friends outside his dorm at

Duke. Looked like he'd enjoyed a fun study break. Meanwhile, Mitch, who attended the University of North Carolina in Chapel Hill, had posted a photo of himself with several other students sitting around a table in the library, along with the hashtag #studygroup. There were some smiling girls in the bunch. I wondered if he'd hit it off with any of them. I'd probably be the last to know. *Sigh.*

My sleuthing complete, I ventured to my room to check on Yeti. Normally, she spent her days napping on the bed, sofa, or windowsill, but this evening she was nowhere to be seen. I felt a small surge of panic, even though I knew she couldn't have escaped the room. The windows were open only a half inch to allow her to enjoy the fresh air, and no one had opened the door to my room all day except me. I retraced my steps and checked behind the shower curtain. She wasn't lying in the tub, either. I exited the bathroom and called, "Yeti? Where are you, girl?"

To my surprise, she peeked out from under the bed, glancing about as if to make sure it was safe to come out. I knelt down next to the bed and patted my thigh. "Did the motorcycles scare you?" She mewed as if to say *yes*, but ventured over to me and let me take her in my arms. I cuddled her and scratched her under the chin. "No need to worry, pretty girl. Those engines are loud but they can't hurt you." Once she seemed reassured, I set her on the bedspread and put a hand on the bed to lever myself to a stand. I rounded up a can of her favorite food and fed her a nice dinner before warming up a can of soup for myself in the microwave. The two of us ate our dinners in companionable silence, and I rinsed our dishes in the small sink at the room's coffee bar.

With a final pat on the head, I told Yeti I'd see her at bedtime.

I returned to the great room to find Rocky lounging in a chair next to the fireplace, a murder mystery novel in hand. I pointed to the book. "Spoiler alert. The butler did it."

He narrowed his eyes. "That seems highly implausible. There's no butler in this story."

I gave him a mischievous smile as I flopped down in a chair next to him and reached down to stroke Molasses. His thick, soft fur was warm from the fire and I sunk my fingers into it. He looked up at me sideways and panted softly, his expression grateful. Yeti rarely showed appreciation for the attention I gave her. She seemed to consider my attention her due. *I suppose that's the difference between dogs and cats. Ego.*

Speaking of appreciation . . . I turned to Rocky. "Thanks again for picking up that load of firewood and stacking it. That's going beyond the call of duty." In actuality, his duties as the sole maintenance staff at the lodge were not well defined. We had a handshake agreement that he'd take care of repairs around the lodge in return for a free room. He planned to stay only until his oldest daughter and her family vacated his home. They'd moved in when Rocky's son-in-law lost his job. Rocky later asked if he could use a room here. Living with a baby had cut into his shuteye, and he figured his daughter and her family could use more space and privacy.

Rocky said, "Happy to help. I enjoy sitting by a fire myself."

Our conversation was interrupted when the phone rang

at the front desk. I stood and scurried over to see that another call was coming in on the outside line. I grabbed the receiver. "It's a beautiful Blue Ridge evening at the Mountaintop Lodge. How may I help you?"

A man's voice said, "Geraldine Burnham's room, please."

To respect my guest's privacy, and also to limit my potential liability, I made it a policy to give out as little information about my guests as possible. To this end, I didn't tell the man on the line that Gerri was out to dinner with the other members of the motorcycle club. I simply said, "I'll transfer you to her room." The call would go to voicemail after four rings.

I returned the receiver to the cradle and retook my seat next to Rocky. I'd worried I might be lonely after my divorce, but fortunately that hadn't proven to be the case. Between Rocky, Brynn, and Patty, I'd formed a new family of sorts. The guests often provided companionship, too, as many chose to hang out in the lodge's great room and often engaged me in conversation, intrigued to learn what it was like to run a mountain lodge. I enjoyed hearing about their lives, learning about the places they were from, their reasons for visiting the area. Some came for the hiking. Others came for the wineries. Now, most were coming to see the foliage.

The phone at the front desk rang again, and again I stood and walked over to answer it. The same man who'd just called for Gerri was on the line again. "I need to speak with Gerri right away," he demanded. "It's urgent. Is she there?"

Pointing out the obvious solution, I said, "Have you tried her cell?"

"Yes," he said. "She's not answering."

I wondered if this man was the same person who'd called her cell phone earlier, the one she'd put off until next week, when she returned home from her ride. *Is Gerri ignoring this man's calls, or are they not getting through?* Cell service could be unreliable in the mountains, even nonexistent in the more remote areas where the towers didn't reach. But Gerri was out to dinner, and the restaurants were generally within zones that got decent reception. I'd be surprised if she was unable to get a call now. "I'd be happy to put you through to her room again."

The caller exhaled so loudly in the mouthpiece that the sound hurt my ear, and I pulled the receiver away. Rocky eyed me, his brows lifting in question. I made a sour face to communicate that I was dealing with a pushy jerk.

The caller barked into the phone. "I didn't ask you to put me through to Gerri's room! I asked if she's there right now. If so, you need to get her on the phone right away."

I wasn't sure how to respond. Out of respect for my guests' privacy, I normally didn't share details about my guests' whereabouts with a caller. After all, I had no idea who was on the phone and what their relationship might be with a guest. But, despite the earlier call for Sadie Hardin, it was rare for someone to call the hotel looking for a guest. I feared the matter might truly be critical. "She's stepped out," I said, hoping it wasn't a blunder to let him know.

"Transfer me, then." Remembering his manners, he added a curt "Thanks."

I put the call through to Gerri's room so he could leave a voicemail. I hoped whatever was going on wouldn't interfere with her plans to ride in the mountains tomorrow.

Half an hour later, a roar of motorcycles sounded again

out front. Rocky and I turned in unison to look out the front windows. When he chuckled a moment later, I turned his way. "What?" I asked.

"That look on your face," he said. "It's wistful. You want to ride with them, don't you?"

"I'd have no idea how to even start a motorcycle," I said, "but it sure looks like fun."

The ladies locked up their bikes again, and a few others joined Katie in covering their rides for the night. After securing their motorcycles, the ladies burst through the door. Several had bottles of foil-topped champagne in their hands. Others had bottles of whiskey, bourbon, and tequila. They must've filled up every square inch of their saddlebags with bottles from the liquor store down in Banner Elk. Reyna carried packages of graham crackers, chocolate bars, and marshmallows, along with metal skewers for roasting them. The ladies apparently planned to pair their cocktails with s'mores.

Erika stopped in the foyer between the two wings and cupped her hands around her mouth. "Lexi!" she hollered. "Come out, come out, wherever you are!" The sound of a door opening came from down the hall. Erika pointed down the corridor. "There she is!"

Bessie raised a bottle of champagne. "You're single again! Let's celebrate!"

Lexi came up the hall, all smiles, ready to have fun with her friends.

I stood and walked toward them. "I don't have champagne flutes, but I'll round up some water glasses."

"Thanks, Misty," Gerri said. "Water glasses will work just fine."

As I reached the woman, I lowered my voice. "A couple of calls came in while you were out. The caller might have left a voicemail. He told me it was urgent."

"I have my doubts about that," she muttered. "But I'll go check."

As Gerri walked down the hall to her room, Rocky stood and addressed the group. "Do you ladies want to celebrate in here, or should I get the fire pit going out back?"

Erika threw a fist in the air and began to chant. "Fi-re pit! Fi-re pit!"

Some of the others joined in, likewise pumping their fists. "Fi-re pit! Fi-re pit!"

Rocky chuckled. "Looks like it's unanimous." He patted his leg to rouse his dog. "C'mon, Mo. Let's get the fire started."

While Molasses ambled out the back door after Rocky, I went to the housekeeping closet and rounded up a divided tray filled with glasses. Gerri came back down the hall, her face puckered in frustration. If the caller left a voicemail, it seemed it wasn't a happy message. She stopped when she saw me. "If anyone calls for me, tell them I asked not to be disturbed."

"Certainly."

She exited through the doors at the back of the lodge, and I followed her with the tray of glasses. By that time, several of the group had already taken seats in the Adirondack chairs that surrounded the fire pit. Others stood about, chatting in smaller groups. Bessie had rounded up Shotgun from her room, and the scruffy terrier lay on the stone terrace at her feet, head up, relaxed but attentive, wanting to be part of the fun. Rocky had the kindling started and added several logs, leaning them up against each other in a pyramid formation. While the woods around us were pitch black, the fire emitted a soft glow. I set the tray down on a table next to the bottles of liquor. Reyna held a bottle of champagne angled away from her as she worked the cork. *POP!* A skittering sound came from the nearby woods.

Erika hooted. "I think you just scared off a bear!"

Katie said, "Could have been an alien."

"Nah," Lexi said. "It was Bigfoot."

The skittering had more likely been a bird in the brush, but I didn't want to ruin their fun by pointing this out. Besides, who was to say it hadn't been a Bigfoot? Numerous people claimed to have seen the human-ape hybrids in the Blue Ridge Mountains. A Bigfoot Festival had even been held in the town of Marion, North Carolina, just fifty miles south of Beech Mountain.

The ladies grabbed glasses and Lexi poured the champagne while Reyna opened the other bottles in quick succession. *Pop! Pop! Pop!*

Dahlia raised her glass. "To Lexi! Congratulations on ridding yourself of Todd the turd."

The ladies lifted their glasses, clinked them together, and called out, "Hear! Hear!" Most sipped their champagne, but Erika guzzled her glass down as if she were in a beer-chugging contest. When the glass was empty, she raised it again and opened her mouth wide to release a loud *burrrrp*! If the popping cork hadn't scared off any bears or aliens, her belch likely had. Gerri and Reyna gave Erika a disapproving look but said nothing. They'd evidently decided to choose their battles with Erika and determined this minor impropriety wasn't worth an argument.

By then, the fire was roaring, and Rocky walked over to stand near me. He leaned in and whispered, "'Love is blind. Friendship closes its eyes.' Friedrich Nietzsche." Not only was the man a whiz with tools, he was also adept with philosophical quotes, a font of worldly wisdom.

Reyna brandished a perfectly browned marshmallow on one of the long metal skewers, like a female conquistador brandishing a sword. "Would either of you like a s'more?"

Rocky and I thanked her but declined the offer, not wanting to intrude on their party.

"We'll leave you to your celebration," I said. With that, Rocky, Molasses, and I went back inside to relax in the great room.

Around eight thirty, the same man called for Gerri again. "I'm not able to transfer your call," I said. "Ms. Burnham has asked not to be disturbed."

He scoffed, muttered a curse, and hung up without saying goodbye. *Sheesh.*

Nine o'clock came, then ten, then eleven. While Gerri, Reyna, Dahlia, and Daisy came inside and returned to their rooms, the rest of the ladies were still whooping it up around the fire pit, showing no signs of slowing down. To save time in the morning, Rocky helped me prepare for breakfast. We set up the serving table, covered it with a tablecloth, and readied the warming trays. When we finished, I found myself stifling a deep yawn. The bikers might not be tired yet, but I sure was.

Rocky glanced out the back window before turning to

me. "I'll make sure the fire gets doused once the last of them comes inside."

His sweet gesture sparked a fresh ember in my heart. "Thanks, Rocky. I owe you one." I gave him a thankful pat on his firm shoulder and stepped out back to check on the women a final time. "Anyone need anything before I head off to bed?"

Fortunately, my guests had no unmet needs at the moment.

I wished them all pleasant dreams and headed back inside to my room. Yeti had warmed up the bed for me. After cleaning up and changing into my nightgown, I slid in next to her and gave her a kiss on her furry cheek. "Night-night, baby girl."

CHAPTER 5

Misty

My cell phone alarm woke me at six. *Ughhhhh.* I'd never been a morning person, which meant I'd spent my sons' early years in a perpetual sleep-deprived fog. The teen years, when they'd stayed in bed until noon, had better suited my natural rhythm. But as the innkeeper of a mountain lodge, I had no choice but to get up early to tend to my guests' needs. It was the tradeoff for getting to live in such a beautiful place.

I forced my eyes open, turned off the alarm, and rolled out of the bed, aiming for the bathroom. I had my morning routine timed down to the second so that I'd be at the front door when the Greasy Griddle staff brought breakfast over. After a quick shower and shampoo, I blow-dried and styled my hair, and got dressed. After brushing my teeth and putting on some basic makeup, I cleaned Yeti's litter box and fed the cat her breakfast. I left her with a scratch under the chin. "See you later, girl." She replied with a swish of her bushy tail.

I stepped out into the dimly lit hallway, closed my door

as quietly as I could, and tiptoed to the great room. No sound came from inside the inn, my guests still snug in their beds. I left the overhead lights off for now, and walked over to the front doors to wait for Patty or her staff to bring the catered breakfast over from the Greasy Griddle.

Outside was still dark, the sun not due to rise for nearly another hour. The diner wasn't open yet and the Greasy Griddle sign wasn't lit up. But through the diner's windows I could see the lights from the kitchen, where Patty was preparing for the patrons who would soon arrive when the diner opened at seven. In the lot next to the diner sat Patty's car, as well as two others that belonged to her staff.

As I stared out the window, a vehicle with its high beams on turned into the parking lot. With the headlights so bright in the darkness, it was impossible for me to make out what type of car it was. Just after turning in, the driver shut off the headlights. Only the yellow parking lights remained on. *That's odd.*

The driver circled in front of the diner and drove to the end of the parking lot, turning to circle back in front of the lodge. An eerie feeling invaded my gut, and I stepped back behind the wood framing around the entry doors so I could watch the vehicle without being seen. The vehicle rolled past the front doors. My eyes had adjusted enough by then to see that the vehicle was a windowless white cargo van with chrome bumpers. There was no license plate on the front of the van. While I'd heard that most states required plates on both the front and back of a vehicle, there were a few states, including North Carolina, that required a plate only on the rear. I assumed this van would bear a North Carolina license plate as it passed, but I could see that it sported a Mississippi plate instead. *Hmm.* While the Blue Ridge Mountains attracted many people from out of state, the vast majority of visitors to our little hamlet came from the neighboring states of South Carolina and Tennessee, or from the southeastern states of Florida or Georgia. Occasionally, I'd see an Alabama license plate, or one from Kentucky, but I couldn't recall having seen one from Mississippi before.

Red brake lights flashed on the back of the van as it rolled to a stop near the row of motorcycles lined up in front of the west wing. *Is the driver checking them out?* Across the parking lot, the door opened on the diner and Patty came out rolling a stainless-steel commercial kitchen cart. Trays filled with breakfast foods filled the shelves on the cart. She turned back to lock the diner's door before heading my way. After she'd taken a few steps, the van began to move again. The headlights switched on just as the van eased back onto Beech Mountain Parkway and turned right to head down the back of the mountain.

The situation seemed strange, but maybe I was just on edge. After all, it hadn't exactly been business as usual since the motorcycle club had arrived. Besides Erika's outburst, there'd been the odd phone calls. First, a caller asked for someone with a name that rhymed with that of a guest, then the rude man demanded to speak to Gerri. But those things likely had nothing to do with the van that had just driven through the lot. The driver had probably simply been considerate and dimmed the headlights so they wouldn't shine through the windows of the lodge and disturb the slumbering guests. But the question remained, why had the driver turned into the lot at all? Maybe they'd been lost and needed a place to stop and consult their GPS or maps app. I supposed I'd never know. Besides, with the van now gone, it was a moot point.

I turned on the overhead lights in the lodge and unlocked the front doors, opening them to let Patty inside. She greeted me with a whispered "Mornin', Misty," as she wheeled her way in. The cart was loaded down with metal trays of southern breakfast staples, including biscuits, gravy, grits, and home fries seasoned with onions and peppers. She'd brought some healthier items, too, including fresh fruit and oatmeal, as well as sweet items such as muffins and pancakes. She'd even brought a white screw-top carafe filled with hot apple cider. *I know what I'll be filling my mug with this morning.*

The two of us scurried about, now well-versed in our setup routine. I got the coffee urns perking, one for regular coffee and the other for decaf. We set out glass pitchers of orange and cranberry juice, as well, and a hot-water dispenser and packets of tea. Patty left a couple of empty bins for bussing the dirty dishes. When we were done, I thanked her and held the doors for her again as she left to return to the diner. Shortly thereafter, just after she entered her restaurant, the parking lot exploded in light as she switched on the Greasy Griddle sign, so bright in the blackness it glowed like a Las Vegas casino marquee.

Returning to the table, I turned the top on the carafe of cider, releasing sweet, spicy-scented steam as I poured some into a mug for myself. The cider was piping hot, sending up a cloud of steam and making the mug nearly too hot to handle. I didn't dare take a sip yet for fear of scalding my tongue. I set the mug down on the mantle to let it cool while I started a fire in the fireplace. The pine logs crackled, filling the room with a crisp and pleasant scent.

Rocky and Molasses ventured into the great room just after seven but, other than Yeti and Patty, they were the first signs of life I'd seen at the lodge that morning. While Rocky took the dog out front for a potty break, I fixed his coffee for him. No cream, lots of sugar. The two of us might only be coworkers at this point, but we'd fallen into a morning routine not unlike a married couple. We had breakfast together each morning, and talked about our plans for the day.

With no guests having yet shown their faces, Rocky and I took seats at one of the best tables by the back windows. Through the glass, we could see a doe and her half-grown fawn grazing along the edge of the woods in the early dawn light. Molasses sat at the window, watching the deer with only a small amount of interest. He'd lived in the mountains long enough that deer no longer brought him much excitement.

While my arrangement with Rocky meant he'd make the lodge's needs his top priority, everything was in shipshape order and there was nothing on his to-do list here. I eyed him over my mug. "What's on your plate today?"

He looked down. "Biscuits and gravy."

I rolled my eyes. "I meant your proverbial plate."

"A vacation rental on Slopeside Road has wood rot. I'll be replacing boards and trim and doing a little touch-up painting there. I'm adding storm doors to a home on Saint Andrews, too."

In other words, he'd be gone most of the day. "Care to

join me in a frozen lasagna for dinner?" Cooking for one was hard. I'd rather not be stuck eating leftover lasagna for the next week.

He cocked his head, brows raised. "Is this a dinner date?"

"Frozen lasagna wouldn't be much of a date, would it?"

He shrugged. "I'm easy. What if I pick up a bottle from the winery in Banner Elk? Would that make it a date?"

"Still no," I said. "People go *out* on dates. Staying *in* doesn't qualify."

He offered a roguish grin. "Whatever you want to call it, I'll be there. With wine."

"Their red blend is my favorite." Truth be told, I was afraid to go on an official date with Rocky. It had been over two decades since I'd had a first date. What if we didn't have fun? It could make our work relationship difficult. Better to keep things casual, right?

Footsteps drew our attention to the lobby. Gerri walked out of the west wing, looking just as sleek in her biker gear as she had the day before. We exchanged greetings before she grabbed a plate and peeked under the lids of the warming trays at the buffet. "What a feast! Everything looks and smells scrumptious."

"I can't claim any credit." I pointed out the front windows to the diner across the way. "The Greasy Griddle caters the breakfast."

She put a spoonful of everything on her plate before heading our way. "Mind if I join you two?"

"We'd love it," I said, looking up at her. "I hope you don't mind if I pepper you with questions about motorcycles."

"As long as you'll pass the pepper for my home fries," she said.

Rocky pulled out a chair for her, and I handed her the shaker. Once she'd sat and seasoned her meal, I inquired about her experience with motorcycles. "When did you start riding?"

She lay her napkin in her lap. "My mom claims I came out of the womb on a minibike, but I was about ten years old before I rode alone. Both of my parents were bikers, though, and they took me along with them all the time when I was little. When I was sixteen, I bought my own bike with money I earned working at a motorcycle dealership. I started out selling clothing. T-shirts, mostly. I was good at it, too. Outsold every other associate."

I took a sip of my cider. "Sounds like you had a knack for sales."

"I did," Gerri replied with a humble shrug. "You just have to listen to the customer, go beyond what they think they want or need and determine *why* they want it or need it. That way, you can steer them in the right direction." She took a bite of Patty's grits and issued an appreciative *mmm* before wiping her mouth. "I remember a guy who came into the clothing department. He was forty or so, seemed ancient to me at the time." She chuckled softly. "He'd just bought his first motorcycle. He wanted to buy studded boots, leather chaps, a logo jacket, the whole nine yards to go with it. He thought all that garb would make him look tough and young and authentic, but I knew it would scream 'midlife crisis.' The experienced bikers would've poked fun at him for being a poser. Know what I sold him?" Before Rocky or I could respond, she answered the question herself. "A bandana, a belt, and a pair of basic boots in brown, not black. The understated style made him look legit. Real bikers don't feel a need to be flashy."

Rocky chimed in. "Bet you saved him some embarrassment."

"I like to think so." Gerri took a sip of her juice. "Some of our repeat customers started asking for me, wanting my opinion. I'd only been working at the store a few months when the manager moved me over to motorcycle accessories. Saddlebags, engine guards, tachometers, light bars. That kind of thing. Got paid a commission and earned a small fortune. My friends were still making minimum wage flipping burgers. Before I knew it, I was selling the motorcycles. I'd barely even reached eighteen at the time. From the motorcycle shop, I moved on to a car dealership. Same thing. Sold lots of cars, and customers gave me positive feedback, said they felt understood rather than pressured. When I wanted an even bigger challenge, I applied at the RV dealership. Been there ever since. Forty-five years."

"That's a long time." I held a forkful of fried potatoes aloft. "You must've enjoyed your work."

"I did. Still do. Went from sales to management, eventually. Hired, trained, and supervised the sales team. Of course, I own the dealership myself now that my husband's gone."

"Still planning to retire at the end of the year?" I asked.

"Nah." She turned to gaze out the window. "There doesn't seem to be any point now. I don't know what I'd do with myself. My husband and I planned to travel the world, but I don't want to go without him." She took a sip of her juice and sat up straighter, as if forcing herself to buck up. "At least I get to travel with the girls in the club. We don't go anywhere we can't reach in a few hours' drive, but that

gives me all of the Carolinas, Virginia, and parts of Tennessee to explore."

"That covers a lot of territory." Rocky raised his coffee
cup in acknowledgment. "I've lived in North Carolina all
my life and there are still places in the state I haven't seen."

"Same here," I said. Between the Outer Banks, sandhills
region, the mountains, and the so-called Land of Waterfalls,
the state offered an endless list of destinations. "Speaking
of the girls," I said, "how long have all of you been riding
together?"

"Reyna and I started riding together in our thirties. Some
of the girls hadn't even been born yet then. The others joined
bit by bit. Bessie's been with us about fifteen years. Before
she adopted Shotgun from the pound, she'd bring friends
along in her sidecar. Dahlia and Daisy have been around
ten years or so. Lexi's been with us about five years. Before
she got her Vulcan, she used to ride this pathetic piece of
junk she'd bought secondhand. Erika's been around for just
a few months." She cast her eyes toward the wings as if to
make sure she wouldn't be overheard, and leaned toward
me. "She's had it hard, so we cut her some slack. But she's
always causing trouble." Her expression turned sour and her
lips pursed. "I'm not sure she's going to last."

I wondered what, exactly, had been hard for Erika, and
how they would force her out of the group if they decided
she was no longer welcome. As Erika had pointed out the
day before, they had no legal right to keep her off a public
road. "What about Katie?" I asked.

"She's our newest member. Been with us about three
months now." Gerri sat back in her seat, her eyes narrowing

slightly. "She's a tough nut to crack. Doesn't talk about her-self much."

I wondered if she'd shared with the group what she'd shared with me when she'd checked in—that her family had included a bulldog when she was a child. Surely one of the other riders had noticed her bulldog keychain, too, and asked about it.

Reyna strolled into the lobby and raised her chin in greeting.

Gerri patted the fourth seat at our table, which sat empty. "Grab a plate and join us, Queen."

I'd heard the riders use nicknames for each other. The woman with the sleeve and neck tattoos was nicknamed Graffiti. They referred to another rider as Razzmatazz. Erika's nickname was Reckless, a seemingly apt moniker. But it was all I could do to keep my guests' real names straight, let alone remember all their nicknames. In the case of Reyna, however, *Queen* was more of a translation than a nickname, given that her name meant *queen* in Spanish.

Reyna filled her plate and came over to our table. Rocky excused himself to get to work, but I poured myself a sec-ond cup of hot cider and went back to the table, eager to hear more from these interesting ladies. I asked them about their favorite roads to ride.

"That's easy," Reyna said. "The Tail of the Dragon."

Gerri concurred. "Three hundred and eighteen curves over eleven miles."

"Some call it 'America's most exciting road,'" Reyna added.

The two went on to tell me that the road known as the Tail of the Dragon was actually part of U.S. Highway 129 and that, depending on which way you were headed, the famous stretch began or ended at the intersection with NC 28. Reyna mentioned that *The Fugitive* had been filmed on the road and at the Cheoah Dam, which was located nearby.

"We just road the Dragon back in July." Reyna pulled out her phone and showed me a pic the group had snapped in front of a shiny metal dragon statue in Deals Gap. She showed me a second photo in front of a tree decorated with colorful parts from motorcycles that had crashed on the road. She referred to it as the "Tree of Shame."

"Yikes!" I said. "I hope the riders didn't get hurt."

Gerri provided a history lesson. "That road has seen a lot of bloodshed. The Cherokee and settlers fought all over the area. The Cherokee later used it to evade soldiers who were trying to round them up and send them off on the Trail of Tears. There was some action out that way during the Civil War, too. Some claim to hear ghosts along the road. That said, the death counts on the road are often exaggerated."

The two went on to talk about other roads in the North Carolina mountains they enjoyed riding, including Moonshiner 28, Cherohala Skyway, Foothills Parkway, and the nearby Shulls Mill Road. Others they identified only by their numbers, like 194, 321, and 221, which Reyna deemed "epic."

I was curious where they'd be headed today and inquired about their plans.

"We'll ride south on the Blue Ridge Parkway," Reyna said. "We plan to hike to Crabtree Falls, then have lunch outside at the Switzerland Inn."

"Sounds wonderful." The beautiful waterfall was located about forty-five miles from Beech Mountain, a little over an hour's drive at typical parkway speeds. I'd hiked to the falls many times myself. I'd also enjoyed many a meal and drink on the Switzerland Inn's terrace, which gives diners a gorgeous long-range view of the mountains. "I suppose the Blue Ridge Parkway will seem relatively tame compared to the Tail of the Dragon." While the parkway had plenty of curves, the ratio of curves per mile came nowhere near that of the famed Dragon. Even so, it would provide them with miles of lovely scenery.

By then, the other riders were emerging from their rooms and filling their plates. Brynn had arrived, too. Though I would've loved to listen to Gerri and Reyna's stories all day, I had to leave the women to their breakfast and get to work. "It was fun chatting with you two."

An hour later, all of the riders had eaten breakfast, put on their gear, and gathered in the lobby for a final briefing before their ride. Gerri ran through the plans, noting that they'd make stops at each lookout point to enjoy the views.

Reyna handed Gerri a bright yellow handheld radio, and carried the other outside to the parking lot so they could test them. Her voice came through the radio a moment later. "Can you hear me?"

Gerri raised the device to her mouth and pressed the button on the side. "Loud and clear."

With phone reception being spotty in the mountains, they'd been smart to bring walkie-talkies. Jack and I had always taken a pair with us when we hiked with our sons, who had much more energy and always ended up far ahead of us. Some models were good for up to sixteen miles, though the range depended on whether there were obstacles such as high ridges.

Gerri turned to Erika and gave her a pointed look. "You're riding in front of me."

Erika scoffed. "I don't need a babysitter."

Gerri repeated her order, her rigid stance and no-nonsense tone making it clear the matter was not up for debate. "You're riding in front of me, or you're not riding at all."

When Erika realized the group had again gathered around to stare her down, she seemed to realize she'd better fall in line. Still, she wasn't going to go down without a snide comeback. She clicked her boot heels together and saluted Gerri. "Yes, ma'am, Madame Mussolini!"

The other riders exchanged looks and shook their heads before heading to the door.

Brynn and I followed them out front, and I called after them. "Enjoy your ride!"

One engine started, then another, then another, each bike purring with its own particular rhythm like a litter of contented cats. With Reyna in the lead, they turned one by one out of the parking lot, the diners in the Greasy Griddle once again watching through the windows as the parade continued. Erika was the penultimate rider, turning onto the parkway on her silver Suzuki just before Gerri followed on the two-tone blue and black Harley Road Glide Special she'd transported in the trailer. It was a beautiful bike, with a wide but low windshield, what Gerri had called a shark nose fairing, and pristine pipes of shiny chrome.

As they rounded the bend and disappeared from sight, I sighed. "Dusting and vacuuming doesn't sound like much fun compared to riding the parkway on a motorbike."

Brynn added a sigh of her own. "Too bad we've got to make a living, huh?"

"Maybe someday we can rent one of those topless three-wheelers and take a drive down the parkway ourselves." Several places in the area rented Can-Ams or Polaris Slingshots.

Brynn cut me a glance. "You'd have more fun taking a romantic ride with Rocky."

I felt the heat of a blush rush to my cheeks, and my assistant chuckled. Thankfully, she changed the subject. "I found a video on YouTube that shows how to make a motorcycle out of towels." Brynn was a whiz with towel art, and had taught me how to make bears, deer, and hawks out of bath towels, hand towels, and washcloths. She waved for me to follow her back inside. "Come on. I'll show you."

CHAPTER 6

Yeti

Though the window was cool when she touched the pads of her paws to it, the rays of late afternoon sun streaming through the glass warmed her. She lay on the sill, soaking in the autumn sunshine, eyes opened just a crack in case that horrid hawk returned. She didn't like it when the raptor circled above, soaring over the woods seeking prey. Even though she knew she was safe inside the lodge, that the enormous winged beast couldn't actually grab her in its sharp-taloned clutches, instinct told her to run and hide whenever the bird appeared. Thankfully, the hawk had stayed at bay today.

The trees' limbs and leaves cast shadows about the grounds and woods, the breeze keeping the shadows in constant motion. *But wait. There's something else in the woods now, isn't there?*

She'd seen two deer at breakfast time, a mother and a juvenile. Several others had wandered by later, too, as well as that big-toothed groundhog who scuttled about as he went to and from his burrow beneath the boulders behind the lodge. But this wasn't one of the woodland creatures . . .

Yeti raised her head and peered out. Through the tree trunks she could see two people. They stood there, their heads together, unmoving. Their behavior seemed a little strange, but Yeti thought much of human behavior was bizarre. Misty enjoyed soaking in a tub of water. Yeti could think of nothing more repulsive. She hated the feel of water on her skin and fur. She was equipped with a nice barbed tongue for cleaning herself, thank you very much. Misty also had a machine that would make an awful noise to wake her up. Why not just sleep until you woke naturally? That's what Yeti did. In fact, she was feeling a little sleepy again now. Lest that pesky hawk return, she hopped from the window to the bed where she could fully relax in comfort.

CHAPTER 7

Misty

I was dusting the windowsill in Katie's room late that afternoon, when movement in the woods behind the lodge caught my eye. With a trailhead not far from the inn, it wasn't unusual to see hikers emerge from the woods or setting off into the trees. These two people were doing neither. Instead, they were standing still, huddled together about twenty feet down the trail, partially obscured by the trees. One of them waved their hand about, as if pointing to the trailhead. They were too far away for me to tell if they were men or women, or to distinguish much more about them other than that they both appeared to be white. I caught flashes of fair faces between the movement of the leaves. They could have been two lovers sharing a kiss or sweet nothings or a secret. As I finished my dusting, the two turned and headed back down the trail, away from the lodge.

I turned from the window and was walking back to my cart when something else caught my eye, something on the floor of Katie's room. At first glance, it appeared to be a black ribbon, but when I bent down and picked it up, it turned out not to be a ribbon at all. Rather, it was a dark hair extension about two inches wide and nearly two feet long, with a clip on the end. *Hmm.*

I'd noticed Katie's blonde roots when she'd checked in, so I knew the dark hair color wasn't natural. But I hadn't realized that she'd also augmented the length and thickness. Of course, there was nothing wrong with filling out a thin head of hair. Hollywood actresses and popular singers used all kinds of accessories to change up their looks, either for roles or for the media, who were always snapping photos. My midlife hormonal changes had caused my hair to thin, though the blow-dryer brush my hairdresser had recommended helped keep it looking sufficiently full and fluffy. Still, it could be a costume of sorts, or a disguise. My mind went back to the cover she'd put on her Kawasaki Ninja motorcycle, the one with the Indian Motorcycle logo. Had she been attempting to disguise her bike, too, or was the cover one she'd simply borrowed from a fellow biker or maybe bought secondhand? It took me only a second to dismiss any suspicions. After all, a change in hairstyle was step one in the getting-over-a-bad-breakup protocol and it only made sense to cover a motorcycle left outdoors overnight so that it would be protected from the elements. None of her behavior was out of the ordinary.

Katie must not have realized the extension had come loose or she wouldn't have left it on the floor where it could get stepped on or vacuumed up. I picked it up for her, carried it into the bathroom, and lay it atop a clean towel next to her curling iron where she'd be sure to find it.

A few hours later, Brynn and I had finished cleaning the

rooms and were emptying the bags on our vacuum cleaners into the larger trash bin in the housekeeping closet when a woman's voice called from the lobby, "Hello? Anyone here?"

I handed Brynn my bag so she could finish the task, and I strode to the lobby. There I found two nearly identical white women. Both had round faces, heavily made-up brown eyes, and hair the color of nutmeg pulled into a low ponytail at the nape of their necks. Both wore tennis outfits—tank tops paired with stretchy tennis skirts, ankle socks, and tennis shoes. To stave off the cool fall weather, they'd donned light-weight windbreakers over their ensembles. Behind them, parked just outside the lodge's front doors, was a red four-door Tesla. A thirtyish man in aviator sunglasses and golf attire leaned back against the front fender on the driver's side, speaking on his cell phone. Behind him, I could see the sky in the distance. It was turning gray and clouds were starting to build. *Looks like we're in for a storm.*

As I drew closer to the two women, I realized they were not quite as identical as they'd seemed on my first impression. One appeared to be about twenty or so years older than the other, though it wasn't her face that gave her away. She'd apparently invested in Botox treatments or some type of miracle cream that kept her face looking young. But the skin on her neck and around her knees had begun to loosen, sure signs of middle age. *A mother and daughter, perhaps? Sisters born far apart?*

I offered a smile. "Hello. How can I help you ladies?"

The older one said, "I'm Andrea Burnham. We're here to see Gerri."

"Are you Gerri's daughter?" I asked.

The woman threw her head back and cackled. Turning

to the younger version of herself, she said, "Did you hear what she asked me? She thinks I could be Gerri's daughter. How hilarious is that?"

I felt my ire rise. Andrea shared the same last name as Gerri and looked to be a generation younger. It had been a reasonable question. Of course, I then remembered that Gerri had said she'd been married only ten years before her husband had passed away earlier this year. Burnham was Gerri's married name. This couldn't be her daughter, then. "Step-daughter?" I ventured.

My second question caused Andrea to throw her head back again and issue another cackle. Much more of her head tossing and the woman would suffer whiplash.

The younger woman offered me a feeble smile and identified herself. "I'm Mariah Burnham. Gerri's daughter-in-law."

"*Step*daughter-in-law," snapped Andrea, giving Mariah a pointed look before turning to me, too. "I'm Mariah's mother-in-law."

If Mariah was Gerri's stepdaughter-in-law, and Andrea was Mariah's mother-in-law . . . I formed a quick mental family tree and realized that Andrea must be the ex-wife of Gerri's deceased husband Norman. *What is she doing here?* "What can I do for you?" I asked, my tone flat.

Andrea raised her right hand and circled a finger in the air. "Is Gerri around? We need to speak with her."

"She's not here at the moment." Gerri hadn't been happy to get the phone calls from the male caller the day before, and I had a feeling she might not be happy about a visit from these two, either. I wondered if the man out front was the one who'd called.

Mariah said, "I didn't see any motorcycles in the parking lot. Is the club out on a ride?"

She'd already put two and two together, so there was no sense hedging. "Yes, they are."

"My condolences," Andrea said. "It must be awful having women like that staying at your lodge."

"On the contrary," I said. "They've been exemplary guests." Okay, taking Erika into account, maybe that was a slight overstatement, but I felt the need to come to the group's defense. By and large the women had been kind, considerate, and appreciative, more so than the typical guest. Many had left generous tips on their pillows. They were also hard-working, self-sufficient women. Among them were a real estate agent, a nail technician, a human resources manager, a college professor, a bartender, a softball coach, and Gerri, of course, who ran the RV dealership.

Andrea's lips pressed in skepticism, but she let it go.

Mariah asked, "Any idea when they might be back?"

"No," I said, "but I'd be happy to take a message for Gerri."

Mariah turned to Andrea, who shook her head. "No message, but thanks," Mariah told me. "We'll wait here for Gerri. That is, if you don't mind?"

Before I could object, Andrea flounced over to the great room and flopped down in a chair in front of the fire. Mariah offered me an apologetic glance over her shoulder and slowly followed her mother-in-law. *Maybe there's some hope for Mariah, at least.*

Brynn came out of the housekeeping closet, saw the women in the great room, and cast me a questioning look. Rather than engage in a rude whisper, I said, "Brynn, these two ladies are Gerri's stepdaughter-in-law and her mother-in-law, Mariah and Andrea Burnham."

Brynn's eyes narrowed as she seemed to be performing the same mental maneuvers I had. "Ah," Brynn said when things clicked into place. "Nice to meet you."

I figured we might as well be hospitable to these folks while they were here. For all I knew they were on good terms with Gerri, and Andrea and I had just gotten off on the wrong foot. I held out my arm to indicate the credenza where coffee and tea were available 24/7. "Feel free to help yourself to some coffee or hot tea while you wait."

Mariah thanked me and consulted Andrea before getting up to pour them both a cup. While Mariah fixed their drinks, Andrea pulled her phone from the pocket of her jacket and began scrolling through social media. After Mariah handed Andrea her drink, she set her own cup on a table and removed her jacket to reveal a thin elastic sleeve that spanned from the middle of her upper arm to the middle of her forearm. *Mariah must be suffering a case of tennis elbow.*

Brynn took over at the desk, while I went to collect the trash from the bins in the great room, making small talk with the ladies as I did so. "Did you two play tennis at the club?"

The Beech Mountain Club offered tennis, pickleball, golf, and swimming, as well as day camps for kids and social activities for all ages. The crisp fall weather would be perfect for outdoor activities.

"We did." Mariah offered a demure chuckle. "Lost every game."

"It's the altitude," Andrea snapped. "I can't catch my breath up here."

She might want to blame her poor performance on the town's elevation but, although Beech Mountain was the highest town in eastern America, it sat at only 5,506 feet. Altitude sickness didn't occur until at least 8,000 feet of elevation. Seemed Andrea was just a sore loser.

Mariah said, "Win or lose, we had a good time. It's so . . ." She looked up, as if trying to find a single word to describe all the wonders autumn brought to the mountains. But no single word could ever do it justice. She settled for, "Beautiful. It's beautiful up here."

"It is, isn't it?" The natural beauty was one of the many things that had brought me here. Most of the town was unmanicured, dwellings tucked among spaces left natural rather than turned into lawns. "Are y'all from Raleigh, too?" If that's where Gerri and her husband had lived, it was likely his extended family also lived there.

Mariah nodded. "We are. Andrea was able to get us a game at the club here." She pointed out the front window. "My husband just finished a round of golf with some locals."

I was still unclear whether they'd come up to the mountains for recreation or to ambush Gerri, but it seemed coincidental they'd just happen to be up here when she was, too. "Are you staying here in Beech?"

"No," Andrea said without bothering to look up from her cell phone. "We're staying at a resort in Blowing Rock for the week. We've booked a two-bedroom suite until Saturday."

Blowing Rock was a beautiful, upscale town that sat along

the Blue Ridge Parkway a forty-five-minute drive away. The town was named after a legendary rock outcropping from which a young Cherokee man allegedly leaped when he was torn between his duty to his tribe and his love for his sweetheart. His heartbroken lover prayed to the gods, and the young man was purportedly blown back up to the rock by an upwind of fate. Whether there was any truth to the romantic tale was anyone's guess, but the rock was a popular landmark and tourist attraction. The view from the rock of the verdant valley below and the distant peaks was awe-inspiring.

Before I could pry further, the front doors opened and the man in the golf outfit walked inside. He removed his sunglasses, folded them, and tucked them into the breast pocket of his golf shirt. Ignoring me, he strode over to the great room and looked down at Andrea and Mariah. "I take it Gerri's not here?"

Andrea pursed her lips. "No."

While Andrea didn't bother with niceties, Mariah looked up at me, held out her hand to indicate the man, and made an introduction. "Misty, this is my husband, Sterling."

The guy glanced my way, but his face remained disinterested. "Hey."

I couldn't be sure, but I suspected his voice was the same one I'd heard on the phone the night before. Returning to my work, I circled to the back of the registration desk to take a seat on my stool next to Brynn. She eyed the trio sitting in front of the fire and jotted a note on a sticky pad, sliding it across the counter toward me. It read, *Oedipus has nothing on Sterling.* She had a point. It was creepy how much Sterling's wife resembled his mother.

Had he chosen her for that reason? I picked up a pen and wrote, *Yep. Ew.*

Sterling said, "I suppose I might as well make good use of my time." He pulled his car keys from his pocket and aimed the fob at the car as he strode back across the lobby. The trunk popped open. He went outside, removed a bag of golf clubs, and carried them into the lodge. After plopping down in a chair, he proceeded to polish his clubs with some type of specialized cleaning bottle topped with a brush to get into the grooves on the clubs. He used a towel to wipe them clean afterward. When he was done, the silver heads gleamed.

Brynn called across the lobby. "Those clubs are so shiny. We should hire you to help clean around here."

She'd meant her comment to be a harmless joke, but the guy responded with a look of such utter disgust that Brynn and I couldn't help but feel insulted. Only Mariah laughed, stifling herself when she saw the irritated looks on the faces of her husband and mother-in-law. *Some people can't take a joke.*

Sterling stood, retrieved a coffee mug from the drink station, and placed it on the floor near the back of the room, laying it on its side. He pulled his putter from his golf bag, placed a ball on the floor, and practiced putting. His ball went into the cup every single time. The guy was good, I'd give him that. *He must play a lot of golf.*

Once again, the air around us seemed to quiver as the sound of motorcycle engines approached. Through the front window, I could see the parade of women returning, Reyna again riding the lead bike and Gerri riding sweep. Oddly, Lexi sat not on her Vulcan, but in Bessie's sidecar with

Shotgun on her lap. Lexi wasn't wearing her helmet, either. The scowl on her face said she was royally pissed. *Something's happened.*

I hurried out front, not only to warn Gerri of the entourage waiting for her inside, but to find out what had happened to Lexi's bike. After Lexi set the terrier down on the asphalt, I held out a hand to help her out of the sidecar. "Where's your motorcycle?"

On her feet now, she threw her hands in the air. "We came back from our hike and it was gone!"

I remembered two of the women mentioning they'd been recent victims of motorcycle theft. *Could Lexi have become a victim, too?* "Was it stolen?"

"No," Lexi said. "Todd the turd had it towed. My helmet was attached to the bike, so that's gone, too."

"But I thought the judge awarded the motorcycle to you at your hearing yesterday?"

"He did," Lexi said, scowling. "But my bike is still in Todd's name. Apparently, he reported it stolen back when I moved out. The judge put in the divorce order that Todd has to cooperate with changing the registration into my name, but there hasn't been time yet to get him a copy of the order."

Erika pounded her right fist into the palm of her left hand. "I'll take a copy to your ex. I'll shove it where the sun doesn't shine!"

Lexi snorted a laugh. "You'd have to pull his head out of that space first." She turned back to me. "When I realized my Vulcan was missing, I tried to call law enforcement, but there was no cell reception at the falls. I had to ride with Shotgun to Little Switzerland and use the restaurant's phone to call the sheriff's department from there." She went on to tell me that while they were on foot hiking to Crabtree Falls, a McDowell County deputy had swung through the parking lot and run the license plates on their bikes. "Motorcycles are stolen more frequently than cars. The deputy said he runs routine checks. Anyway, he told me their database listed my bike as stolen property, so they'd seized it."

"Can't you just have your lawyer send them a copy of the divorce decree?"

"I asked the same thing," Lexi said. "They said title determines ownership and, since title is in Todd's name, he's the only one their impound will release it to."

Behind Lexi, Katie seemed to be having trouble getting the cover on her motorcycle. When Bessie noticed, she stepped over to help. Once the green Ninja was covered, Katie turned around, her left arm crooked awkwardly up in front of her. *Uh-oh.*

"Are you okay?" I asked.

"I slipped on some wet rocks at the waterfall and fell."

My maternal instincts turned on automatically. "Let me see your hand."

Katie had trouble removing the glove from her left hand, and grimaced when Bessie gingerly tugged it off. Underneath, her wrist had swollen into a goose egg. *Ouch.*

"That's awfully swollen," I said. "It could be broken. You should drive down to the urgent care clinic in Banner Elk and get it looked at."

Katie shook her head. "I appreciate your concern, but I think it's just bruised. It'll be okay once the swelling goes down."

I wasn't sure if she was trying to be tough, or if the real issue might be that she didn't have good health insurance. Either way, it was her decision to make, even if I disagreed with it. "I'll get you some ice." I hustled inside and rushed to my room, where Yeti watched me fill a small plastic bag with ice cubes. I hurried back to the lobby. Gerri stood with her hands on her hips, engaged in a showdown with Andrea and Sterling Burnham. Mariah remained seated, though she'd slid to the edge of her chair and perched there, worrying her lip with her teeth.

Although Gerri spoke at normal volume, her tone was pure fury as she addressed Sterling. "I told you I would address your request when I returned to Raleigh. You had no business coming up here and interrupting my vacation!"

Sterling scoffed. "We're on vacation, too."

Gerri crossed her arms over her chest. "Do you really expect me to believe that's a coincidence? That you just happened to come up to the mountains while I'm here?"

Andrea huffed. "We're staying at a resort in Blowing Rock. That's nowhere near you."

Yet they'd arranged to play tennis and golf right here in Beech . . .

Gerri stared Sterling down. "From now on, all requests for distributions from the trust must be put in writing." She looked from him to Andrea. "If either of you come to Camper Country or my home, I'll get a restraining order."

Mariah rose tentatively from her seat as Sterling turned to me. "Are you going to let her talk to us like that in your lodge?"

I had no interest in getting in the middle of a family dispute, but if pressed I would certainly side with the person paying for a room here. And who, frankly, I liked better. "I think it's best you all leave now."

Brynn came from behind the registration counter to stand next to me. Likewise, Erika stepped up beside Gerri and pounded her right fist into her left hand again. Gerri frowned and reached over to push Erika's hands down in a gesture that said there was no need for threats of violence.

Sterling scoffed. "Such hospitality." Sarcasm dripped from his words. "I'll be sure to let everyone I golf with this week know how the staff at the Mountaintop Lodge treats people."

I felt my ire rise. *How the heck did my lodge and I get dragged into this?*

Andrea and Sterling stormed out to the Tesla. Mariah rounded up the putter Sterling had left leaning against a chair, slid it into the golf bag Sterling had forgotten, and slung the bag over her shoulder as if serving as her husband's caddy. She followed them out, but not before whispering "Sorry" to Gerri and giving me an apologetic look, as well.

Sterling slid into the driver's seat while Andrea climbed into the passenger side, leaving Mariah to open the back door herself. She'd barely sat down before Sterling hit the gas. Mariah pulled her leg into the car and grabbed for her door handle. Luckily, the bikers who remained outside were either on the walkway or by their motorcycles, out of the way of the car.

Gerri turned to me. "I suppose I owe you an explanation."

She didn't really. Her personal life wasn't my business. But I had to admit I was curious, so I didn't discourage her.

"Andrea was my husband's ex-wife," she said. "Norman

was forty and she was twenty-two when they met years ago. She'd been doing a little local modeling and was hired for a print ad for the RV dealership. When she came to Camper Country to do the photo shoot, Norman fell for her pretty face. They married six months later. It didn't take long for Andrea to show her true colors and Norm realized she was a gold digger. By that time, she was pregnant with Sterling, so Norman stuck around. She spoiled that kid beyond rotten. He's the only thing she's ever cared about other than herself."

Honestly, that didn't surprise me. Loving your children was as much instinct as choice.

"Norman tried his best with the boy," Gerri said, "but it was a futile effort. Sterling and his mother are cut from the same cloth. Norman finally gave up and filed for divorce. Andrea blames me for it, calls me a home-wrecker, but there was nothing going on between Norman and me while he was married. He didn't even ask me out on a date until well after his divorce was final." She let out a long, soft breath. "'Course I'd always thought my boss was a great guy, that his wife didn't appreciate him the way she should." She was quiet for a beat, as if lost in reverie, before she spoke again. "Norman was extremely generous in the divorce. Even Andrea's attorney said so. He gave her the house, which was paid off. He gave her half of the other assets, even though he'd acquired some of them before they'd met and she hadn't worked a day since they'd married. On top of that, he paid monthly alimony."

The divorce settlement did indeed sound generous.

Gerri wasn't done. "Norman covered every penny of Sterling's college expenses, too, though the kid graduated by the skin of his teeth. Norman gave him a job as a salesman at Camper Country, but Sterling spent his time sitting in his cubicle, playing video games on his computer. He never grew up and took responsibility for himself. My husband finally fired him, thought the kid needed a taste of the real world."

"Tough love?" I said.

"Exactly. When Norman made his will, he left the dealership to me and all of his other assets in trust to his grandchildren, Sterling and Mariah's kids."

I was pretty sure I could see where she was going, why Sterling had come up here with his wife and mother in tow to harass Gerri. "Let me guess. You're the trustee?"

She nodded, but then a grin claimed her face. "Those two kiddos are adorable. Sweet, too. They take after their mother, thank goodness. They call me 'Ree-ree.' 'Gerri' is hard to manage at their ages. They're just two and three, born back-to-back."

"The toddler years are so fun," I said, thinking back to when my boys were that young, playing with their wooden trains. Of course, every age was fun with kids, just in different ways.

Gerri's grin dissolved as she continued. "Norman knew I love those little ones like they were my own grandchildren, that I'd do what's best for them. He said I was the only one who would stand up to Sterling, make sure he didn't bleed the trust dry to pay for his own expenses or his mother's. Andrea blew through her divorce settlement, and the alimony stopped when Norman died. Sterling doesn't have his act together and bounces from job to job. Mariah's smart, though. She's not afraid of hard work, either. She's got a job with a biotech company in Research Triangle Park and does pretty well for herself, but she'll need an advanced degree if she wants to move up into management. Of course, she can't afford to go back to school unless Sterling steps up to the plate, and that's not likely to happen. Sterling has already asked for trust funds to help pay for the twins' Montessori preschool, and now he's had the nerve to ask for funds to cover the family's country club membership. He says the membership benefits Norman's grandkids by making sure they're running in the best social circles." She pursed her lips. "He just wants his golf paid for. He'd never acknowledge it, but he's essentially stealing from his own children."

A loud boom of thunder sounded outside, as if God himself were sharing his opinion on the subject. A moment later, the remaining riders scurried inside.

Daisy wiped her cheek. "I felt a raindrop!"

A couple of the other ladies did the same. "Me, too!"

Katie came in, her arm still limp, and I remembered the bag of ice in my hand. I rushed over. "Here's your ice."

"Thanks." She took the bag from me and held it to the goose egg on her wrist. "I hope it's better by morning or I might have to sit out tomorrow's ride."

Dahlia said, "At least you won't be alone. I'm going to have to stay here at the lodge tomorrow to teach an online class and grade papers."

Reyna stared out the window. "If this storm doesn't pass by morning, we might *all* be stuck in the lodge tomorrow." Realizing how her words sounded, she turned to me. "Not that it isn't a wonderful lodge. It's just that we want to be out on the road."

I gave her a smile. "Understood."

It was quitting time for Brynn, and she gathered her things to go. She covered her head with a copy of the *High Country Press* she'd snatched from the display in the lobby as she ran to her Prius. Another clap of thunder sounded, and the drops turned to a soft but steady rain.

With the guests returning to their rooms to freshen up, I figured it would be a good time to get my lasagna in the oven. I went down to my room, heated the toaster oven that sat atop my coffee bar, and slid the frozen pasta inside to bake. I set the timer on my phone for fifty minutes and picked up Yeti, carrying her out to the lobby with me. With it raining outside, I didn't have to worry about her trying to sneak out the doors. She knew better.

She strutted back and forth on the check-in counter until deciding to lie down at the spot closest to the window, where she could look outside. A large drop gathered size and speed as it slid down the outside of the glass, and she reached out a paw, trying to grab it.

I stroked her head. "You're on the wrong side of the window, girl."

While most of my guests armed themselves with umbrellas and braved the rain to head over to the Greasy Griddle for dinner, Gerri and a small contingent loaded into her Yukon to drive down to Banner Elk in search of gourmet fare.

Rocky pulled up in his truck and parked. My heart pitter-pattered along with the rain when he emerged with a paper bag in his hand, the shape indicating it was the wine he'd promised to bring to our dinner. He let Molasses out of the back, and the two of them hightailed it into the lodge. While Molasses headed on to flop down in his favorite spot in front of the fireplace, Rocky stopped on the mat inside the door to wipe his feet and shake the water from his shoulders and hair. He raised his nose in the air. "Do I smell lasagna?"

"Yep," I said. "Go wash up and meet me at my room."

Ten minutes later, the two of us were sitting across from each other at the small, square table in my room, plates of lasagna and glasses of red wine between us. I'd dumped a bagged salad into a bowl, too. Molasses lounged on my sofa, while Yeti glared at the dog from atop the bed.

Rocky raised his glass in toast. "To our first date."

"It's not a date," I reminded him, raising my glass anyway.

"Okay, then," he countered. "To frozen lasagna."

We clinked our glasses and dug in. After he'd taken a couple of bites, I said, "Aren't you going to compliment me on the meal?"

"No. It's mediocre at best." When my jaw dropped, he grinned. "I didn't come for the food. I came for the company. And that's top notch." He shot me a wink.

I felt my cheeks heat with a blush and raised my wine glass to my lips to hide it. After taking a sip, I said, "You missed a lot of drama today." I filled him in on the impoundment of Lexi's bike, Katie's wrist injury, and the confrontation between Gerri and her stepson.

"You want me to stick around tomorrow?" he asked. "In case her stepson comes back?"

It wouldn't be fair for me to ask him to put off his handyman projects. "I can't ask that of you, but if they show their faces I'll call the police." Despite Andrea and Sterling's sense of entitlement, the lodge was private property and I had every right to exclude troublemakers.

We turned to other topics and before we knew it, we'd

cleaned our plates. I wrapped up the leftover lasagna and handed some to Rocky to take down to his room. "Here you go," I said. "Consider it a party favor."

Molasses slid down from the sofa, and the three of us left the room. Rocky returned to his own room to put the lasagna in his fridge, while I added a log to the fire in the great room and stoked the embers. Not long thereafter, the women who'd gone over to the Greasy Griddle for dinner came back across the parking lot, huddled in groups of two or three under umbrellas. Erika didn't bother trying to stay dry. Rather, she ran ahead of the group, stomping in the puddles along the way like a carefree child. A bolt of lightning lit up the sky behind her, making her look like a dark specter, the grim reaper in a black leather hoodie. By the time she burst through the doors of the lodge, she was dripping wet. Her wild abandon might be admirable if it didn't seem to always pose risks to others. Lest she leave a slippery trail behind her, I met her on the doormat with a towel and the rolling mop bucket with the built-in wringer. Katie had already fallen and hurt her wrist. I didn't want any of my other guests to end up injured.

The ladies and Shotgun gathered in the great room. Not long after, Gerri and the group who'd driven down to Banner Elk for dinner also returned. While the women played games, sipped cocktails, and enjoyed each other's company, the terrier basked in the warmth of the fire.

Before heading to bed, I suggested indoor activities they could enjoy the next day if the rain didn't let up. "The Mast General Store down in Valle Crucis is a fun place to shop. There are two wineries nearby, too. Linville Caverns is another option." While my ex had felt claustrophobic in the caverns, my sons and I had enjoyed touring the cave many times over the years. The ladies couldn't all fit in Gerri's Yukon, so I also noted the closest car rental outfits.

Reyna thanked me for the suggestions, and I bid the group good night, crossing my fingers the rain would dissipate by morning.

CHAPTER 8

Yeti

Her curious ears pricked on instinct, yanking the cat from her slumber. Yeti lifted her head to listen. The gusty winds and blowing rain from earlier in the night had finally stopped rattling the windows. Other than the *drip-drip-drip* of the rain from the edge of the roof outside and the steady rhythm of Misty's slow, deep breaths next to her, the lodge was quiet. So, what had woken her?

That's when she heard the noise again, the crack of a small stick outside. Something was walking outside the lodge. *A deer? A bear? A squirrel in search of a late-night snack? A person?* The cat had no way of knowing. But when a small crack sounded again, this time farther away, she realized it didn't much matter what—or who—was sneaking around the lodge, because the source of the sound seemed to be leaving. Though she remained curious, she knew she'd be unable to see through the closed shutters that blocked her view out of the window. No sense wasting precious sleeping time worrying about what was going on outside the lodge when she could be happily dreaming sweet dreams curled up on Misty's spare pillow.

CHAPTER 9

Misty

Midweek was normally a slow time at the lodge, and Brynn's typical days off were Wednesdays and Thursdays. But with the motorcycle club visiting this week, Brynn had agreed to take off Monday and Tuesday of the following week instead. We had only a few guests on the books those nights, and I'd be able to handle the cleaning and administrative duties on my own.

Thankfully, the storm passed during the night and Wednesday morning dawned bright and sunny. Nevertheless, I warned the ladies of potential hazards as they ate their breakfast in the great room. "Wet soil loosens roots and can bring trees down," I advised. "If you hear a cracking sound, look out. It could be a tree falling." I warned them about runoff, too. "Be careful if you take another hike. What's normally a harmless creek can become a roaring river after a deluge like we had last night."

Erika cut me an irritated look. "Enough nagging! Jeez."

Gerri frowned at Erika. "Misty is only looking out for

her guests. She has more experience in the mountains than we do."

Lexi glanced out the window, her expression wistful. "I won't have to worry about falling trees and raging rivers since I don't have my bike to ride."

Across the table from Lexi, Katie gingerly touched her injured wrist as if to assess it. The goose egg was gone, but a telltale bruise encircled her wrist like a thick, purple tattoo. "Take my Ninja, Lexi. I won't be able to ride today. I can barely move my hand."

Lexi brightened. "You'd let me ride your bike?"

Katie shrugged. "Why not? You're a good rider. We shouldn't both miss out."

"Thanks!" Lexi said. "I'll take you up on that offer."

Daisy turned my way. "Dahlia's staying here to work today. Want to take her spot on the back of my motorcycle?"

"Really?" A thrill rushed through me, but it was short-lived. There was no way I could ride with these ladies all day. There was too much work to do at the lodge. "As much as I'd like to go," I said, "I have to decline. It takes two of us to get the guestrooms cleaned."

Brynn, who was dusting the shelves, turned around. "Go." She made a shooing motion at me with the duster. "I can stay late if I need to. You won't get an opportunity like this again."

Reyna clenched it. "No need to clean the rooms today. We're big girls. We can make our own beds and reuse our towels. In fact, why don't you both come? Brynn can ride with me."

Brynn and I exchanged a glance. "You mean shut down the lodge?"

"Why not?" Reyna said. "We're your only guests, right? What's it gonna hurt?"

Rocky had been applying WD-40 to a squeaky hinge on the front door. He cast a glance back at me. "I agree with Reyna. As Atticus Finch said, 'What good are wings without the courage to fly?'"

"You're right." I turned to my assistant. "Let's play hooky!"

"Woo-hoo!" Brynn threw her fists into the air and broke into a happy dance.

Gerri said, "You can't ride in a dress, Brynn, but I've got Norm's gear in my trailer. You can wear his helmet and leathers."

Reyna leaned over to take a better look at my attire. "Your hiking boots and jeans will work, but you'll need a thick jacket."

Dahlia said, "Misty can wear mine." She went down the hall to her room and returned a moment later with her stylish jacket and her helmet.

I slid into the jacket, instantly feeling tough and sexy. "It's heavier than I expected."

"It's one of the best jackets on the market," Dahlia said. "It's lined with Kevlar."

"Kevlar?" I repeated. "The stuff they use to make bulletproof vests?"

"Mm-hmm," she said. "Same stuff. Protects a rider from getting road rash if they slide across the pavement."

Yikes! I hoped I wouldn't put the jacket to the test today.

Rocky's eyes had gone wide and his mouth gaped. It was the same look Danny had given Sandy in *Grease*, when Danny first spots her in the black leather pants, smoking a cigarette. "The bad girl look works on you."

I didn't bother fighting my grin.

Rocky cocked his head. "You know how to ride a motorcycle?"

"No. Daisy will be doing the driving," I explained. "I'll be sitting behind her."

Erika grunted. "It's called riding b—"

Gerri slapped her hand over Erika's mouth. "I'm sure they've heard the term."

Patty came in the door to collect the breakfast items, took one look at me in the jacket, and said, "Did you join the motorcycle club?"

I told her about my plans to ride with the girls.

"Lucky you!" she said. "Wish I could take the day off and play."

I wished she could come with us, too, but someone had to keep her diner running and none of the staff working today had been trained to manage the place.

A half hour later, Rocky, Patty, and Molasses stood in front of the lodge, watching as the Dangerous Curves and their newest temporary members—Brynn and yours truly—prepared to set off. Katie had given Lexi a brief primer on the particulars of her Ninja. While Lexi wore mostly her own gear, she'd donned Katie's lime-green helmet since her own was still attached to her Vulcan at the impound lot. Reyna had Rocky snap a pic of the group with her phone. After she posted it to social media, I texted a link to my sons and ex-husband with a message that read *Look who's joined a motorcycle gang* along with the winky-face emoji.

I climbed on behind Daisy. She started her engine and the bike began to vibrate underneath us. My heart raced. *I'm really doing this!* The group exited the parking lot in its usual lineup, with Reyna at the front and Erika riding at the back of the group just before Gerri, who took up the rear. As Daisy pulled out onto Beech Mountain Parkway, I turned my head and smiled back at Rocky and Patty, though I doubted they could see the smile through the helmet's tinted faceplate. I didn't dare take my hands from around Daisy's waist to wave goodbye.

Down the mountain we went, banking left and right with the curves, like a roller coaster. The ladies' obsession with motorcycles made sense to me now. I felt so alive! So free! I had to fight the urge to whoop.

As we made our way down the parkway, we passed the defunct Archer's Mountain Inn. The small inn had closed down years ago and been listed for auction by the bank. Unfortunately, the building suffered a fire while sitting vacant. While trees obscured most of the driveway, I caught a glimpse of a white cargo van backed up against the chain that stretched across the drive to prevent trespassers from entering the property. While the van resembled the one that had circled through my dark parking lot the morning before, I couldn't tell if it was the same vehicle. There wasn't much to distinguish the common vans other than license plates, and there was no plate on the front of this vehicle. What's more, dozens of such vans were in the area at any given time. Contractors of all types drove them: plumbers, woodworkers, flooring specialists.

Could someone be at the inn, looking things over with thoughts of fixing it up? If the inn reopened, it would be competition for my lodge. Even so, I'd be happy to see the place given new life. It seemed a waste for the building to sit idle and deteriorate.

As we executed a hairpin turn below the inn, I could see that the white van had moved forward and was now stopped at the end of the driveway, preparing to turn onto Beech Mountain Parkway. Without a turn signal blinking, it was unclear whether the driver intended to turn left to go up into town or right to follow us down the mountain. An instant later, my view of the van was gone as we descended around another bend.

We drove on and I enjoyed the rush of the wind and the warmth of the autumn sun, the wonderful feeling of being a part of the world around me rather than separated by a climate-controlled cage of metal and glass. We reached the Blue Ridge Parkway and headed southwest. Our initial destination was Craggy Gardens. Afterward, we'd have lunch in Burnsville, then stop on our return trip at Mount Mitchell, where we planned to hike to the summit for a photo. I could hardly wait to text more pics to my boys and show them how fun their mom could be.

We passed the turnoff for Crabtree Falls, where Lexi's bike had been seized yesterday. Now that we were on a section of the road the Curves had yet to explore, we made several stops, turning into the scenic overlooks and climbing off the bikes to enjoy the views. Though none of the vistas were new to me, I was seeing them with new eyes today. I'd never ridden the Blue Ridge Parkway on a motorcycle before, and it gave the experience an entirely different feeling.

We were at the Table Rock Overlook, helmets in hand as we enjoyed the view, when the sound of a motorcycle approaching pulled our attention to the north.

Lexi's eyes narrowed. "That sounds like my Vulcan." Sure enough, a few seconds later, a pearly white and turquoise Vulcan came into view. Lexi stomped her foot and spat a curse. "Todd must've sprung it from the impound."

Lexi's ex had the nerve to pull into the overlook and zip past us, beeping the horn all the while. *Beep-beep-beep-beep!* Some of the ladies raised their middle fingers and hurled insults at him, questioning his parentage, declaring the composition of his brain matter to be scatological in variety, and proclaiming in British parlance that he was the type of man with a proclivity for self-pleasure. As he zipped past me, I spotted the handles of adjustable hiking poles sticking out of a bag affixed to the top of the gas tank.

Erika raised her insulated metal water bottle over her head, but Gerri grabbed her forearm before she could fling the bottle at Todd's back. "Violence never solves anything."

Erika scoffed. "It does if you do it right." She yanked her hand out of Gerri's grip, but refrained from throwing the bottle.

Todd hooked a left as he exited the overlook, turning back the way he'd come. He beeped the horn again as he drove out of sight and Lexi spat another curse.

Gerri offered the younger woman some sage advice. "Don't rise to his bait. If he doesn't abide by the judge's order and transfer the bike to you, he'll be held in contempt and face jail time."

"Jail, huh?" Lexi's angry face relaxed a bit. "It would serve him right to get locked up."

"Let's get a pic," Reyna said, waving for everyone to gather near the sign that identified our location.

I'd snapped the photo the day they'd arrived at my lodge. I'd have been glad to take one now, too. "Want me to take it?" I offered.

"No," Reyna said. "You need to be in the photo. Brynn, too." She looked around the outlook parking lot, searching for someone who could take the photo for us.

At the far end of the outlook was a group of four college girls dressed in green and gold UNC Charlotte sweatshirts. Each wore a cheap cardboard birthday party hat and held up a bottle of wine from the Linville Falls Winery. The redheaded, freckle-faced girl in the middle sported a big button that read Official Adult and held a selfie stick out in front of them. "Everyone say Chardonnaaaaay!" She drew out the last syllable in a singsong way before snapping the pic. They headed to their car, a bright yellow convertible Mustang with the top down.

"Excuse me!" Reyna called to them. "Would y'all mind taking our picture?"

"Sure!" The redhead collapsed the telescoping metal pole on the selfie stick, handed it to her friend along with the bottle of wine she held, and walked over, swaying on her feet and bringing a strong odor of wine with her. *Just how much wine has this girl drunk?*

I pointed to the Official Adult button. "You turned twenty-one today?"

"Yesss!" She pumped her hands in the air. "I'm a grown-up now! Last of all my friends." With her drunken slur, the word *last* sounded like *lashed*. "We skipped class to celebrate."

I wasn't sure skipping classes, especially ones their parents had likely paid good money for, was something a true adult would do. I was also concerned this girl was beyond tipsy. *She's not driving, is she?*

She took the cell phone Reyna held out and stepped into place in front of us. "One, two, three!" she called out.

We smiled for the photo.

As she handed the phone back to Reyna, Gerri walked over and gestured to the convertible. "Do y'all have a designated driver?"

The grin dropped and the girl's upper lip quirked in irritation. "Don't worry about us, *grandma*. We'll be fine." With that, she returned to the car, climbed in, and shouted "woo-hoo!" as they zipped out of the parking lot.

Gerri frowned as she watched their car head down the parkway. They were headed in the same direction we were. It was a good thing they'd be in front of us rather than behind us. It was easier to avoid a drunk driver from the back. "You think they'll be okay?"

The group held a quick discussion. We had no idea whether the driver was inebriated and, even if she was, our cell phones had no reception. We couldn't call law enforcement. All we could do is keep a sharp eye out in case we rode up on them and hope for the best.

We donned our helmets, climbed onto the bikes, and continued on. As we rode through the Craggy Gardens Pinnacle Tunnel, the roar of the motorcycle engines echoed inside the space, making me thankful the helmet muffled the sound. My ears would be ringing for days, otherwise. Shortly thereafter, we reached the turnout for the Craggy Gardens Visitors Center. Named for the craggy rocks and beautiful flowers that covered the mountains in summertime, the area was just as rugged and beautiful now dressed in its autumn foliage finery. One by one the bikers exited and pulled to a stop in the parking lot. Daisy and I were near the middle of the group. We climbed off the bike, removed our helmets, and walked over to join the others standing at the hip-high stone wall that prevented sightseers from falling over the edge of the precipice. The view was spectacular, a blanket of orange, gold, and red as far as the eye could see.

Brynn's stomach growled loudly and we all laughed as she looked down, put a finger to her lips, and said, "Shhh." It was nearing noon by then and, after this stop, we planned to go for lunch in the nearby town of Burnsville before backtracking to Mount Mitchell.

After a moment or two, Reyna turned around. "Where's Gerri?"

CHAPTER 10

Misty

Lexi tucked the lime green helmet she'd borrowed under her arm and glanced around. "I don't see Erika, either."

Reyna's face clouded with concern. "They should be here by now."

Bessie said, "You think Erika went after Todd? She's always spoiling for a fight."

"I hope not." Reyna put two fingers in her mouth and issued a shrill whistle, just as she'd done after arriving at my lodge two days ago. The ladies gathered around, and Reyna proceeded to count them, skipping over me and Brynn. Everyone was there except Erika and Gerri. Reyna pulled her phone from a zippered pocket in her jacket and consulted the screen. "No bars." After returning the phone to her pocket, she unclipped the yellow handheld radio from her belt, raised it to her lips, and pushed the talk button. "Where you at, Gerri?" She got only silence in return.

Bessie bent down to pour water into a small plastic bowl for Shotgun. While he lapped it up, she stood. "Unless Gerri's stopped somewhere, she won't hear the radio over her motor."

Reyna raised her hands helplessly. "There's no cell reception out here, so I can't call her phone and hope it will vibrate to get her attention."

An engine roared to our left, and we turned to see Erika racing into the lot. I was no expert on motorcycles, but she seemed to be going much too fast. Sure enough, she overshot the parking space. She braked hard—*SCREECH!*—but she was unable to stop in time. Shrieks and screams joined the sound of the engine. Three of the women jumped out of the way in just the nick of time as Erika careened over the sidewalk. Her front tire slammed into the stone wall and her rear tire bucked up before the bike bounced a few inches backward.

"Holy crap!" Lexi cried. She rushed over to Erika. "Are you all right?"

"I'm fine!" Erika snarled as the rest of us gathered around. She slid off her bike, removed her helmet, and looked down at her front fender, which bore gouges and scratches from the rough stones. "My fender's another story." She was lucky the impact hadn't popped her tire or mangled her fender bad enough to prevent her from riding.

Reyna was nearly purple with rage. She pointed her finger in Erika's face. "You're damn lucky everyone got out of your way in time! That was the last straw. You're out of the Curves!"

I'd expected Erika to argue with Reyna, maybe even call the older woman a name. What I hadn't expected was for Erika to burst into tears. Nobody else seemed to have expected it, either. They cast glances at one another while

Erika buried her face in her hands and sobbed. No one offered her consolation. They were more concerned with Gerri's whereabouts.

Reyna put her palm on Erika's forehead and forced her to look up. "Where's Gerri?"

Erika looked out at the parkway and wiped her nose on her sleeve, sniffling. "She was right behind me." She paused a moment before adding, "Last time I checked."

Reyna seethed. "When was the last time you checked?"

Erika looked down at her boots. "Last time we stopped, I guess."

Reyna's hands fisted at her sides and she rose up on her toes, as if having to fight to keep from throttling the reckless young woman. "We're supposed to watch out for each other!"

Erika began blubbering again. We left her and walked to the other side of the parking lot. With the parkway being curvy and lined with woods, we could only see a short way back the way we'd come, a tenth of a mile at most. We waited for five minutes, then ten, then fifteen, anxiously staring down the road, our ears straining to catch the sound of a motorcycle engine. When an engine sounded far off, Daisy said, "That sounds like her Harley!"

Our relief was short-lived when the motorcycle came into view. It was a Harley similar to Gerri's, but it was solid black and ridden by a man with a beer belly resting on his thighs. Reyna tried the radio again, but still got nothing.

Brynn asked, "Could she have run out of gas?"

"No," Reyna said. "We all had full tanks. We filled up at the end of our ride yesterday."

I pointed to the small visitor center that housed a gift

shop and bathrooms. If something bad had befallen Gerri, the staff might have heard something. Surely, they'd have a landline telephone. "Should we go inside and see if they can help?"

Reyna said, "Good idea."

Everyone followed us into the small building, including the still-sniffling Erika, crowding the space. Reyna stepped up to the counter. "Our sweep rider hasn't shown up."

The female clerk winced. "That doesn't sound good."

Reyna said, "Have you heard of any problems on the parkway?"

"No," the woman said, "but news travels slow out here sometimes."

"Can you put us in touch with law enforcement?"

"Of course."

The woman turned her desktop phone around on the counter so Reyna could use it to dial 9-1-1. Reyna explained the situation to the dispatcher. She listened for a moment before thanking them and hanging up the phone. "A tree came down a mile back. They've got officers en route."

Erika looked at me, her expression chagrined. *Looks like this 'nag' was right about the rain bringing trees down.* I turned my attention back to Reyna. "Was anyone hurt?"

"There's no reports of injuries." The ladies murmured in relief, but Reyna wasn't so quick to join in. "If Gerri's stuck behind a fallen tree and she's not hurt," Reyna said, "she would have tried to reach us by radio. She'd know we'd be worried when she didn't show up here." She raised the radio to her lips and again attempted to contact their friend. "Gerri? You there?" She released the button and listened for a response. Once again, none came.

Bessie's eyes shined bright with worry. "What do we do now?"

Reyna waved for the women to follow her. "We ride back, look for her."

It was the only option we had, really. We climbed back onto the motorcycles.

Erika bit her lip and addressed Reyna. "Can I ride with y'all to look for Gerri?"

Reyna exhaled sharply, but acquiesced. "Just know this is your last ride with the Curves."

Erika nodded, fresh tears welling up in her eyes.

We returned to the road, heading back the way we'd come. Erika road at the back, following at a distance. It didn't take long before we found ourselves at a standstill behind a long line of cars filled with fellow leaf peepers. When the drivers realized the road was blocked, many of them performed three-point turns on the two-lane roadway, reversing course and driving past us to head back in the direction of Craggy Gardens. As the line shortened, we were able to move forward. When we neared the fallen tree, orange warning signs and cones blocked our progress. The sound of chainsaws filled our ears and the smell of fresh-cut wood filled our noses. Reyna climbed off her motorcycle and walked to the edge of the roadway, attempting to see what lay on the other side of the fallen tree. But whatever she could see, it wasn't Gerri. She turned back to the group and shook her head.

There was no use trying to reach Gerri by radio again. We'd never be able to hear over the sounds of the saws. All of us pulled out our phones. None had service. No surprise there. Without reception, the ladies couldn't even send Gerri a text.

Though it took only a matter of minutes for the road crew to clear the fallen tree, it felt like hours. Eventually, a man in a hardhat waved us through. The ladies started their engines and rode in formation, slowing near each scenic turnout to see if Gerri might be there waiting. She wasn't. *Could something have gone wrong with her motorcycle?* Maybe she'd broken down. But an engine failure wouldn't explain why she hadn't used the radio to contact Reyna. *Could she have lost the radio along the way? Had it fallen from her belt without her realizing?* I kept an eye out for the bright yellow radio along the road, but saw nothing.

When we'd backtracked ten miles or so, Reyna pulled over and tried the radio again. Still no luck. I had a single bar on my cell phone now, and dialed the lodge in the hopes that she might have left a message on the landline's voice-mail. No such luck.

We rode back to the lodge, hoping to find Gerri there, but she was still AWOL. While Reyna and I called law enforcement and local hospitals to see if Gerri might have been in an accident or suffered a sudden health problem, Daisy rounded up Dahlia and Katie. They were shocked to hear that their club's matriarch had gone missing. The Dangerous Curves convened in the great room to determine their next course of action.

Reyna looked around the group. "Gerri's not in the hospital, and law enforcement says there's been no reports of any accidents along the parkway involving motorcycles. They said there's no point trying to ping her phone out there. Cell service is so spotty, they can't triangulate in the mountains."

Katie wrapped her arms around herself in an instinctual self-calming action, grimacing when the motion seemed to cause pain in her injured wrist. "What should we do? It seems wrong to just sit here and wait to see if she shows up."

As much as I hated to say it, it seemed that only one possibility remained. "What if she went off the road and nobody saw it happen? It would explain why she's not in the hospital and why law enforcement doesn't have any reports of a motorcycle accident." It would also explain why she wasn't responding to Reyna's attempts to contact her via the handheld radios. There were many spots along the road where she could have veered off into the woods and be difficult to spot among the trees. There were also places where she could have run off the road and plummeted down the side of a cliff, though I wasn't about to mention that horrific possibility.

Bessie cuddled Shotgun to her chest, clearly using her dog for comfort the same as I often did with Yeti. "Should we retrace our steps again?"

"Yes," Reyna said. "Everyone keep an eye on the woods and look for debris on the roadside, anything that would indicate a motorcycle crashed there."

I had what I hoped might be a good idea. "I could take someone in my car with me. If one of you continuously speaks through the radio, we could listen for it." If Gerri were lying on the side of a cliff out of sight of the road, the radio chatter might be the only way to find her.

Brynn pulled her purse from the drawer. "Let's take my Prius. It's a hybrid so it's quiet. We'd have a better chance of hearing the radio."

"Smart thinking, Brynn." I gave her a soft, grateful smile.

We strategized and decided to drive stretches of the parkway between the last turnout where everyone had seen

Gerri and the Craggy Gardens overlook. Odds were, if she had indeed gone off the road, it had happened somewhere along that stretch. While Dahlia agreed to remain at the lodge in case Gerri returned or a call came in, Katie asked if she could ride along with Brynn and me.

"Of course," Brynn and I said in unison.

We climbed into Brynn's Prius. The car bore the soft scent of the sage Brynn was fond of. She'd recently smudged the lodge with the stuff to clear it of bad juju. I wasn't sure what to make of her Wiccan practices, but the idea of a female deity—the Goddess—was intriguing, along with the fact that Wiccan rituals were often tied to nature's rhythms. I, too, found spiritual comfort in the natural world, which was one of the many reasons I'd moved to the mountains.

We drove to the last scenic stop before Craggy Gardens. I rode in Brynn's passenger seat and Katie rode in the back on the driver's side, both of us keeping a close eye on the roadside on either side of the vehicle. We saw no skid marks, broken motorcycle parts, or spots where the ground had been clearly disturbed, nothing that would indicate a bike wreck had occurred. Reyna remained at the turnout with the radio, while the Curves rode ahead of the Prius toward Craggy Gardens. We stayed far enough back that we'd be able to hear the radio over their engine noise.

Luckily, with it being late afternoon and midweek, traffic on the Blue Ridge Parkway was light. We rolled slowly along, nearing the spot where the tree had come down. The only sound was our stomachs growling. None of us had eaten lunch, and our tummies were letting us know they were none too happy about it.

We were rounding a tight turn when a faint, disembodied

voice off the to the left caught our attention. It was Reyna, calling, "Dangerous Curves search team, do you hear me? Hello, search team! Can you hear me?"

Brynn pushed the button to activate her car's warning lights and veered across the southbound lane, which was thankfully empty, to park on what little shoulder there was. She'd had to pull so close to the trees that neither she nor Katie could open their doors. Instead, they climbed out on the passenger side with me.

Reyna's voice came again, louder now that we were out of the car and didn't have the tire sound impeding our hearing. "Search team, can you hear me?"

We looked around frantically.

"There!" Katie shouted, pointing.

The yellow radio lay a few feet away atop a bed of last year's fallen leaves. Katie instinctively held her hurt wrist curled up in front of her to protect it, rushed forward, and scooped up the radio. She pushed the talk button with her thumb and responded to Reyna. "We found Gerri's radio!" She gave them the number of the mile marker we'd just passed so they'd know where we were.

Reyna's voice came back. "We're at the visitors' center. We'll use their phone to call for help and then be on our way."

Anxiety clogged my throat and I had to gulp to force it down. I took the radio from Katie and said, "Stay there. There's not a safe place for all of you to pull off the road here."

Reyna hesitated a moment. She probably didn't like being told to stay away but, at the same time, she must've realized it made more sense for them to remain where they were. "Okay. But stay in touch. We want to know what's happening there."

"I will." I slid the radio into the breast pocket of my shirt.

Brynn and I exchanged an anxious glance and continued a few steps farther into the woods.

It was Brynn's turn to point this time. "There's her motorcycle!"

The black and blue Harley lay crumpled on its right side at the base of a tree, surrounded by broken bits of metal, plastic, and glass. My eyes moved along the ground, tracing the path of destruction to its inevitable conclusion. Gerri lay a few feet farther back, at the base of another tree. Momentum must have carried her over the handlebars of her bike and through the air. She lay on her belly, arms crooked above her shoulders, her head turned to the left.

At the sight of her motionless body, my hands reflexively covered my mouth. "Oh no!" Once I could gather my wits, I hurried forward, slipping and sliding on the leaf-covered slope.

Brynn and Katie were right behind me. I bent down to take a look. With Gerri wearing a helmet and fully decked out in riding gear, including gloves, it was impossible to tell what condition she was in. I saw no blood, but that didn't mean she hadn't been horribly hurt. At best, she seemed to have been knocked unconscious. But she'd been lying here for hours. Things didn't look good. I reached out and lay a tentative hand on her shoulder. "Gerri?"

No response. Lest we exacerbate internal injuries she might have suffered, we didn't dare try to roll her over or move her. While Brynn checked her wrist and neck for a pulse, I lowered my face to the ground and looked through the cracked plate of her helmet. Her eyes were closed, as if she were dozing. My gaze moved just a few inches higher and saw that her helmet bore signs of a horrific impact, a roundish dent surrounded by a web of thin cracks. No doubt she'd been thrown headfirst into the tree and suffered a severe brain injury.

Brynn sat back on her heels and shook her head. "No pulse."

I turned to look at the two of them. "Her helmet is shattered in front, too."

At least she'd gone fast. As they say, she'd probably never known what hit her or, in this case, what she'd hit—a yellow birch tree, seemingly aglow with its golden leaves as if to tell us Gerri had ascended to heaven now.

Katie fell to her knees on the forest floor and put a hand over her mouth to stifle her sobs. Though she might be the newest member of their group, seeing their matriarch like this had to be shocking and horrifying. Still kneeling, Brynn eased over and put an arm around Katie's shoulders. "Let's get you back to my car so you can sit down." She helped the young woman to stand.

I stood, too, though I planned to stay by Gerri's body. Dead or not, it seemed wrong to leave her here in the woods all alone. I turned back and watched Brynn and Katie pick their way through the woods to the road. Once they were out of sight, my gaze moved to Gerri's motorcycle. Though the front was smashed and the sides were dented and scuffed, as if she'd ping-ponged among the trees before hitting the one where the bike lay, the back fender was essentially intact. It made sense in light of the fact that, with the motorcycle in motion, the primary point of impact would have been the front of the bike. Oddly, though, there was a shallow, narrow dent spanning the fender. The dent was accentuated by a streak of silver across the blue paint. *How did that dent get there?*

Rather than try to stand on the slippery slope, I crawled back to the bike. I glanced around for something metal that the back fender might somehow have hit, something that could have left the silver stripe. All I saw was the brown and gray bark of trees, the brown decomposing leaves, and patches of orangish-brown dirt. There was no guard-rail on this stretch of road, either, or Gerri never would have ended up in these trees. She'd have crashed on the pavement.

I took out my phone, snapped several photos of the fender from different angles, and sat back to think. As I did, a sick feeling slithered into my gut.

Erika's Suzuki is silver. She'd arrived at the Craggy Gardens overlook minutes after the others—minutes she hadn't accounted for. She'd been riding much too fast when she'd turned into the parking lot, too. She was an experienced rider. She should've known better. *Had she been trying to put distance between herself and Gerri's body?* Maybe she'd even crashed into the stone wall on purpose, to hide evidence of a collision with another motorcycle. Maybe she'd bumped Gerri's bike and sent the woman and her bike reeling. It seemed a plausible theory, yet a critical question remained. *If Erika bumped Gerri's motorcycle with her own, had it been an accident or on purpose? Were we dealing with manslaughter or murder?*

CHAPTER 11

Misty

Fifteen minutes later, Brynn led a seasoned Buncombe County deputy sheriff through the woods to Gerri's body. In the interim, I'd whispered to Gerri, vowing to do everything in my power to find out what had happened to her and ensure justice was done. She'd brought her motorcycle club up to my lodge, trusted me to take care of them. I owed it to her, to all of them.

On seeing the body, the deputy took off his hat as if in reverence, revealing a bald head. The skin on his head furrowed as he bent down and put two fingers to Gerri's neck. I noticed that his name badge read Gillespie.

After a few seconds, he looked up at me and Brynn. "I don't feel a pulse. 'Course, it's the medical examiner's office who makes the final determination."

He stood, pulled out a small notepad and pen, and asked us a series of questions. What road conditions had been like earlier in the day when Gerri had disappeared; how experienced a rider Gerri was; whether we'd seen anyone driving recklessly on the parkway. We answered the best we could.

"Other than Katie and Dahlia," I said, "the rest of the women in the motorcycle club are waiting at the Craggy Gardens Visitors Center. There's a woman with purple hair named Erika. She rides a silver Suzuki Katana. When we were taking our ride earlier, she was late showing up to the Craggy Gardens. Everyone but her and Gerri had arrived minutes before." I explained how she'd raced into the parking lot several minutes after the rest of the group and slammed her front tire into the stone wall.

His eyes sparked with interest. "Are you saying you think she might have damaged her bike on purpose? To hide evidence of a collision?"

I exhaled a shaky breath. "I don't know what to think, but it seems like a possibility. Gerri admonished Erika a couple of days ago for riding recklessly, and she grabbed Erika's arm earlier today to keep her from throwing a metal water bottle." I filled him in on the details. "Erika doesn't like to be told what to do."

Brynn's head bobbed as I spoke, and when I finished he summed Erika up in four words. "She's a loose cannon."

I nodded in agreement. "She hasn't accounted for why she was late, either. The group was more concerned about Gerri's whereabouts." I motioned for him to follow me over to Gerri's bike. I pointed to the long dent on the back fender. "See? That looks like silver paint."

He crouched down and took a closer look. "Could be. Could be just that the paint came off and the metal is showing through. But the whole bike is a shambles. Hard to say when the damage might have happened. A part that came loose from the bike might have scratched the fender." He stood and pointed at the trail of engine parts and motorcycle pieces behind the bike. "There's several pieces of chrome that could've caused the dent and the silver coloration."

He could be right, of course. He had much more experience in criminal investigation than I did, but my gut told me the damage to her back fender was no accident.

"There's someone else," I told him. "A guy named Todd. He's the ex-husband of one of the riders, a woman named Lexi. Their divorce was just finalized on Monday. She says her ex didn't show up for the hearing. The judge awarded her a Vulcan motorcycle, but it's still in her husband's name." I told him how an officer in McDowell County had impounded the bike the day before. "Her ex has the bike now. He rode up when we were stopped at an overlook about an hour ago and harassed her."

"A Vulcan, huh?" he said. "Any chance either of you know the license plate number?" He looked from one of us to the other. Both Brynn and I shook our heads.

"I can radio the women and see if I can get it for you." I pulled out the radio and contacted Reyna again. "Can you ask Lexi for the license plate number on her Vulcan?"

Reyna's voice came back through the radio. "Sure."

There was a moment of silence before Lexi's voice traveled over the airwaves, providing the number. "Is law enforcement going after Todd?" she asked.

The sheriff gestured for me to hand him the radio. He pressed the talk button and, after identifying himself, said,

"I'll put out a be-on-the-lookout. If anyone sees him, they'll detain him for questioning. You got a phone number for him?"

Lexi came back with a sigh. "Not anymore. Our mobile account was in my name so I had his service turned off a couple of days ago."

In other words, there'd be no way to reach Todd by phone, even if he happened to be in a place with cell service.

The deputy handed the walkie-talkie to me and proceeded to use his own radio to contact dispatch. "Get me a BOLO on a Kawasaki Vulcan motorcycle." He rattled off the license plate number. When the dispatcher came back asking for a description, he looked to me for an answer.

"Turquoise and white," I said.

He returned his radio to his belt and cast a glance back at the road. "The fact that there are no skid marks on the pavement tells me that Ms. Burnham didn't even try to brake. If I had to hazard a guess, I'd say the most likely scenario is that she swerved to miss a deer or some type of little varmint and inadvertently veered into the woods. Happens frequently out here, especially this time of year. Hell, she might've even come upon a bear." He pointed to a pile of scat a few feet away. It was filled with half-digested nuts and berries. "See? There's bears all over these woods."

He made a valid point about deer. They were pretty creatures, but their instincts were sorely lacking when it came to avoiding cars and roadways. Bears seemed to have a little more sense in that regard, though collisions with bears weren't entirely unheard of, either. "Motorcycles are much louder than cars," I pointed out. "They can be heard from a long way off. Wouldn't they be more likely to scare a bear away than a car?"

"Could be." He was quiet for a moment as he ran his gaze over my tight face, assessing. "Don't you worry, Ms. Murphy. I've only been thinking out loud here. I'm far from reaching any firm conclusions yet. We've got the BOLO out on the Vulcan. I'm gonna take a close look at the road up there and the bike Erika was riding, see what her friends have to say about her and what she's got to say for herself. Okey dokey?"

I exhaled in relief, feeling a little embarrassed that I'd insinuated he wasn't taking the investigation seriously enough by suggesting Gerri had swerved to avoid an animal. "Thanks, Deputy."

He pulled out his cell phone and snapped several photos of Gerri's bike and the trail of debris it had left in its wake as she careened toward her death.

When he finished, we returned to the roadside. Brynn and I slid back into the car with Katie. Her eyes were rimmed in pink and wet with tears. Her voice was soft, and broke when she spoke. "What are they going to do with Gerri?"

Brynn retrieved a fast-food napkin from the console of her car and handed it to Katie in the back seat so the girl could wipe her tears. "The medical examiner is on their way. They'll take care of things."

While we waited for someone from the M.E.'s office to arrive, I radioed Reyna and gave her an update to share with the group. Meanwhile, Deputy Gillespie walked slowly up and down both sides of the road, scouring the area for any debris that might indicate a collision had taken place on this stretch. He bent down a couple of times to pick things up, but when he returned all he'd found were a twist-off bottle top, a pair of mangled sunglasses, a metal tire gauge, and a single men's sneaker, nothing that appeared at all connected with what had happened to Gerri. Nonetheless, he slipped them into clear plastic evidence bags and stashed them in the trunk of his cruiser.

A vehicle pulled up behind us, a flashing light atop the roof. Although the car was white instead of black, it was clearly a hearse. Two male workers in scrubs emerged and spoke to the deputy. He pointed into the woods. While the new arrivals went to retrieve Gerri's body, Deputy Gillespie came to the window of Brynn's car. She rolled it down.

"Stick around." The deputy angled his head to indicate the staff from the M.E.'s office. "They'll want a statement from the three of you once they're done."

We waited while the medical professionals tended to Gerri's body down below. They returned a few minutes later carrying a stretcher covered in a white sheet. The lump underneath was a once-vibrant woman who should have had many more years ahead of her. The sheet shifted as they slid her into the back of the hearse, and I caught a final glimpse of her lace-up biker boot. Emotion closed my throat. *This is where the road stops for her. The club's ride or die has died.*

The M.E. staff asked us just a few simple questions. The first was, "How did you find the body?"

I cleared my throat—*ahem*—and explained how we'd cruised slowly down the parkway, listening, as Reyna spoke through the other radio unit. "When we heard Reyna's voice, we pulled over."

"Did Ms. Burnham have any health issues that you're aware of?"

I looked to Katie.

Katie raised her shoulders. "She never mentioned anything to me. Reyna would probably know."

The deputy chimed in, noting that he planned to follow up with the riders waiting at the Craggy Gardens visitors center. "I'll ask the other ladies about Ms. Burnham's medical history and let you know what I find out." Turning to other matters, he asked, "Any property on the body?"

One of the men handed him a clear plastic bag that contained a wallet and a cell phone. With that, they climbed back into the hearse and left, taking Gerri's body with them.

The deputy radioed for backup, stashed Gerri's property in his cruiser, and retrieved a roll of yellow cordon tape from his trunk. He tied the loose end of the tape to a tree just ahead of Brynn's car. He unspooled the tape as he walked back thirty feet or so, slowing once to circumnavigate a tree so that the tape would be held taut. Once he was satisfied he'd blocked off all of the relevant area, he used his teeth to tear through the tape and tied off that end, as well.

A few minutes later, flashing lights once again came up the parkway. This time, it was another patrol car from the Buncombe County Sheriff's Department. Once the cruiser pulled to the side, Deputy Gillespie stepped over to the window to speak to the other officer. With the windows down on Brynn's Prius, we could hear their conversation.

"Keep an eye on this area," he said. "It could be a crime scene."

Katie sat bolt upright in the back seat and leaned forward

to stick her head between us. "Did he say 'crime scene'? I thought Gerri's crash was an accident."

Brynn and I exchanged a glance. Katie had been back at the lodge when Erika drove her motorcycle into the wall at the lookout, and she'd been sitting in the car when I'd shared my suspicions with the deputy. I wondered if any of the ladies waiting for us had become suspicious of Erika. I didn't want to be the one to point a finger at my guest. Neither did Brynn, apparently, as she said nothing. Finally, I said, "The deputy said it *could* be a crime scene, not that it definitely is one. He probably can't make a firm conclusion until he's taken everything into consideration, like Gerri's medical history and all of that."

"Oh." Katie sat back in her seat, dabbing at her eyes with the napkin. "That makes sense, I guess."

Deputy Gillespie followed us in his cruiser as we made our way to Craggy Gardens. There, I introduced him to Reyna. Like all of the others in the group, she looked shocked, her face streaked with tears.

"Sorry about your friend." The deputy dipped his chin in solemn reverence to the new matriarch of the Dangerous Curves, but got right down to business. "The medical examiner's office has asked me to gather more information. Can you tell me if Ms. Burnham had any health problems that could have contributed to her accident? She ever had a heart attack or stroke? High blood pressure? Or low blood pressure, maybe?"

"No," Reyna said. "She's never had a heart attack or stroke. We see each other regularly. I would've known. Far as I know, her blood pressure has been fine, too. She takes calcium for osteoporosis, but that's the only heath problem she's ever mentioned to me."

His gaze roamed over the group. "Did anyone notice whether Ms. Burnham's motorcycle had any pre-existing damage when y'all headed out this morning? I'm talking anything big, but also just minor dings and scrapes."

Reyna shook her head vehemently. "Gerri kept that bike in mint condition. She trailered it up to the lodge and stored it back in the trailer overnight. If that bike got so much as a smushed gnat on the windshield, she'd clean it off immediately."

The other ladies agreed. Bessie said, "That bike was her baby."

The deputy motioned for Reyna to follow him to a spot a hundred feet or so away, where they could speak privately. As a sign of respect, I turned to look in the other direction. I noticed Katie watching the two, though. Erika also kept an eye on them. As she stared, she gnawed her thumb like she was a coyote with its leg caught in a steel-jaw trap.

After a few minutes, Deputy Gillespie returned and addressed Erika. "Let's take a look at your motorcycle."

Erika's eyes flashed, but was it in alarm or mere surprise? "You want to see my motorcycle? Why?"

"So, I can clear you," the deputy said matter-of-factly. "It's routine to take a close look at the last person to see someone alive when there's been a potentially suspicious death."

"Suspicious death?" Her face contorted with emotion and her eyes went wide. "You think somebody killed Gerri *on purpose*?" Her voice rose several octaves. "And you think that person might be *me*?"

He held up his palms. "Let's not get ahead of ourselves here. At this point, I'm just gathering information."

She snapped her mouth shut, and her jaw flexed as if she was biting back words she wanted to spew. She was uncharacteristically quiet as she led him to her motorcycle. He bent down to inspect her front fender. After taking a look, he snapped several photos with his phone. He questioned her for several minutes. At one point, she raised a hand and circled it in front of her face. *I wonder what that's about.* He extended a hand and she gave him her helmet. He held it in both hands, the faceplate turned upward. He turned the helmet to and fro in the waning sunlight, seeming to be examining it. He snapped a photo of the helmet, as well, before handing it back to her. He leaned in and took a close look at her clothing. Spotting something on her shoulder, he snapped another photo. He said something else, and Erika led him over to show him the spot where she'd crashed into the stone wall. As my gaze followed him, I spotted something on the stone I hadn't noticed earlier. A streak of silver paint where her fender had made impact. He crouched down before the wall and snapped several more pictures.

The other ladies began to whisper among themselves.

Bessie leaned toward Daisy. "Does he think Erika ran Gerri off the road?"

"Maybe," Daisy said softly. "Do *you* think Erika ran Gerri off the road?"

"I don't know what to think," Bessie admitted.

"Me neither," said Daisy. The rest of the group concurred. All of them seemed to think Erika might be capable of such a horrible, impulsive act. They just weren't sure whether she'd actually done it.

Evidently, Deputy Gillespie was just as indecisive. He dismissed Erika, and she headed our way. The ladies all straightened up and tried to look innocent, as if we hadn't just been talking about her.

Erika wasn't fooled. She stopped in front of the group. "I know what you all think of me. That I'm a reckless, out-of-control loudmouth." She paused for a moment, as if expecting someone to deny it, to try to spare her feelings. But things had moved well beyond that now. "But I didn't hurt Gerri. I'd never do that! I didn't like when she told me what to do, but at least it meant she gave a crap. She was like a mother to me. I feel bad for giving her such a hard time." She burst into fresh sobs, crooking her arm and raising it to cry into her elbow. A few seconds later, she lifted her face. "The reason I was late to the lookout was because a bird dropped a load on my helmet. I could hardly see with the white poop all over my faceplate. I had to pull over and clean it off." She pointed to a smudge on her shoulder. "See? That's bird poo, too."

We all closed in to take a look. Sure enough, there was a whitish smudge on her jacket, too. But was it thick enough to be bird excrement? It was nearly translucent. Of course, if she had cleaned her helmet, she might have attempted to clean her jacket, too. What remained might only be a thin remnant. Then again, maybe Erika had concocted a lie about bird droppings after Reyna mentioned that Gerri wouldn't abide so much as a smashed gnat on the windshield of her motorcycle.

Reyna turned to me and Brynn. "Could that be what caused Gerri to crash? Was there bird stuff on her helmet?"

"I didn't notice any," I said, "but I could only see one side of her face."

Bessie said, "Maybe she drifted off the road when she was trying to wipe it off."

Daisy offered another possibility. "She could've been blinded by a leaf. A couple of them blew up against my chest as we were riding."

It was a plausible theory. Though the leaves had yet to begin falling en masse, an errant leaf came down here and there. If a large one had come down at just the right moment and stuck to Gerri's faceplate, she could have been blinded. The leaf could have been knocked off the faceplate once she'd crashed, been thrown from her motorcycle, and slid across the forest floor.

The deputy called the other women over, one at a time, and spoke with each of them privately, too. When he was done, he asked Reyna, "Do you know how I can reach Ms. Burnham's next of kin?"

Reyna looked lost for a moment. "She's a widow, and she doesn't have any kids . . . I suppose her next of kin would be her stepson?"

Sterling Burnham. My heart sank. The selfish guy probably wouldn't shed a single tear on learning that Gerri had died. Never mind that his father had loved the woman. I could just picture the entitled, spoiled Sterling sitting there in the lodge, polishing his golf clubs . . .

Oh, my gosh! His golf clubs! Could the silver dent on the back of Gerri's bike have been caused by one of Sterling's clubs?

Reyna continued to inform the deputy. "Her stepson's name is Sterling Burnham, but I don't know how to get in touch with him. He's from Raleigh, but he came up to the mountains this week, too."

I joined the conversation. "Sterling and Gerri had a heated conversation at my lodge yesterday afternoon." I gave Deputy Gillespie the rundown. "Before Gerri and the other ladies arrived back at the lodge, he and his wife and mother had waited at my lodge for an hour or so. They'd been at the Beech Mountain Club. The women had played tennis while Sterling played a round of golf. When they were waiting at my lodge, Sterling brought his golf clubs inside and cleaned them."

The deputy stared at me a moment, processing my words, then gave me a small nod to indicate he understood what I was implying—that a golf club could have left the silver streak on Gerri's rear fender.

I gestured to the deputy's cruiser. "I know that Sterling called Gerri on her cell phone Monday night. If he isn't listed in her contacts, you should be able to get his number from the list of recent calls."

Deputy Gillespie returned to his cruiser and retrieved Gerri's cell phone. He powered it on but the screen requested a passcode. He eyed Reyna. "Any chance you know her passcode?"

"No," Reyna said, "but I might be able to guess. Try zero-five-two-three, that's her birthday, May twenty-third."

He tapped the numbers into the screen and shook his head. "That's not it."

"Her husband's birthday was November thirteenth. Try one-one-one-three."

Again, the code failed.

Reyna said, "She and Norman were married on April second. Maybe that's it."

The deputy said the numbers aloud as he tapped them

on the screen. "Zero-four-zero-two. That worked. I'm in."
He went to her contact list and apparently found Sterling
Burnham. He gave me a nod. "He's in here. Thanks." The
deputy turned back to Erika. "You okay with letting me remove your front fender? I assume it's going to have to be
replaced anyway."

Uh-oh. Is he taking her fender into evidence?

Erika opened her mouth as if to argue. Being contrary
seemed to be an automatic response for her. But then she
seemed to think better of it. "Okay," she said hesitantly,
"but I don't have any tools to get it off."

"No problem," the officer said. "I carry a toolbox in my
trunk." He pulled a key fob from his pocket and pressed a
button. The trunk of his cruiser popped open. He rounded
the car and reached into the trunk to remove a red metal
toolbox. He carried the toolbox over to Erika's motorcycle, donned a pair of blue latex gloves, and proceeded to
use some type of wrench to remove the damaged fender.
Once he had, he carried it over to his cruiser and placed it
in his trunk, along with the toolbox. He turned to address
the group. "I'll be in touch." With a final dip of his head in
goodbye, he climbed into his cruiser and drove out onto the
road, heading back toward the accident scene.

Reyna's lip trembled as she turned to Kris. "Why don't
you ride sweep?"

Kris nodded.

The ladies put on their helmets, climbed on their motorcycles, and started their somber procession out of the
parking lot. Erika glanced back before heading out onto
the parkway, but she'd never see Gerri behind her again.
Kris followed her onto the road, and Brynn drove behind

the line of bikes, leaving plenty of space between the motor-cycles and her Prius for safety.

We rode for a few minutes in silence. Flashing lights gave us a grim greeting as we approached the spot where Gerri had driven off the road. Her broken bike was being loaded onto a flatbed tow truck. Deputy Gillespie stood beside the truck. He raised a hand in acknowledgment as the Curves rode slowly by. Once we'd passed him, I cut my gaze to the side mirror of Brynn's car. In the reflection, I saw him step over and yank on the cordon tape, pulling the end from the tree. How long would it be until we knew whether the site had been the location of a horrific accident or a murder? Would a killer be staying under the roof of my lodge to-night?

CHAPTER 12

Misty

Katie leaned her head against the window in the back seat, sniffling occasionally and staring out the window with red-rimmed eyes. Her vacant expression made me wonder if she was actually seeing anything at all. The question was answered when a white van with chrome bumpers passed us heading in the other direction, and she sat bolt upright and gasped. She turned so quickly to look after the van that she smacked her forehead on the window.

In light of her reaction, I looked after the van, too. I could see that the back bumper bore the standard North Carolina license plate that had the words "First in Flight" superimposed in red over a blue image of the historic plane the Wright Brothers had flown at Kitty Hawk, North Carolina, all those years ago. Because the Wright Brothers had invented their aircraft in Dayton, the state of Ohio touted itself as the "Birthplace of Aviation." I'd even heard that Ohio had issued thousands of license plates with an image of a banner mistakenly attached to the front of the

Wright brothers' plane rather than the rear. It was an easy mistake to make. The plane was oddly shaped. That hadn't stopped the North Carolina Department of Transportation from lightheartedly trolling the Ohio DMV on social media, though, stating that Ohioans wouldn't be familiar with the plane because *"they weren't there."*

Katie's hand went to her chest as she exhaled in relief.

Still turned around in my seat, I eyed her closely. "Are you okay, Katie?"

She swallowed hard before speaking, but when she spoke, she didn't meet my gaze. "Yes. I thought I saw someone I knew, but it wasn't him, after all."

"Who?" Brynn asked, eyeing Katie in the rearview mirror.

I'd been curious, too, but I thought it would be rude to ask since Katie hadn't offered the information. Brynn could be blunt, but that bluntness often came in handy. If this information could have anything to do with what happened to Gerri, we needed to know it.

Katie rested her head against the back of the seat and closed her eyes. "Just an old boyfriend."

Was it a coincidence that a white van had driven through my parking lot in the early morning hours yesterday, and that Katie had been startled to see a white van here on the parkway? I supposed it only mattered if the old boyfriend was from Mississippi, like the plates I'd seen on the van at the lodge. I fished for information. "An old boyfriend from Raleigh?" I asked. "Or from somewhere else?"

Her head came off the back of the seat, her eyes popping open at the same time. They gleamed as she looked at me. But was that fright in them, or just the remnants of her tears? "Raleigh," she said, a little too emphatically, as if speaking the word loudly and clearly would be more convincing.

Hmm . . .

Brynn again eyed the young woman in her rearview mirror. "You gasped. Are you afraid of the guy?"

"No-no-no!" Katie insisted, raising her hands defensively. "He was a deadbeat, but he wasn't abusive. It just surprised me is all. My mind was on Gerri and I overreacted. I guess I'm on edge."

It was understandable, I supposed. My nerves felt raw and frayed, too. Still, her reaction had seemed to be more one of panic than surprise. Despite her protestations, I couldn't help but think she'd left a bad relationship behind. My maternal instincts took hold again. I turned, reached over the seat, and patted her knee. I wished I could offer more to the disconsolate young woman, but a pat was all I had at the moment.

We arrived back at the lodge, a solemn and somber bunch. By then, it was dinnertime, though none of the ladies seemed interested in venturing out again. They gathered in the great room to mourn their friend together. As I got the fireplace going, the women shared both tears and tales about Gerri from over the years.

Reyna said, "I've lost count, but Gerri and I must've taken two hundred rides together. Maybe more." She gulped to swallow her emotions. "I never expected today to be our last."

As the ladies grieved, Brynn rounded up a cedar smudge stick, held it in the flames of the fire to light it, and waved it around the space, holding a bowl underneath to catch the ash that fell. The aroma was clean and had a calming effect.

Dahlia lifted her nose to the air. "What is that scent?"

"Cedar," Brynn said. "It banishes fear and gives courage."

Reyna said, "I could use some courage right now. I don't know how we'll go on without Gerri." She closed her eyes and inhaled deeply.

Brynn continued around the room. "Wiccans believe that when a person passes on they go to the Summerland. It's a place of eternal sunshine and peace, with green fields and flowers."

I wasn't sure how I felt about the Wiccan version of Paradise or Heaven. Summers were wonderful, but there was much to enjoy about the other seasons, too. After all, it was the gorgeous autumn colors that had brought these women to the mountain in the first place. My version of the afterlife would include all four seasons.

Bessie stroked her terrier's back. "Wherever Gerri is now, I hope that there are lots of fun roads to ride."

When Brynn finished smudging, she sneaked out quietly, reaching out to give me a supportive squeeze on the shoulder when she left.

Rocky returned from a handyman gig. He wore a smile as he and Molasses came through the front door. On seeing my troubled face, his eyes darkened. When I cut my eyes to the women, he looked their way and noticed them crying, wiping their eyes, one of them rubbing another's back to comfort her. Erika sat alone outside on the back deck in a self-imposed exile, staring up at the sky. The sun had begun to go down and the temperatures had dropped. *She has to be cold out there.* Was she imposing a penance on herself? If so, was it for Gerri's death?

Rocky strode quickly over to the desk and whispered, "What happened?"

I motioned for him to follow me out front where we could speak privately. Once the doors closed behind us, I filled him in on the day's events. Lexi's ex-husband, Todd, retrieving her motorcycle from the police impound lot and harassing her at the outlook. Erika arriving late, roaring into the lot, and crashing into the stone wall at the Craggy Gardens Visitors Center. Gerri failing to show up at the scenic turnout. Brynn, Katie, and I finding Gerri's body along the side of the Blue Ridge Parkway. The narrow, silver dent on Gerri's blue back fender. Deputy Gillespie taking Erika's front fender into evidence. My theory that a golf club could have caused the dent in Gerri's fender. The possibility that Gerri's death could be nothing more than an unfortunate accident, perhaps caused by an errant groundhog, deer, bear, or leaf.

Rocky heaved a deep breath. "That's a lot to process. And here I was, hoping you'd be telling me about all the fun you had today."

The doors to the diner opened across the parking lot, releasing the sounds of conversation and clinking silverware as well as the aroma of warm cornbread and vegetable stew, tonight's special. "I'll go get dinner for the ladies. They could use some comfort food." I pulled out my cell phone and rang the diner. When Patty answered, I asked, "Any chance you can fix me up with stew, cornbread, and blueberry pie for my guests?"

"It would be my pleasure," she said. "You planning to start serving dinner now, too?"

"Just for tonight. Something's happened."

"Uh-oh," she said on an anxious inhale. "Everything okay?"

"Not at all," I replied. "I'll be right over to explain."

Rocky and I went back into the lodge. While he took Molasses to his room, I informed the ladies that I'd return in a few minutes with dinner for them.

Reyna gave me a soft smile. "Thanks, Misty. You're a thoughtful hostess."

Providing them with supper seemed the least I could do. *If only I could also provide them with some answers . . .*

Rocky returned to the lobby and we walked over to the Greasy Griddle together. Patty ushered us to a booth in the back corner. She slid in after me, while Rocky took a seat on the other side of the table. She turned to me, her face drawn tight. "Tell me what's going on, Misty."

For the second time in a quarter hour, I found myself running through the events of the day. When I got to the part where we found Gerri's body, Patty crossed her hands over her heart. "No!" When she realized her patrons had looked her way in alarm, she clasped her hands atop the table and forced a stiff smile. "What happened?" she whispered.

"We can't be sure," I said. "The deputy seems to think it was most likely an accident."

"Wouldn't be the first," Patty said. "People crash on these mountain roads all the time. They drive too fast for the curves or conditions. They cross the center line sometimes, too. Maybe someone came at her from the other direction and drifted into her lane. Maybe she was trying to avoid a head-on collision and veered off the road."

I grimaced. "I'd hate to think someone could force her to swerve and not bother to stop and see if she was okay."

Rocky said, "Maybe they didn't even realize they'd forced her off the road. The driver could have been looking down at a cell phone."

Patty said, "True. Or maybe they rounded another curve and couldn't see what happened behind them. They might have just assumed she'd swerved back onto the road." She slid out of the booth and stood. "Whatever happened, I think we could all use something to calm our nerves."

She circled around the counter, bent down behind it for a moment or two, and returned to the booth with three steaming mugs in hand. They contained her delicious hot apple cider. But that wasn't all. Each mug held at least two fingers of bourbon, too. We sat in silence for a moment, sipping the hot brew, letting the liquor work its magic.

Patty draped a consoling arm over my shoulders. "I'm so sorry, Misty. This is heartbreaking all around. I know how hard you work to ensure your guests enjoy their stay."

It was true, I did work hard, and the vast majority of my guests went home with happy memories of their time in the mountains. I only wished the same could be said of the ladies in the motorcycle club.

As I took another sip of the spiked cider, my mind went back to another group of ladies, younger ones, the college girls with the wine at the lookout. The drunken redheaded birthday girl had called Gerri "grandma" in a sarcastic way, and the selfie stick she'd used had a metal telescoping handle. Might she have swung at Gerri with the selfie stick as they were driving down the parkway in the open convertible? It seemed farfetched. After all, we hadn't spotted the girls' car as we'd continued down the road. Even so, they might have pulled off the road to get gas or take a potty break, and we could have passed by them without noticing. They could have ended up behind us. Maybe the redhaired girl had been just playing around and swung the selfie stick, not truly intending to hit Gerri, but in her drunken stupor had accidentally hit Gerri's back fender and caused the motorcycle to veer out of control.

I raised the possibility to Patty and Rocky. "Do you think the birthday girl could have been responsible for the crash?"

Patty winced. "Could be. If so, that girl didn't just end Gerri's life, she ruined her own."

Rocky let out a long breath. "Young people do stupid things sometimes. Of course, they aren't alone. Older people do stupid things sometimes, too."

My head bobbed in agreement. "Things can get out of control before they realize what's happening."

How many movies or TV series were there that showed a bad situation snowballing, otherwise good people getting inadvertently sucked into horrible situations? Many came to mind, including *Breaking Bad*, *Good Girls*, and *The Flight Attendant*. Jack and I had watched all of those series together. Captivating stories, but not exactly happy feel-good material. But people could get ahead of themselves, too, just as the deputy noted when speaking with Erika at Craggy Gardens. Maybe that was exactly what I was doing here, jumping to conclusions. I took another sip of the hot cider, letting the warm liquid calm and soothe me.

Changing the subject, I raised my mug and asked, "How are your cider sales going?"

"Fantastic." She raised her right arm, made a fist, and flexed her muscle. "My biceps have never looked better and I've sold more than enough to cover the cost of the apple press."

I raised my mug again, this time in salute. "You're a smart businesswoman."

She lifted her mug in reply. "Takes one to know one."

CHAPTER 13

Misty

From outside came the buzz of an approaching motorcycle. I looked out the window to see Lexi's ex-husband turning into the parking lot on her Vulcan.

"That's him!" I pointed. "Lexi's husband!"

As Todd reached the front of the lodge, he braked, turned the handlebars in tight, and stuck out his left leg to perform a series of tight donuts on the asphalt. The Vulcan's back tire screeched as he circled, sending up a cloud of gray smoke and leaving dark circles of burnt rubber behind on the pavement. The breeze carried the acrid smell across the parking lot, and it seeped into the diner as two patrons opened the door to exit. Several people fanned their faces to clear the air of the burnt rubber stench and muttered about the "idiot," "showoff," or "crazy biker" in the lot.

A second later, Erika bolted out of the lodge with Lexi and Katie on her heels. Spotting the women in pursuit, Todd straightened the handlebars to ride out of the lot. But he was too late. Erika reached him and grabbed him from behind in a bear hug around the chest. Katie grabbed the handlebars to seize control of the bike. By the time the petite Lexi caught up to the two bigger women, Erika had dragged Todd off the bike and tossed him onto the pavement. Good thing he was wearing a helmet to protect his head or he might have gotten a concussion. Katie turned the motorcycle off. Though we could now hear the diner's patrons murmuring in surprise, we couldn't hear what Lexi said as her mouth flapped. It was an easy guess that she'd called Todd a few choice names. She pulled her leg back and kicked the man she'd once loved as hard as she could in the gut. He clutched his stomach and writhed on the pavement.

"Call the police!" Rocky shouted as he slid from the booth.

While he ran outside, Patty leaped from the booth, darted behind the counter, and grabbed the phone hanging on the wall behind it to summon law enforcement. I wriggled out of the booth and dashed after Rocky. By the time I reached him, he'd subdued the melee and was standing between the parties with his arms stretched out, palms raised, like some sort of sports referee. Lexi was bent over, hands on her knees, her chest heaving with emotion. Erika and Katie stood near the motorcycle they'd retrieved for their friend. They, too, appeared emotionally wrought, their faces slack, their cheeks stained with tears. Todd, wisely, had remained on the ground, though he was now curled up in the fetal position with his arms clutching his shins. He'd worn jeans with rips in them, and the skin on his knee bore a raw scrape from where Erika had tossed him to the asphalt. The girl was rough around the edges, but she'd make a good bouncer or bodyguard.

Patty soon hustled up to my side. "The police are on their way."

With the Beech Mountain Police Department headquarters located only a half mile up the road, it didn't take long before a cruiser with sirens wailing and lights flashing turned into the lot. Rocky waved an arm over his head, and the patrol car turned in his direction, braking to a stop a few feet away. The officer emerged from his cruiser and closed the door behind him. "Got a call about a fight?"

Now that a police officer was on site to ensure the ladies couldn't give him his due, Todd rolled onto his hands and knees and pushed himself to a stand. He pointed at Erika and Katie. "Those two attacked me!"

Rocky raised a palm to silence Todd. "For good reason." Rocky met the cop's eyes and acknowledged me with a lift of his chin. "Misty can give you the rundown."

Once again, I found myself telling the story of the day's events. When I got to the part where Todd stalked Lexi down the Blue Ridge Parkway and badgered her at the overlook, the officer frowned. "He drove over here to badger her again." I pointed to the series of black circles marring the pavement in front of my lodge. "See those marks? Not two minutes ago, he was doing donuts out here."

"On *my* motorcycle!" Lexi cried, throwing up her hands. "The judge awarded it to me in our divorce hearing on Monday."

Before I could go further and tell the officer about Gerri, he apparently put the clues together himself. He noted the license plate on the motorcycle before staring pointedly at Todd, his eyes narrowed and his hand resting on his belt, ready to grab a weapon if necessary. "You're the guy every-one's been looking for."

"What?" Todd jerked his head back, as if to dodge a strike, and his face puckered. "Why would anyone be look-ing for me? All I did was drive through an overlook where Lexi happened to be and honk my horn."

Lexi growled. "It's *my* horn!"

Todd rolled his eyes at Lexi before turning back to the police officer. "So, what? Y'all think I'm stalking her?" His tone said he thought the very idea was ridiculous.

The officer gave Todd a wry look. "Well, you did just ad-mit to following her into an overlook, and now you're here at the lodge where she's staying."

Todd opened his mouth to argue but then stopped him-self, as if realizing that maybe he was the one who was be-ing ridiculous.

The officer cocked his head. "A woman died on the Blue Ridge Parkway today. The Buncombe County Sheriff's De-partment wants to talk to you about it."

"Whoa-whoa-whoa!" Todd waved his hands as if doing so would somehow clear up the confusion he felt—*or was pretending to feel*. His eyes narrowed to a mere squint. "Did you say someone *died*?"

Erika replied before the officer could. "It was Gerri!" She made a motion as if pounding her fists on an invisible table. "Gerri died, you idiot!"

"Gerri?" Todd's eyes popped wide and his mouth fell open. "Oh, my God," he expelled on a breath. He looked sheepish now, remorseful even. He looked askance at Lexi. "I'm sorry, Lex. I had no idea about Gerri or I never would have acted this way."

Is he telling the truth? Or was he the cause of the woman's demise? Maybe Gerri had seen him coming up from behind on Lexi's Vulcan and had tried to prevent him from getting past her to harass Lexi again. Maybe that's how Gerri ended up crashing. But if that were the case, would Todd have come here and made an ass of himself like this? If he'd hurt her, even inadvertently, it seemed that he'd have tried to put some distance between himself and the mountains as quickly as possible. Then again, maybe he knew that fleeing on Lexi's motorcycle would only make him look more guilty. Maybe his coming here was a stunt to deflect suspicion, nothing more than smoke and mirrors.

Todd looked down and toed the ground with his boot. "I feel like a total jerk."

Erika snorted. "You *are* a total jerk, *Turd.*"

Todd sent a scorching look Erika's way before unzipping his jacket and reaching into it to remove an envelope from an inside pocket. "This is the title to the Vulcan," he said to Lexi. "I had to bring it with me to get the bike out of impound. I'll sign it over to you right now."

Patty whipped a pen from her apron and held it out to him. "Here you go."

Todd removed the title from the envelope, lay it against his thigh to sign it, and returned the pen to Patty. He held the signed title out to Lexi. "I'm sorry," he said again. "Not just about Gerri, but about"—he paused for a moment—"everything."

I watched his face. To the guy's credit, he looked regretful, heartbroken even. He'd made some really stupid choices, and now he was paying the price.

Lexi's expression said his apology was too little, too late, but she didn't say so out loud. She had much bigger things on her mind at the moment.

The officer took Todd's arm before the guy even realized what was happening. "I'll give you a ride to the station. You can talk to the sheriff there."

Todd's expression was bewildered, but he went along as the cop led him to his cruiser and put him in the back seat. The officer was about to close the door when Todd glanced over at the Vulcan. "Wait! My tank bag is still on the bike."

"I'll get it." Lexi walked over to the motorcycle and removed the black vinyl bag from the tank. There were no straps, and by the way she tugged it off it appeared to have been held to the tank by magnets. The bag was zipped shut. She carried it over and handed it to the police officer. He unzipped it and rummaged through it, probably looking for evidence or weapons, before handing it to Todd.

Todd cast a glance out the back window as the patrol car rolled out of the parking lot. Lexi watched the car go, continuing to stare at the empty road once it had rounded the curve out of sight. I wondered what was going through her mind. Was she trying to figure out what she'd ever seen in the guy? Or was she trying to determine if her ex could be responsible for Gerri's death?

Erika wondered the same thing, although she wondered out loud. "Hey, Lex? You think Todd killed Gerri?"

Lexi continued to stare at the empty road for a few more beats. "No," she said finally, turning to look at Erika and Katie. "Not on purpose, anyway."

Katie appeared thoughtful and offered the same theory

I'd considered. "If she saw him riding up behind her, she might have tried to keep him from passing her, maybe weaved back and forth in the lane or something."

Lexi could only shrug in reply. *If only someone had seen something . . .*

As the girls headed back to the lodge, Patty angled her head to indicate the diner. "Let's get your guests that supper."

Rocky and I followed Patty into the Greasy Griddle. Patty loaded a large bread basket with corn muffins and filled a Crock-Pot with vegetable stew. I carried the basket to the lodge, while Rocky carried the Crock-Pot and Patty followed with a ladle, bowls, soup spoons, and pads of butter. We set the dinner up on a table in the great room, along with a stack of napkins.

I gazed around the group; everyone looked absolutely lost and devastated. I wished I had some words of wisdom for them, something that would bring them solace. But where I fell short, Rocky stepped in. "Cicero said, 'The life of the dead is placed in the memory of the living.'"

Consoled, however slightly, by the thought that Gerri would continue to live on, even if only in their memories, the ladies rose quietly and stepped toward the table. Once they had served themselves, Rocky and I ladled out bowls of stew for ourselves and grabbed a couple of corn muffins. We stationed ourselves at the front desk and ate in silence.

Just after seven, a Buncombe County Sheriff's Department cruiser pulled up in front of the lodge. Deputy Gillespie climbed out and headed into the lobby.

While some of the women from the motorcycle club had retired to their rooms to mourn privately, a few others had remained in the great room. Bessie was one of them. Both her head and Shotgun's popped up over the back of a chair when she heard the deputy say, "Good evening, Ms. Murphy."

I slid off my stool and cast a glance into the great room. The night had grown too cold to sit on the deck, and Erika had come inside and taken a seat by the fireplace. Her eyes seemed to flash with alarm when she saw that the deputy had come to the lodge, but it could have simply been the reflection of the flames.

"Hello, Deputy Gillespie." I introduced him to Rocky, who'd stayed at the desk to provide me with emotional support. The two men shook hands over the counter.

Bessie set Shotgun on the floor and he padded along behind her as she walked over. Eager to hear what the deputy might have to say, the other ladies followed her—all but Erika, that is. She stayed by the fire, staring into the flames, though her rigid posture told me she was likely listening in.

"Do you have news for us?" Bessie asked the deputy. "Did Todd having something to do with what happened to Gerri?"

"I questioned him," Gillespie said, "but he says the only time he saw Ms. Burnham was when he drove through the outlook where you ladies were stopped."

I chimed in. "Where did he claim to be in the afternoon, after he drove through the outlook and before he came here?"

"Riding some of the side roads. Says he hiked for a short

while at Grandfather Mountain, too, then grabbed a burger and a beer in Banner Elk."

Bessie asked, "Were you able to verify his alibi?"

"I called the restaurant. They confirmed a guy fitting his description had stopped in, but it was well after you ladies first contacted law enforcement to let us know Ms. Burnham was missing. Any hikers who might have seen him on the trail at Grandfather Mountain would be long gone by now." The deputy raised a shoulder. "Without some real evidence pointing his way, I couldn't take him into custody."

Bessie's face puckered. "But that doesn't mean he's innocent."

"No," the deputy agreed. "It doesn't. But if he had killed Ms. Burnham, whether intentionally or by accident, he'd have to be a darn fool to come up here and do donuts in the parking lot."

Bessie and the other ladies exchanged glances. Clearly, they thought Todd was indeed a darn fool. Heck, I did, too.

Deputy Gillespie said, "I finally got in touch with Sterling Burnham. I'd left a voicemail earlier but he was out golfing and had turned the ringer off. I haven't broken the news to him yet. An unexpected death is not the kind of thing we normally inform people about by phone." He turned his attention to me. "Hope you don't mind, but I've asked him to meet me here at the lodge so we could discuss the matter. It would've taken me another half hour to drive to Blowing Rock, and I was already on my way to Beech Mountain to question Todd when we spoke. I figured your lodge would make a good meeting spot and, if he had any questions for the ladies, he could ask them while he's here."

My guess was that the deputy wanted to break the news of Gerri's death to Sterling in person not only because it was such a sensitive subject, but also because he wanted to be able to judge Sterling's reaction, see if the man did anything to give away his guilt. I, too, was curious how Sterling would react. After all, with Gerri gone, he might have a better chance of getting his hands on his children's trust funds. I wondered who would succeed Gerri as trustee. Had her husband named an alternate should she be unable to serve? If not, would Sterling seek to be appointed? Or maybe Mariah?

The deputy asked, "Has anyone been in Ms. Burnham's room today?"

"No," I said. "Ordinarily, Brynn or I would have been in the room to clean, but the ladies gave us the day off so we could ride with them."

"Good," he said. "I don't want anybody going in there until I can catalog Ms. Burnham's property. Okay?"

"Sure." I reached down, unlocked the drawer that held the keys to the guestrooms, and handed him the spare set to Gerri's room. "Here's the key to Gerri's room. It's Room Two at the end of the hall." I pointed down the west wing.

"Thanks." He pocketed the keys. "I'd like to speak to Lexi first. Which room is she in?"

"Ten." I pointed down the west wing again. "It's that way, too."

He headed down the hall. A moment later, we heard a *rap-rap* as he knocked on her door. When she opened it, he said, "Mind if I come in for a moment?"

"Sure." She stepped back to allow him into her room and shut the door behind him.

Meanwhile, Bessie hustled down the hall to roust Reyna and let her know the deputy they'd spoken with at the outlook had come to the lodge. Shotgun trotted down the hall after Bessie, then trotted after the two women as they came up the hall and sat down in the great room to wait for the deputy to return.

A few minutes later, Deputy Gillespie emerged from Lexi's room. He thanked her before coming back up the hall. Reyna watched him with eagle eyes as he walked over and stopped at my desk. "When Sterling arrives, is there somewhere I can speak privately with him?"

He had the keys to Gerri's room, but it appeared he didn't want to speak to Sterling there. The deputy probably didn't want to risk the room being disturbed before he had a chance to take a look at it. "Unless you're allergic to cats," I said, "you're welcome to use my room."

"Nope," the deputy said. "Not allergic. Almost wish I was. The wife keeps collecting homeless critters. We had five cats at last count."

I handed him my key. "She sounds like a lovely lady." Deputy Gillespie was a nice guy, too, for allowing her to rescue the strays.

Sterling's red Tesla pulled up in front of the lodge. Sterling was at the wheel and Andrea sat in the passenger seat. The back seat was empty. *Mariah must've stayed at the resort.* Knowing the two had caused problems for their ride or die, the Curves in the great room looked none too happy to see the mother and son.

Sterling and Andrea climbed out of the Tesla and walked inside, perplexed expressions on their faces as they approached the desk. Sterling was dressed in golf attire similar to what he'd worn here the day before, but Andrea had ditched her tennis outfit for a classic cable-knit sweater in a pretty pumpkin color, dark jeans, and high-heeled ankle boots, a youthful yet classy look.

Deputy Gillespie introduced himself, then held out a hand to invite them down the hall. "Let's go on down to Room One so we can have some privacy." The trio headed into my room. No doubt Yeti was wondering why three complete strangers had dared to trespass on her realm.

CHAPTER 14

Yeti

How dare these strangers trespass on her realm!

Yeti stared the three down as they took seats around the square table where Misty ate her meals, but they ignored her. She debated lying on the bed and turning her back on the interlopers, but decided that showing them who was boss was a better idea. She hopped down from the dresser and leaped up onto the table, flopping down right in the center, claiming it as her domain. She gazed around at them, swishing her tail in a sinister manner, daring them to try to move her. The tall man with no hair reached out and stroked her side. *Maybe he's not so bad.* As for the other two? Well, they could hiss off.

The man who was petting her spoke to the other humans in a soft, calm voice for several seconds. Yeti couldn't understand what he said, but whatever it was, it seemed to upset the others. The woman issued a series of squeaky sounds, and the man slumped back in his chair, slowly shaking his head. After a moment, the hairless man said something else. The woman exhaled a quivering breath, rose from the table, and walked to the door. She glanced back before stepping out into the hall and closing the door softly behind her.

The two men engaged in a back and forth. The hairless man's voice remained calm, but the voice of the other one went up and down in pitch and volume. Yeti knew this meant he was upset. He pulled out his phone and showed his screen to the hairless man. The hairless man made some notes on a pad of paper as the other man spoke. After another minute or two, they stood to go.

Yeti escorted them to the door, twitching her tail as they went. Later, when Misty returned to their room, Yeti would be sure to let her know that she had not appreciated the intrusion.

CHAPTER 15

Misty

Rather than join the members of Gerri's motorcycle club in the great room, Andrea opted to take a seat on a bench in the lobby when she returned from speaking with the deputy in my room. While she didn't shed a tear over Gerri's death, she wasn't smug about it, either. She stared at the floor in quiet reflection, perhaps trying to come to terms with what Gerri's passing would mean for her son and grandchildren, for the trust Gerri had managed. Maybe she was even finally acknowledging to herself that Gerri had not been to blame for the demise of Andrea's marriage to Norman Burnham, that Gerri had not been a home-wrecker but merely a convenient scapegoat, that Andrea's marriage failed due to her own shortcomings and because it had been based on little more than an initial physical attraction.

She looked up and caught me watching her. Rather than pretend I hadn't been, I said, "For what it's worth, Gerri said nice things about your grandkids. She said they were adorable and sweet."

Andrea's face softened. "They take after their mother. If they'd taken after their dad, they'd be little hellions."

We shared a small chuckle. It was the first sense I had that Andrea wasn't totally blind where her son was concerned. But I had to wonder, if he'd been a "little hellion" once, might he have been a big hellion, today? Had he caused Gerri's crash? At this point, did Andrea even suspect that Gerri's death could have been anything but an accident?

Deputy Gillespie and Sterling Burnham returned from my room. As Andrea began to stand, the deputy raised a palm and said, "Hold tight." A cloud passed over her face as she slowly lowered herself back down to the seat. The men walked out the front door and over to the Tesla. Sterling used the fob to pop the trunk open and removed his golf clubs. The deputy looked them over carefully, glancing up a time or two to make inquiries.

Andrea looked from the men to me. "I wonder what that's all about?"

I feigned ignorance with a shrug. "I have no idea." *What a lie.* I had lots of ideas, the big one being that Sterling had driven his Tesla down the Blue Ridge Parkway early today in search of Gerri, swung at her with his golf club, and hit the back of her motorcycle, causing her to veer off the road.

When the two came back inside, the deputy motioned for Andrea to follow him to my room again. Sterling took a seat on the bench his mother had vacated. Like her, he took advantage of his time on the bench to engage in solemn thought, but unlike his mother he seemed less contemplative and more anxious. Two or three times his heel started to bounce, as if to burn off nervous energy, but each time he seemed to catch himself, to realize what the nervous reflex might imply, and stopped it.

A quarter hour later, Andrea and Deputy Gillespie came up the hall. Sterling stood to join them.

The deputy looked from one of them to the other. "Thanks for your cooperation. And, again, I'm very sorry for your family's loss."

Sterling said, "Will you contact us once you figure things out?"

"I will," said Gillespie. "But like I said, at this point it's looking like it was probably just a tragic accident. Will you two be making her funeral arrangements?"

Sterling and Andrea exchanged a glance. The looks of surprise on their faces told me they hadn't given the issue any thought yet.

Andrea turned back to the deputy. "If I'm not mistaken, Gerri has a brother somewhere. South Carolina maybe? Mariah will know. She was closer to Gerri than either of us. Anyway, if he doesn't want to make the arrangements, I'm sure Mariah would be happy to take care of them."

Though Andrea's tone was matter-of-fact, I had to wonder if she might have felt some jealousy that her daughter-in-law got along well with her ex-husband's new wife. I also had to wonder about Mariah and Gerri's relationship. If the two were close—or at least amicable—might Mariah have been especially angered or hurt that Gerri hadn't agreed to honor Sterling's request that the trust pay for her family's country club membership? Mariah seemed to enjoy playing tennis. After all, she'd played enough to develop a case of tennis elbow, as evidenced by the elastic support I'd seen on her arm before. *Could Mariah have been the one to hurt Gerri?* I also wondered if I wasn't the only one wondering whether Mariah was responsible. Her absence was odd, wasn't it? Why wouldn't she have come along with her husband and stepmother tonight? Could they have left her behind on purpose to protect her, so that they could find out what the deputy might suspect without subjecting her to questioning?

"Speaking of Mariah," I said, "where is she tonight?"

Andrea said, "She's back at the resort, putting her feet up."

"Worn out from playing tennis?" I asked.

"No," Andrea said. "No tennis for her today. She spent the day shopping."

The town of Blowing Rock had several upscale boutique stores, as well as great art galleries, but when I ventured there my favorite place to shop was the outlets. I'd bought much of my family's hiking and ski apparel there at big discounts. "I've found some great stuff for next to nothing at the outlets."

"Mariah's become quite the bargain hunter, too." Though Andrea offered a small smile, her lip quirked, as if the thought of discount stores was repulsive or beneath her. *She's obviously never had to get by on a middle-class income.* Of course, the same could be said of Mariah. Her family's income had always been subsidized by Sterling's father, until his death earlier this year. *Have they been under severe financial stress since?* I got the impression they were living beyond their means. With Sterling unemployed, the family's support would have fallen entirely on Mariah's shoulders. Money trouble could push people to the edge. But could the young mother have gone so far as to kill her stepmother-in-law? Had Sterling's anxiety been not on his own behalf, but his wife's? I realized all my musing was likely for naught, and nothing more than my active imagination coming up with stories and scenarios. After all, the deputy had told Sterling that Gerri's death had likely been an accident and, at this point, it was starting to look like that might be the simple, sad truth.

With a final "goodbye," Sterling and Andrea walked out to the car. Sterling opened the passenger door to help his mother inside, and circled around to the driver's side. He cast one last look at the lodge before sliding into his seat. A second or two later the car's headlights came on and they drove out of the lot.

Deputy Gillespie came over to the desk. "May I speak with you in your room, Misty?"

"Of course." I turned to Rocky.

Before I could even ask him to watch the desk for me, he said, "I'll hold down the fort."

"Thanks." I put a hand on his shoulder and gave it an appreciative and affectionate squeeze.

At the door to my room, the deputy returned my keys. I unlocked the door and we went inside, taking seats at the table.

He said, "Did you hear me tell Sterling that we're looking at Ms. Burnham's death as an accident?"

"I did."

"Well, that wasn't exactly the truth. We've found some new evidence that clearly points to murder or, at the very least, involuntary manslaughter."

My brows rocketed toward my hairline as the deputy pulled out his cell phone and showed me a photo of a motorcycle helmet. It was the same color as Gerri's, and bore the same damage that I'd seen on the front of her helmet when we'd found her. But when she'd been lying in the woods, only the front and left side of her helmet had been visible. This image showed the right side. It bore evidence of a strike with a metal object of some sort, a silver swipe about four inches long. With the surface of the helmet being curved, it was unclear how long the metal object would have been. The object had only impacted the outermost edge of the helmet near her ear. The remaining surface that curved back inward toward her face and the back of her head was thus undamaged.

My mind whirled. "So, someone did hit her? Like I'd thought?"

"It appears that way. But this stays between us for now." He pointed to me, then himself. "Understood?"

"Yes sir." I thought back to earlier, how I'd thought the silver mark on Gerri's back fender had been from Erika's motorcycle. But, as far as I knew, Erika hadn't brought anything with her that she could have stuck Gerri's helmet with.

When I said as much, the deputy said, "I found a metal tire gauge along the roadside. It's possible the gauge was used to strike her helmet, but it's small. I'm not sure it would have caused damage. Plus, with it being so short, it would've required whoever hit her to drive up very close alongside her."

My mind went to the knife throwers I'd seen at the Renaissance faire. "Could they have thrown the tire gauge at her?"

He angled his head to and fro. "I suppose that's possible. I'd considered that it could be Sterling Burnham hitting her with a golf club, like you insinuated when we first spoke, but he showed me his equipment. None of it was bent or appeared damaged. That said, he might have used a club that he subsequently ditched somewhere. He claims to have an alibi, though. He says he played a round of golf with three other men in Blowing Rock this morning, and that he had a late lunch and drinks with the other golfers afterward. I'm not crossing him off my list until I check with the resort and verify that he was on the course and at their tavern afterward."

"What about his mother?" I asked. "Could she have borrowed his car and gone after Gerri with one of his clubs?"

"She's got an alibi, too," he said. "She had a late-morning lesson with a tennis pro. She showed me the email confirmation on her phone. Of course, I'll verify her alibi, too." He cocked his head and eyed me intently. "Did you see anyone else today with any kind of metal pole?"

I mentally ran through the day, from the time the Dangerous Curves left my lodge with Brynn and me tagging along, until now. *White van at Archer's Inn . . . Todd circling through the Table Rock overlook . . . The college girls snapping photos . . .* As I wracked my brain, two possibilities popped into my mind. "Lexi's ex-husband Todd had hiking poles in his bag when he drove through the overlook. I saw the handles sticking out of that bag on his gas tank. They must've been too long to fit fully inside. But when he drove to the lodge tonight, they weren't there."

"Interesting," said the deputy. "I searched his bag and didn't see hiking poles, either. He's got some explaining to do."

I told him what Lexi had said earlier, that she didn't think Todd had killed Gerri, at least not on purpose.

The deputy said, "She told me the same thing. She may very well be right, but it could also be a defense mechanism."

"A defense mechanism? What do you mean?"

"I mean, if her ex killed Gerri, then Lexi would be guilty by association, in a sense. The assumption would be that Todd was coming after Lexi, and Gerri somehow got in the way. Lexi might not want to think it was Todd who caused Gerri's death because she'd feel responsible. That would be a tough load to bear."

It sure would be. "There were some girls at the Table Rock overlook, too," I said. "College students from UNC Charlotte. They'd been to a winery. I can't speak for the others because I didn't get near them, but the birthday girl was half-sloshed. She used a selfie stick to take a photo of her group. Gerri asked if they'd designated a driver, and it seemed to irritate the girl. She called Gerri 'grandma' in a snide way and said they'd be fine." *Could the marks on Gerri's helmet and motorcycle have been caused by the selfie stick?*

"Any chance the girl gave you her name?" he asked.

"No." I didn't recall her friends using her name, either. "All I know is that today was her twenty-first birthday. That's why they'd gone to the winery. To celebrate."

"That's good intel," he said. "Knowing her birthday will narrow things down significantly."

"Her friend was driving a yellow convertible Mustang," I added. "A recent model."

"That will narrow things down too," Deputy Gillespie said. "Thanks for the information."

"This is probably nothing," I said, "but Reyna and Gerri brought some metal skewers with them. The group used them to roast marshmallows around the fire pit out back Monday evening. Also, Dahlia has a metal cane. She's got low vision. It's not one of those typical canes that blind people use, though. She called it an ID cane. She wears it in a holster on her belt. It's used as a signal to other people that she's visually impaired. She wasn't on the ride today, though. She stayed back at the lodge to grade papers. Her sister Daisy is the one I rode with, so I know she didn't use the cane to strike Gerri." Of course, none of the women on the ride, other than Erika, seemed to be a viable suspect. They'd all been riding ahead of Gerri and had shown up to the stops one right after the other.

"Would Erika have had access to Dahlia's ID cane?"

"I don't know," I said. "Dahlia only seems to use it when she's in public and needs to signal others that she's visually impaired. I assume she keeps it in her room the rest of the time, but the ladies have been going in and out of each other's rooms since they arrived. Some have even left their doors propped open. It's been like a big slumber party."

He nodded as he absorbed the information.

As he turned to leave my room, I held out a hand to stop him. "Before you called me back here, I was wondering about Mariah. She's Sterling's wife." My stomach seemed to squirm inside me. I felt guilty even suggesting she might be the one who'd caused Gerri's death, but I'd feel even more guilty if I didn't do everything in my power to avenge my guest. "It seems strange that she didn't come with here with Sterling and Andrea."

"I wondered about her, too." A grin tugged at the deputy's

lips and his gaze assessed my face. "Maybe you're in the wrong business, Misty. Maybe you should be a detective instead of running a mountain lodge."

"No way," I said. "I took a cake decorating class with a friend and could never seem to master the piping bag. My frosting ended up all over the place." I held up my hands and wiggled my fingers. "These hands were not made for working with a gun."

The deputy chuckled. "Of all the women here, Reyna was the closest to Gerri, correct?"

"Yes, sir."

"I'm going to see what, if anything, she can tell me about Mariah."

The two of us walked back to the lobby. I noticed that Lexi had come out of her room and rejoined her friends.

As I retook my seat beside Rocky at the front counter, the deputy approached Reyna. "May I speak to you in your room?"

"Certainly." She stood and led him down the hall.

They returned ten minutes later. I wondered what more the deputy had learned about Gerri's relationship with her stepdaughter-in-law, but I couldn't very well ask.

Gillespie headed down the west wing and disappeared into Gerri's room, closing the door behind him. After a few minutes, he came out with her car keys in his hand. He went outside and searched her SUV and trailer, as well. He came back inside and handed the keys over to me. "You can clear out her room if you'd like, but hold these keys and her other property in safekeeping until we determine who to turn it over to."

"How will you figure that out?"

"I'll check with the court in Raleigh, get the name of the attorney she hired to file her husband's will for probate when he passed away. She likely used the same lawyer to prepare her will."

Now he had me wondering who Gerri's heir or heirs might be. She had no children of her own. Might she have left her property to the brother Andrea had mentioned? What if she'd left her property, including the RV dealership, to someone else? Might that person have wanted her dead so that they could get their hands on her money and other assets?

The deputy donned his campaign hat, turned to the women gathered in the lobby, and tipped the hat in a good-bye gesture. "You ladies take care now."

The instant the door swung closed behind him, the lodge filled with scraping sounds as the ladies pulled their chairs in tight. If I perked up my ears, I just might find out what Lexi and Reyna had discussed with the deputy, after all.

CHAPTER 16

Misty

Lexi was the first to share with the other women. "The deputy asked me all kinds of questions about Todd. Whether he had a violent temper. Whether he'd ever threatened me. That kind of thing. He'd obviously run a background check because he mentioned that Todd had a clean record."

Reyna said, "He asked me about Sterling first. Same kinds of questions he asked Lexi about Todd. Whether Sterling had a temper. Whether Gerri had ever mentioned him threatening her or acting violently."

I found myself straining to listen in. Rocky had pulled up a website that sold tools, but I think he was only pretending to peruse it and was actually listening in, too.

"I told him that Sterling has acted like a spoiled, pompous ass," Reyna said, "but that he'd never threatened her or gotten physical, as far as I know. He asked about Andrea, too. She's a you-know-what with a capital B, but Gerri never mentioned her throwing a punch or tossing out a threat. She seemed to stick to insults." She straightened just a bit. "He even asked about Mariah. I told him that Gerri and Mariah got along well, that Mariah often played the mediator when her husband or mother-in-law ended up at odds with Gerri. She was the only one with the sense to realize that antagonizing Gerri wasn't in their interests."

Bessie's eyes narrowed. "The deputy seems to be doing a lot of digging for someone who thinks Gerri's crash was an accident."

Reyna said, "I thought the same thing." In my peripheral vision, I could see her turn to look my way. "Hey, Misty! What did the sheriff ask you?"

I'd been advised to keep the information about the damage on the right side of Gerri's helmet secret, so I couldn't share that tidbit. Instead, remembering that he wanted everyone to think he was sticking with the accident theory, I said, "He just asked my opinion on Gerri, whether she seemed healthy and mentally acute. I told him she seemed sharp as a tack and pointed out she was in great shape for a woman her age."

Reyna's expression appeared dubious. So did Bessie's. "That's all you talked about?" Bessie said. "You were gone several minutes."

I flung out a hand in a dismissive gesture. "You know how these investigators are. They ask you the same question ten different ways."

Reyna and Bessie still appeared far from convinced, but at least they didn't push me further.

Reyna turned back to the group. "It's been an exhausting day. I say we all head to bed early tonight, and ride out to Mount Mitchell tomorrow. Gerri would want us to enjoy ourselves. Besides, a ride would do us good, help us clear our heads."

The ladies stood to return to their rooms. I raised a hand from behind the desk and called, "Good night, everyone!"

As Katie walked down the hall, I found myself staring at the long, dark hair hanging down her back, courtesy of the synthetic hair extensions. My mind went back to the white van we'd passed on the parkway, how she'd gasped on seeing it. She'd said that she'd thought she'd seen an old boyfriend at the wheel, but that she'd been mistaken. But had her explanation been as fake as her hair? Had she actually seen the boyfriend? If so, did she have reason to fear him? Or was there something else going on? Could the white van have something to do with what happened to Gerri?

I turned to Rocky. "Come down to my room."

He gave me a mischievous grin. "It's going to take a lot more than some lousy frozen lasagna for me to give in to your charms."

I rolled my eyes. "Just come."

Once we were in my room, I closed the door behind him. Keeping my voice quiet, I told him about Katie, how she'd reacted on seeing the white van pass us on the Blue Ridge Parkway. "I'm wondering if she was being truthful. I saw a van like it backed up in the driveway of the Archer's Inn this morning. Right after we passed by, the driver pulled to the edge of the drive, but I couldn't tell which way they intended to turn. There was a white van with chrome bumpers in the parking lot early yesterday morning too," I said. "Of course, those white vans all look alike to me, so it could be nothing more than coincidence."

Rocky's brows drew inward. "Are you sure all the vans had chrome bumpers?"

"Yes, I'm sure. I've overheard the Curves talking about adding this or that piece of chrome to their bikes. One jokingly called another a 'chromosexual' because she added so much of the metal to her motorcycle." I shrugged. "I guess their discussions made me more aware of chrome."

"Chrome is actually pretty rare on vehicles anymore," Rocky said. "It's heavy, so chrome bumpers negatively impact gas mileage. It's more expensive than the alternatives, too. Most bumpers are plastic these days."

"The vans I saw were probably all older vans, then?" I said, thinking out loud.

"It would seem that way," Rocky said. "Plus, the fact that they all had chrome bumpers makes it more likely they were all the same van."

"But they couldn't be," I insisted. "The one in the lot here had a Mississippi license plate, but the one we passed on the parkway had a North Carolina plate."

"What about the one at Archer's Inn?"

"I couldn't tell," I said. "It was backed into the driveway. There was no license plate on the front."

Rocky stroked his beard as he thought things over. "You know, Molasses woke me up growling last night. He was staring at the window, then a few seconds later he turned to look at the door. I heard a sound like someone opening the exterior door at the end of the hall. I didn't hear footsteps in the hall afterward, so I figured one of the ladies had stepped outside, maybe to smoke a cigarette. But what if the noise was something else?"

"Do you know what time this happened?"

"No," he said. "I didn't check the clock. Didn't seem important at the time."

"Let's check the security camera feeds."

We returned to the front desk and logged into the site where we could view the footage from the lodge's security cameras. There were two fish-eye cameras inside, one aimed down either hall. We'd recently added exterior cameras after an unfortunate incident involving the death of a yoga instructor on the property.

We watched the recording from the interior cameras first, starting it when the ladies retired to their rooms. We saw Bessie come out of her room an hour later carrying a book. She carried it down to Kris's room and returned it to her before taking Shotgun out the exterior door at the end of the eastern hall to relieve himself. Bessie and her dog returned right away and went back to their room. There was no action again until one thirty, when Erika tiptoed out of her room in the western wing. She held a pack of cigarettes in one hand, her room key and a lighter in the other. She exited the door at the end of the wing. The poor quality of the camera image and the reflection of the glass door made it difficult to see through the door to the outside. Ten minutes later, Erika came back inside and returned to her room.

I turned to Rocky. "You think that's what Molasses heard? Erika going out to smoke?"

"Maybe," he said. "But unless Erika walked around to the front of the lodge, that wouldn't explain why Molasses was looking at our window when he first started growling. I'm also not sure I'd hear the sound of the outside door all the way at your end of the hall. I thought the sound came from the exterior door at the end of my wing."

Befuddled, we continued to watch. At 3:08, a dark, blurry image appeared outside the glass door at the end of the eastern wing. It was there only a moment and then disappeared.

"What was that?" I asked.

Rocky frowned. "I couldn't tell for sure. Could have been a person but, judging from the color, size, and shape, it could've been a bear."

Bears were known to amble about the town at night, getting easy snacks from bird feeders or garbage cans that weren't properly secured. Residents constantly captured bear footage on their home security cameras, or on their cell phones. Some bears even ventured out in broad daylight. The bear theory seemed to have some merit until thirty seconds later, when the same blurry image appeared at the door of the western wing.

A creepy feeling invaded my gut. "That's no bear." It was too much of a coincidence. Someone had been checking the doors, trying to get into my lodge.

I quickly changed the feed to the exterior camera mounted on the front of the building. Sure enough, a person emerged from the side of the lodge, hunched over as if to trying to be less visible. The person wasn't large, but judging from the way they moved, they appeared to be male. He hustled across the parking lot to a white van with chrome bumpers waiting in the shadows. There didn't appear to be a license plate on the front of the van. The guy climbed into the driver's seat, but the interior light didn't turn on. Either it was broken, or he'd intentionally turned it off. Without light, it was impossible to tell if anyone else was in the van. The red flash of brake lights and the burst of smoky fog from the exhaust pipe told us he'd started the vehicle, though he didn't turn on the headlights. A few seconds later, the van drove out of the lot. It was too far away and too dark in the parking lot for us to make out the license plate. The driver didn't turn the headlights on until he was fifty feet down the road.

"You think he was just looking for a restroom and was trying to be discreet?" I belonged to an innkeepers' association and received a monthly newsletter via email. The most recent edition had an article addressing the topic of van dwellers and people with small campers squatting in the parking lots of hotels and motels. Doing so saved them the cost of a campsite and offered the convenience of a public restroom in the inn's lobby—assuming they could access the lobby, of course. Some innkeepers had even reported such folks attempting to score free breakfasts at inns that offered the amenity to their guests.

Rocky pointed to my hand, which rested on the mouse. "Take it back a few minutes."

I dragged the time stamp back until we saw the van come up the road, approaching the lodge. The headlights went off just before it turned into the parking lot. The driver parked, and nothing happened for several minutes. *Weird.* Was he waiting to see if there'd be any reaction at the lodge, whether anyone spotted him driving in?

A couple more minutes went by before the driver's door opened and the guy slid out, gently closing the door behind him as if to avoid making noise. He bent over and darted toward the lodge. I'd hoped we'd be able to tell more about him now that he was closer to the camera, but he wore one of those thick, fleece-lined bomber-style hats with a big tuft of fake fur on the forehead, wide ear flaps that came down on the sides, and a strap under the chin. The ear flaps covered his cheeks and obscured his face. It was cool on the mountain, but not cold enough yet that someone would need a winter hat. *He planned for this.* That thought made my stomach twist.

He reached the row of motorcycles and began to lift the covers to look under them. We watched as he made his way down the row. When he lifted the one with the Indian Motorcycle logo, he hesitated for a few beats. Looked like he'd found Katie's green Ninja to be of particular interest. My gut twisted even tighter. Had he been specifically looking for Katie's motorcycle to verify whether she was staying at the lodge? Could he be the ex-boyfriend she'd mentioned? If so, was he stalking her?

He pulled the cover back down. To my surprise, he turned back to the van and raised his hand in a thumbs-up signal. *That's odd, isn't it? Don't stalkers usually work alone?* Maybe I'd misread the situation. Maybe something else entirely was going on here. I turned to Rocky. "Someone must be in the van." *A partner in crime, perhaps?*

Rocky had apparently reached the same conclusion. He gestured at the screen. "Looks like they were thinking about boosting a bike. Maybe more than one."

"Good thing the ladies secured them." Thieves would need bolt cutters to get through the chains or keys to unlock the wheel locks.

The guy in the hat didn't bother looking under the covers of the remaining motorcycles. Rather, he darted along the front walkway and tried the front door. Without a key, he couldn't get it open. *Thank goodness!* Who knew what he might have done if he'd gotten inside. Would he have tried to force the women to give him the keys to their motorcycles and the locks? Or would he and the person in the van have done something much worse?

He scurried along the outside of the east wing, still hunkered down so as not to cast a shadow when moving past the windows. He crossed right in front of Rocky's room at the end and circled around to the side. I switched the camera feed to the unit mounted over the exterior door on that side. Sure enough, the guy stopped in front of the door and reached out to try it, too. He found it locked as well.

I swallowed hard and manipulated the feeds so that we saw him circle around the entire lodge, trying each exterior door.

Rocky shook his head. "The guy was determined, I'll give him that."

But exactly how determined was he? "Do you think he'll come back?"

Rocky inhaled a deep breath. "Hard to say. Seems he might have unfinished business."

The cargo van was big enough to hold two or three motorcycles at once, and the bikes would be hidden from view in the bay. It would be the perfect vehicle for this type of crime. Two of the women from the club had mentioned having their bikes stolen recently. Could someone be targeting this particular group? It dawned on me then that, if the guy and his cohort were here to steal motorcycles, Katie could be involved. Maybe the bad ex-boyfriend had been a ruse, and maybe the change in hair color and style were to disguise herself to the motorcycle club. I recalled Gerri telling me that Katie was their newest member, and had joined the Dangerous Curves about three months earlier. The motorcycle thefts had taken place not long thereafter.

Of course, Katie's possible involvement in the thefts was all conjecture at this point, and I was hesitant to share my thoughts without some solid proof. Maybe instead the people in the van were motorcycle thieves looking for a particular type of bike and Katie's Ninja fit the bill. Maybe that's why the guy in the hat stopped looking under the covers once he'd spotted her green Ninja.

"Tell you what," Rocky said, sliding off the stool and pulling his car keys from the front pocket of his jeans. "I'll park my truck longways behind the motorcycles. If the guys in the van come back with the intent of trying to steal a bike, they'll have a much harder time with my truck in the way."

"Great idea," I said. "I'll get my keys and pull my car up on one side, and we can lay the bear statue down across the other." My ex-husband had a carved wooden bear statue delivered to my lodge the day I'd bought the place. The bear was nearly as tall as me. If we laid the bear on its side, it would make a good roadblock. If nothing else, our safety measures would let the people in the van know that we were on to them. They'd be stupid to take a chance on trying to steal the bikes now. Even so, I'd keep the lodge locked during the daylight hours for a while. That way, nobody could wander inside without a key.

Rocky pulled his truck behind the motorcycles, and I drove my Subaru Crosstrek up on the left of the bikes, pulling it clear up onto the walkway as an extra measure. Once the vehicles were in place, the two of us wrangled the heavy bear over and gently lowered it down onto its side. Seeing the bear lying there lifeless gave me flashbacks to finding Gerri's body, and I vowed once again to ensure that her death was avenged. I wasn't sure who was responsible—Erika, Todd, the drunken birthday girl, the van men, Sterling, Andrea, maybe even Mariah—but I wouldn't rest until Gerri's killer was behind bars.

CHAPTER 17

Misty

Rocky and I moved our cars early Thursday morning, when it was still dark, and wrangled the bear back into place, standing him up next to the front door.

None of the bikes were missing that morning. We reviewed the security camera feeds, but the van hadn't returned to the lodge last night. Maybe they'd driven by on the main road, seen my car and Rocky's truck forming a barrier around the bikes, and realized they'd been spotted earlier. Or maybe Katie had become aware of our precautionary measures and warned her cohorts to stay away. Whatever the reason, we decided not to alarm the ladies with what we'd seen on the security camera footage from two nights ago. The would-be thieves' efforts had been thwarted. They were probably well on their way by now, searching for easier targets.

The day dawned bright and sunny, as if the earth had missed the news that Gerri Burnham had died and was simply going about its daily business in blissful ignorance. Of course, I continued my daily routine, too. Greeting Patty at the door when she brought breakfast over. Having coffee with Rocky. Wishing my guests a good day as they headed out to enjoy the mountains. Fortunately for Katie, her wrist felt better this morning, so she'd be able to ride with the others. As she walked out the door, I couldn't help but wonder about the young woman.

I watched through the front windows as Erika climbed onto her bike and headed off alone, riding slowly and safely, like she'd lost her mojo. The other ladies paused by their motorcycles, forming a circle with their arms draped over each other's shoulders. They leaned in and closed their eyes, sending up prayers for their dearly departed matriarch. As their circle broke, a few of them wiped fresh tears from their eyes.

Shortly after the women left, Rocky headed out to handle a leaky faucet for a local who lived down the backside of the mountain, near the Buckeye Recreation Center. After that, he had a gig replacing several stair treads at a roundhouse near the ski resort. He wouldn't be back until late afternoon, maybe even dinnertime if he got any other handyman calls. Brynn arrived for her workday, and the two of us rounded up our housekeeping carts and started our rounds.

Rather than spend the day dreading the task, I decided to start with cleaning Gerri's room. I unlocked the door and hesitated a moment on the threshold, feeling as if I was invading a sacred space, a shrine of sorts. Gerri had spent the last night of her life in this room. I was glad it was a happy one spent with her friends, anticipating a fun ride the following day. *If only we could have foreseen what would happen to her . . .*

The first thing I did was gather the things that the deputy had left behind after searching Gerrie's room. I returned her makeup and lotion to her toiletries case, and put her clothing and shoes back into her suitcase along with the mystery novel she'd been reading. Alas, she'd never discover whodunit. The deputy had taken her cell phone at the crash site, but I unplugged her charger and slid that into her suitcase, too.

I walked over to the closet and used the universal code to take a look inside the safe. It was empty. That wasn't a surprise. While Gerri's motorcycle was bright with bling, I couldn't recall her wearing any jewelry since she'd arrived at the lodge. In fact, few of the women wore much jewelry. Earrings were probably incompatible with a tightly fitting helmet, and riding gloves would be likely to snag on rings, which could also stretch the material. I closed the safe and placed the luggage by the door, where it would be ready for someone to pick up later. Now that everything was packed, I closed my eyes and sent up a silent plea for justice for Gerri before setting about my cleaning routine.

After I finished with Gerri's room, I rolled my cart down the hall to Erika's and heaved a sigh as I entered. The girl was an absolute slob. She'd left candy wrappers and potato chip bags all over the place, not bothering to throw them in the trash can. Judging from the greasy fingerprints on the pillowcase, she'd used it to wipe her hands after eating the chips. I'd have to spray the pillowcase with stain remover and let it soak awhile to eliminate the oily stain. She'd left her worn clothes scattered all over the floor, too. I had to wade through dirty socks, wadded panties, a discarded sports bra, a pair of rumpled jeans, and an equally rumpled long-sleeved T-shirt to get to the bed to make it. There was no way I could vacuum with her clothing all over the floor, but there was also no way I was going to touch her undergarments with my bare hand. I slid my hands into latex gloves, picked up her clothing, and deposited it on the now-made bed. I proceeded to dust the room as best I could, working around the items she'd left on the night tables and dresser. A cell phone charger. A pair of Bluetooth earphones. A spare pair of riding gloves. After vacuuming the room, I spritzed and wiped down the mirror and window.

The bedroom complete, I entered the bathroom. The countertop was littered with personal care items. Toothbrush. Toothpaste. Nail file. But two items stopped me in my tracks. A tube of sunscreen and a bottle of leave-in conditioner. My mind flashed back to the white smear on the shoulder of Erika's jacket, the one she claimed was bird poo. Had she been honest when she said she was late to Craggy Gardens because she'd had to stop to clean the bird mess from her helmet? Or had it been a lie, concocted on the spot? Maybe an errant glop on her shoulder had inspired the story—an errant glop of sunscreen or leave-in conditioner that she had inadvertently gotten on her jacket while applying the products to her skin or hair.

Normally, I only moved a guest's items for cleaning purposes but, today, I was on a mission to identify Gerri's killer. If fulfilling that mission meant I had to invade a guest's privacy a little, then so be it. I picked up the tube of sunscreen and squeezed a small dollop into my hand. The particular brand Erika wore was extra thick and contained zinc oxide. I tapped my finger to the top of the goo and spread a smear in my palm. *This could very well be what I saw on her shoulder yesterday.*

I wiped off the sunscreen with a washcloth and tested the leave-in conditioner. The conditioner was more ivory than white in color, and less thick than the sunscreen. I couldn't rule it out as the source of the smudge on Erika's jacket, but if I'd had to bet, my money would be on the sunscreen. Still, it was possible that she'd told the truth, that she'd truly been a target of an aerial bombing by a wayward bird. The woods in the area were home to dozens of bird species, some of them quite large, like the Cooper's hawk, eastern screech-owl, or wild turkeys—which, contrary to popular myth, were perfectly capable of flight though they were often seen pecking for food on the ground. Any of those birds could have released a large enough load to coat a helmet's faceplate.

I finished Erika's bathroom and moved on to the next guestroom, which two of the riders were sharing. They were far neater than Erika, having left their belongings in neat stacks or piles atop the tables and dresser. They had, however, left their television on. I couldn't blame them for forgetting to turn the TV off, what with their club's ride or die having lost her life the day before.

A volleyball game played on the television, two college teams serving and spiking, the young, athletic girls giving it their all. As I went to turn off the TV, the banner across the bottom caught my eye. Each end featured a cartoon bulldog mascot, though they varied quite a bit in appearance. The one on the left was Uga, the University of Georgia's mascot. He wore a spiked collar, had a bad underbite with upward-pointing fangs sticking out of his mouth, and appeared to be snarling. His eyes were narrowed, too, making him appear mean and aggressive. The bulldog on the other side of the banner had droopy jowls and a determined look on his face, still tough but decidedly less menacing. He looked just like the one I'd seen on Katie's keychain when she'd checked in. According to the banner, he was the mascot for Mississippi State.

I involuntarily took a step back as the realization hit me. The bulldog on Katie's keychain. The Mississippi license plates on the white van with the chrome bumpers that had been outside my lodge the morning after she arrived. Her gasp on seeing a similar van pass us on the Blue Ridge Parkway. It was all too much to be mere coincidence, wasn't it?

Maybe the guys in the van had gone after the rider of the green Ninja yesterday, not realizing that it wasn't Katie on the bike, but Lexi. Maybe Katie was working with the guys to help them steal the bikes, and she'd gasped on seeing the white van pass by because she thought they'd unwisely been indiscreet in openly revealing themselves. Had Gerri realized the men might be following her girls and done something to hold them back? Is that how she'd lost her life? It was all so unclear and confusing!

I continued on my rounds until I reached Katie's room. Leaving my cart in the doorway, I grabbed the duster and glanced around, desperate for answers. Could there be some clue here that would either implicate or exonerate her, tell me whether we were dealing with a bad ex-boyfriend or something more?

Like the other bikers, Katie had brought only the essentials with her, along with a backpack to transport them in. The bag lay on top of the dresser. Curious as I might be, I wasn't about to unzip the bag and snoop around inside it. Rummaging through a guest's private property would be crossing a line.

I stepped closer to the dresser and eyed the bag. As I ran my gaze over it, I caught a reflection in the dresser mirror. Even if I'd wanted to open the backpack, I wouldn't have been able to. Katie had put a small luggage lock on the bag. The thin cable strung through the two zipper pulls would prevent the backpack from being unzipped. But while she'd ensured the bag couldn't be opened, she'd left a tiny gap about a half inch wide between the pulls. So long as I didn't open the backpack, there was nothing wrong with me shining a light in it, right?

I pulled my cell phone from my back pocket, activated the flashlight, and aimed it at the gap. In the mirror, I could see the reflection of something green and red inside the backpack. *What is that?* I turned off the flashlight and held my cell phone camera close to the gap to snap a pic. I enlarged the image to get a better look. To my surprise, the image looked right back at me. It was Andrew Jackson's left eye, complete with the wild, bushy brow. A red rubber band bisected his nose, apparently holding a large roll of bills together. While Katie had paid cash for her room, claiming her wallet had been stolen, this big wad of cash nonetheless raised my suspicions. It seemed like a lot of money to be carrying around.

I mentally ticked off the evidence against her. Katie had

dyed her hair and worn extensions to change her look, and she'd attempted to stay out of the photos Reyna had taken and posted to the Curves' social media accounts. She hadn't provided a driver's license or credit card when she'd checked in, and she'd joined the motorcycle club only a short time ago. Was she who she claimed to be? Was her name even really Katie Martin? Could she be the Sadie Hardin the guy who called Monday night had been looking for? I felt fairly certain she was involved in the motorcycle thefts, even if only tangentially. But could she somehow be involved in what happened to Gerri, too?

While I didn't have the resources to get to the bottom of things, there was someone who did. *Deputy Gillespie.* Leaving my cart in the hall, I rushed down to the registration desk, circled around it, and opened the drawer where I filed the signed lodging agreements. I riffled through them until I found the one Katie had signed, and pulled it from the file. I dialed the deputy's number. I got lucky. He answered on the fourth ring. The background noise told me he was on the move in his cruiser.

"Good morning, Deputy," I said. "It's Misty Murphy from the Mountaintop Lodge. I think I might have stumbled across something that might be relevant to the murder investigation."

"Give me a second to pull over." He was silent for a moment, then said, "Okay. I'm off the road now. Fill me in on what you've got."

I told him about Katie's bulldog keychain, how she hadn't presented any identification on check-in, and how I'd just spotted what appeared to be a big wad of cash in her backpack. "She said her wallet had been stolen. She paid for her stay in cash. I figured it was okay since the only other guests would also be members of the motorcycle club. But she's the newest member of their group. I'm not sure how well they really know her." I told him about the vans I'd seen at the lodge, at the closed inn, and on the parkway, about Katie's reaction when the van drove past us, how she'd said she thought she'd seen an old boyfriend but been mistaken. I also told him what Rocky and I had seen on our security camera footage. "We assumed the guys in the van wanted to steal the motorcycles. Two of the women in the club have had their motorcycles stolen recently. I'm wondering if Katie might have something to do with it." *Could Katie have joined the motorcycle club to gather information about the women and their motorcycles to make it easier for her cohorts to snatch the bikes?* I wondered if she knew where the other ladies lived, where they stored their bikes when they weren't riding them. I also wondered if the cash might be her share of the profits on the sale of the stolen bikes.

"Have you confronted Katie?" the deputy asked. "Told her any of this?"

"No," I said. "She's not here. The club went out for a ride to Mount Mitchell." It seemed like positively identifying the woman was step one. Then we could try to figure out whether she was involved with the guys in the van. *Could she be part of a motorcycle theft ring? Had Gerri become suspicious and thus a threat to the thieves?* It seemed possible. "I've got the license plate number for her Ninja. Can you run that and see if it's registered to a Katie Martin?"

"I sure can."

I read the number off the registration form. The clicks of his fingers typing on his laptop keyboard came through the phone. A moment later, he said, "Well, I'll be. You're on to something, Ms. Murphy. That bike's not registered to a Katie Martin. It's in a similar name, though."

"Might that name be Sadie Hardin?" I asked.

"How'd you know?"

"A man called the lodge Monday night shortly after the club arrived. He asked for Sadie Hardin and seemed surprised when I said we had no guest by that name."

"Did you mention to him that you had one with a similar name?"

"No," I said. "It didn't seem wise. I try to keep guest information private, let them decide what they want to share."

"Good call."

"What address did she use for her vehicle registration?" I asked. "I wonder if it's the same one she gave me." I rattled off the Raleigh address on the registration form.

"Yep," Gillespie said. "That's the one she used to register her vehicle. Hold on a second." More clicking noises came through the phone. "I see a North Carolina driver's license in the name of Sadie Hardin at that address. Let me check Mississippi's records, too." More clicks met my ears before he said, "I've got four hits." He mumbled, reading their birthdates out loud, before saying, "I found her. There's a Sadie Hardin licensed in Mississippi with the same birthdate as the Sadie Hardin licensed here in North Carolina."

"Is her hair dark or blonde in her driver's license photos?" I asked.

"Blonde."

"The young woman staying here has dark hair," I said, "but it's dyed. I noticed her blonde roots when she was checking in and bent over to pick up her things. I found a dark hair extension in her room, too."

"Sounds like she might be trying to disguise herself," the deputy said. "Of course, you women love your hair dye. My wife's always switching things up. Getting highlights and whatnot."

His remark was somewhat sexist. After all, many men dyed their hair now, too. But he had a point. The difference in hair color could just be a young woman shaking things up. Women liked to change up their look now and then, and the change was often instigated by a bad breakup. We wanted to become someone new, no longer be the woman who'd been dumped. But the young woman at my lodge had another distinctive characteristic. *Her height.*

"Is she tall?" I asked. "The girl staying here stands nearly six feet."

There was a beat of silence as the deputy consulted the records. "Five eleven. Not many women are that tall. Heck, most men are shorter than that."

"It has to be her, then, doesn't it?"

"Not necessarily," he said. "It could be a coincidence. Let's not jump to conclusions."

I felt my ire rise a little. Concluding that the woman staying at my lodge and the woman in the DMV records were one and the same hardly felt like a leap. It felt like a logical deduction. Even so, he had a point.

"I'd like to run her fingerprints," Gillespie said, "see if we can get a positive ID and determine if she's got priors. Can you get me something from this woman's room? It can't be anything that belongs to her or I'd need a search warrant. But as the lodge's owner, you have the right to enter the room to remove your own property. Maybe a water glass or the hair dryer?"

"I can go do that right now."

"Good," he said. "Wear gloves so you don't leave your own prints on the item. Put whatever you can get me in a plastic bag. I'll be by later to pick it up."

The deputy hadn't mentioned Todd. I wondered about the missing hiking poles, whether the clue had led anywhere. "Is Todd in custody?"

"No, we haven't been able to pin anything on the guy, at least not yet. When I asked him about the poles, he told me he stopped in the parking lot at the trailhead after hiking yesterday. He claims he leaned his poles up against the kiosk while he drank some water, and then got into a conversation with another hiker and accidentally left them behind. He says he didn't even realize he'd forgotten the poles until I called to ask about them. An officer from the Seven Devils Police Department agreed to run by the trailhead for me and take a look this morning, but I haven't heard back from her yet."

I wondered if the officer would find the poles and, if she did, would one of them show signs of damage? I also wondered if Todd's story was even true. Maybe he'd struck Gerri with a hiking pole and then ditched them someplace along the way. He could have tossed them out along the parkway somewhere where they'd never be found. There were long stretches of road where the woods were especially thick and wild, essentially inaccessible.

We ended the call and I rolled my cart down to Katie's—or Sadie's—room. On the off chance that any of the bikers returned early, I wanted it to look like I was cleaning the room, not pilfering from it. I unlocked the door and stepped inside. To my dismay, Katie/Sadie hadn't touched the water glasses on her coffee bar. The mugs were undisturbed, too. Though she'd used the towels, I figured it would be next to impossible to get a fingerprint from moist fabric. The hair dryer was still tucked away under the countertop, its cord wrapped neatly around the handle, unused. She'd likely turned on a lamp, but it would probably be difficult to lift a complete fingerprint from the small knob. *Hmm* . . .

It was then I remembered the thing that brought me here in the first place. *The television.* It had been playing the Georgia Bulldogs versus Mississippi State Bulldogs volleyball game. My gaze went to the dresser, where I always placed the TV remote after wiping it down. It wasn't there. I turned around. There it was, on the bedside table. *Good.* That meant she'd used it, left evidence of her true identity behind. Even so, I knew not everyone was in the law enforcement database. She'd only be in the system if she'd been arrested before. There was a good chance that Deputy Gillespie might not get a hit on her fingerprints. I supposed he'd press her directly, then, if he had to.

I donned a fresh pair of gloves, picked up the remote by the top end where I'd be less likely to disturb any prints that might be on it, and slid it into a plastic trash bag. Leaving my housekeeping cart at the door, I hurried down the hall and locked the remote control in the key drawer at the front desk. I looked up to see a red Tesla rolling to a stop in front of the lodge. To my surprise, neither Sterling nor Andrea sat at the wheel, but Mariah did. Even though Reyna had told me that Mariah and Gerri had been cordial, my heart couldn't help but do a nervous *bump-bump* on seeing the woman. Andrea had said Mariah had been shopping most of the preceding day, so the woman seemed to have an alibi for Gerri's murder. But I couldn't forget that Mariah none-theless had a motive to kill Gerri—getting her hands on the trust funds. She might even have had a means—Sterling's golf clubs. *Why is she here?*

I'd kept the front doors locked after my guests left this morning, so I walked over to the door and met Mariah there. Though it was still sunny, the temperature had fallen and the wind had picked up. She'd dressed accordingly, wearing a black track suit. The dark color and the fact that the track suit had a hood made her look like an athletic grim reaper.

"Hello, Mariah," I said. "What can I help you with?" Rather than allow her into the lodge, I stepped outside, into the brisk autumn day. A cloud seemed to pass over her face, which already looked stricken. I supposed she'd expected at least a lukewarm reception and, here I was, making her stand outside like some sort of unwelcome door-to-door solicitor.

"I was hoping to speak with Reyna." She glanced over to where the Curves had parked their motorcycles before. The space was empty now. "They went out on a ride?"

"Yes. They figured Gerri would have wanted them to go, and sitting around here wallowing in grief wouldn't do anyone any good."

Mariah nodded almost imperceptibly. When she spoke, her voice was soft and broke. "I wish I'd been here last night when the deputy gave everyone the news."

Since she'd brought up the subject, I felt free to ask, "Why weren't you?"

A tear escaped her eye and ran down her cheek. "My mother is watching our kids back home. We do a video call each night at their bedtime. I didn't want to miss it. I had no idea Gerri had died or I would have come."

I found her explanation a little specious. "Why did you think law enforcement would summon your husband if it wasn't an emergency?"

She wiped another tear and looked away. "I thought maybe he'd pushed Gerri again about the trust and that she'd called to report it as harassment or something." She turned back to me. "Sterling sometimes . . ." She looked up, as if searching for a word that would make her point yet not denigrate her husband. She went with "oversteps." She released a shaky breath. "He thinks he's being a good father, doing what's best for his children . . ."

She didn't finish her sentence, but she didn't have to. Clearly, she didn't agree with his methods, even if she admired his purpose. Her statement had me wondering again if Sterling was the one who'd killed Gerri. He seemed to have a poor sense of boundaries and a well-developed sense of entitlement.

She worried her lip. "What did the deputy say? I mean, I know he said it looked like Gerri's crash was an accident, but do they know why she lost control of her bike?"

Is she fishing for information? Trying to find out what law enforcement might suspect? Maybe Sterling sent her here to gather intel, to see if law enforcement realized the mark on Gerri's helmet was caused by a golf club. If he had sent his wife here to gather information, did that mean she knew he was responsible for Gerri's demise? Or might he have kept her in the dark? Of course, it was always possible that Mariah was genuinely concerned about Gerri and was simply trying to make sense of the situation.

"The deputy mentioned the possibility that a bear or deer might have been on the road, and that Gerri swerved to avoid hitting them. October is the most active month for bears and deer in this area."

Mariah glanced over at the empty parking spots again. "Do you have any idea when they'll be back?"

"No," I said. "They didn't give me a time. I expect it will be before dark, but they might be planning to have dinner on their drive back to the lodge."

"I can't be gone that long," she said quietly, looking down.

"Why not?"

Her gaze returned to my face. "Sterling doesn't know I'm here. Neither does Andrea. They're golfing together today. They wouldn't be happy if they knew I came here to talk to Reyna about Gerri." She exhaled a sharp breath. "It's just silly family politics."

Divorce could indeed make things awkward, test alliances and cause jealousies. But it was in everyone's best interest to get along. Too bad Sterling and Andrea didn't understand that.

She said, "Will you tell Reyna that I came by? And that I was heartbroken when I heard the news?"

I gave her a nod. "I'd be happy to pass along the message."

"Thank you."

Though her words had a finality to them, she made no

move to go, as if wanting or needing something more. She stared at me and her face started to wobble. A few seconds more and she totally broke down, sobbing into her hands, her shoulders jerking. Her sorrow seemed sincere, and I suddenly felt cruel keeping her outside.

I put a hand on her shoulder. "Why don't you come in for a little bit? You can sit by the fire until you pull yourself together."

She nodded. I held the door open for her and she went inside. She walked slowly over to the great room, took a seat by the fire, and cast a hopeful glance my way. I realized she wanted someone to talk to. With Reyna gone, I supposed that task fell to me. I had a real job to do, cleaning the rooms, but my maternal instincts wouldn't let me leave this sad young woman just sitting there alone.

I walked over and sat down, too. "Were you and Gerri close?"

She nodded, gulped down a sob, and sniffled. "She was only Sterling's stepmother, and she didn't come along until he was nearly grown, so the two of them weren't close. But Gerri and I really connected. She gave me a lot of good advice." When she sniffled again, I plucked a tissue from a box on a nearby table and handed it to her. She dabbed at her eyes and nose before continuing. "I could go to Gerri with anything. She was like a second mother to me."

A second mother? I had my doubts about that. With Mariah working full time and Sterling discouraging his wife from engaging with the woman, it seemed unlikely that Mariah and Gerri could spend enough time together to develop a strong bond. *Mariah is laying it on a little thick, isn't she?* I wondered again if she might have had something to do with Gerri's crash. I decided to see if I could catch her in a lie. But first, I needed to gain her trust.

"That's wonderful that you two had such a good relationship," I said. "What types of things did she give you advice on?"

"Everything." Mariah raised her hands slightly, palms out, in an all-encompassing gesture. "Work. Marriage. Kids. Money. She knew what it was like to want to build a career."

I took it that Andrea did not. According to what Gerri had told me on Tuesday evening, Andrea had stopped working once she'd married Norman. Being a homemaker wasn't a bad thing, of course. I'd spent many years as primarily a stay-at-home mother who worked seasonal part-time gigs to supplement the family income. Running this lodge was my first real job in two decades. But I could understand where Mariah was coming from. She had career goals and ambitions, and that was something Andrea could not relate to.

Mariah went on. "My kids adored Gerri as much as she adored them. You should see how their faces light up"— she corrected herself—"*lit* up when they'd see her. They called her Ree-Ree. They had a hard time pronouncing her name. She was always so patient with them. She'd get down on the floor and play dolls and trains and have tea parties." She gulped back a sob. "I'm really going to miss her."

"Sounds like she was a great woman," I said. "I know the ladies in the club had a lot of love and respect for her."

Mariah was quiet for a bit. It seemed that she'd just needed someone to talk to about what she was feeling, to get things off her chest. She stood to go. "Sorry I unloaded on you. I just don't have anyone else to turn to right now."

I gave her a soft smile. "I was happy to listen. We women need to support each other." As I walked her to the door, I said, "Did you find some good deals at the outlets yesterday?"

"I only went to the Carter's store," Mariah replied, "but I found some cute things for the kids. Seems they grow a size every time I turn around."

She hit only one shop yesterday? Andrea had implied that Mariah had spent the entire day shopping. Had she been trying to cover for Mariah? Had Mariah just slipped up by admitting she hadn't been shopping all day? And if she hadn't been shopping, where had she been?

"Kids certainly do grow fast," I said. "I've got two boys and they'd always outgrow their clothes before they wore them out."

Mariah paused a moment before responding with a question. "How did you know I went shopping?"

I lifted one shoulder casually. "Andrea mentioned it. I told her that I liked shopping at the outlet mall in Blowing Rock. She said you enjoyed bargain shopping, too."

Mariah frowned slightly, as if she knew Andrea looked down on her for it.

I decided to do a little more fishing, see if I could get anything else out of her. "Andrea mentioned that she had a lesson with a tennis pro yesterday. Do you plan to take a private lesson while you're at the resort, too? Seems like a great way to improve your game."

Mariah's head cocked slightly. "Andrea said she had a lesson yesterday?"

"Mm-hmm. I understand Sterling played a round of golf and then had a nice meal and drinks at the tavern."

Her head was still cocked, but she nodded. "He'd play a round every day if he could. It's what he lives for." She righted her head and managed a feeble smile.

"Other than visiting the Carter's outlet," I said, "what did you do all day while they were gone?"

Mariah froze. *I'd been too obvious, hadn't I?* Her answer was evasive. "Oh, you know. Just puttered around the resort."

Puttering. Sure. But had she taken Sterling's putter to Gerri's helmet?

CHAPTER 18

Yeti

The two men were back in the woods. She'd been watching them for several minutes now as she lay, unmoving, on the windowsill, her eyes mere slits. They'd come up the trail, then turned back and returned the way they'd come, only to venture back toward the lodge again a few minutes later, as if they were attempting to familiarize themselves with the trail. She'd walked back and forth in the lodge when she and Misty had first moved in for the same reason, to get to know her surroundings. It was instinctual. Not only had Yeti been curious about their new home, but she felt inherently driven to find places to hide, either for self-protection or stealth. One never knew when they might need a secret place to crouch so that they could pounce on an unsuspecting mouse. The opportunity to prey upon a small rodent had yet to present itself, but she'd hunted down a fair share of spiders and dust bunnies. Maybe the men in the woods were doing the same, preparing to capture some prey. But what, exactly, did they plan to prey upon?

CHAPTER 19

Misty

I walked Mariah outside and bade her goodbye. As long as I was outside, I figured I might as well check the mail. I strode to the mailbox on the roadside, pulled the door open, and retrieved the contents—my electric bill, a box of individually wrapped leaf-shaped maple candies I'd ordered to put on the guests' pillows, and the most recent edition of my favorite woman's magazine. The cover promised both tried-and-true diet tips and delicious dessert recipes. I just might have to try their pumpkin pie recipe at Thanksgiving next month. The crust bore a beautiful leaf-shaped border. I wasn't sure I could pull it off, but maybe I could get some baking tips from Patty. She was a whiz in the kitchen, a natural chef and baker.

As I turned back around, I noticed Yeti lying on the windowsill in our room. She faced the rear of the lodge. Her head rested on her paws and she appeared to be asleep, but I knew better. The very tip of her tail twitched. Something had her agitated. Probably a hawk. She cowered anytime the shadow of a large bird moved across the landscape. I put a hand over my eyes to shade them from the sun and looked up into the sky. I saw nothing but fluffy white clouds. If there had been a bird, it must have flown off already. But then my eye caught movement in the woods. Two people made their way down the trail, heading away from the lodge. They'd probably hiked up from the small parking lot at Perry Park on Tamarack Road. The park was a half-mile drive down the winding road that weaved through the town, but only a quarter mile away via the trail. Even so, it wasn't an easy quarter mile. The terrain was steep and rocky. Tree roots posed a tripping hazard. You had to watch your step or you could take a tumble. That said, it was a beautiful hike.

I went back inside the lodge and locked the door behind me. After stashing the candy, bill, and magazine at the front desk, I returned to my cart and spent the next two hours cleaning and mulling over the clues and suspects. *Could the killer be Katie, also presumably known as Sadie? Todd? Had it been Mariah? Sterling? Andrea? What about Erika? Someone else entirely?* When I finished cleaning the rooms, the lodge smelled fresh and sparkled, but I was no closer to figuring out who had killed Gerri.

I pulled a large garbage bag from my cart and rounded up the one from Brynn's cart, as well. Venturing outside again, I carried the bags to the metal bear-proof bin. As I turned to head back into the lodge, movement in my peripheral vision caught my eye. The strong autumn wind had caught the scarecrows and threatened to pull them from the stakes they were tied to. Realizing they'd be less vulnerable if they weren't out in the open, I decided to pull the hay bales over in front of the lodge where the building would block the breeze.

I strode over to the scarecrows and took hold of the twine holding the bale together. I was tugging at the hay bale, making very slow progress, when Deputy Gillespie turned into the parking lot. He parked his cruiser nearby, climbed out, and walked over to help me. "Where do you want this?"

"Thanks—there, by the flowerpot." I pointed to a spot in front of the lodge.

Being far stronger than me, the deputy moved the hay bales and scarecrows with ease.

"Thanks, Deputy," I said. "You're a lifesaver." Well, maybe not a lifesaver, but he'd certainly saved my back. Sometimes I missed the days when physical activity didn't come with repercussions. But I'd never want to go back to a time when I didn't know everything I knew now. I'd learned some hard but valuable lessons over the years, and they'd made me better prepared to handle the things life sent my way. Of course, they hadn't exactly prepared me to investigate a murder. But while Patty had a natural knack in the kitchen, I seemed to have a natural knack for solving crimes.

The scarecrows now protected from the wind, the deputy walked back to his cruiser. He popped the trunk and removed Erika's dented and scraped fender.

Looks like the lab is done with it. My hopes rose that he'd tell me he'd identified the culprit. "Did the paint on Erika's bike match the paint on the back of Gerri's motorcycle?"

"We don't know yet," he said. "The lab took a sample

from Erika's fender, but they haven't completed their analysis. Mind getting this back to her?" He held the fender out to me.

"No problem." I took Erika's fender from him and we continued on into the lodge. After setting the dented part on the registration counter, I offered the deputy a warm drink. "Coffee? Tea? Cider?"

"I wouldn't mind a cup of coffee," he said.

I headed for the drink station. "How do you take it?"

"Black."

A straightforward, unadulterated brew seemed appropriate for someone who dealt in facts.

I fixed him a cup from the urn. After handing him the coffee, I said, "I had an interesting visitor earlier."

"Oh, yeah? Who?" He raised the cup to his lips and took a sip as he waited for his answer.

"Mariah Burnham."

"Mariah Burnham?" he repeated. "Hmm." Wrinkles formed at the edge of his eyes as they narrowed. "What did she want?"

"Consolation, information, or both." I gave him the rundown. "She told me she'd only gone to the Carter's outlet, but yesterday Andrea said that Mariah had been out shopping all day."

The deputy reached the same conclusion I had. "Maybe Mariah didn't realize Andrea had made up an alibi for her. Or maybe Andrea was simply mistaken. I phoned the resort earlier today. I confirmed that Sterling played a round of golf yesterday morning and had a late lunch in a restaurant on site. I also confirmed with the tennis pro that Andrea had a one-hour lesson that started at eleven. If Andrea went to her lesson and returned to their suite later to find it empty, she might have made assumptions about Mariah's whereabouts."

He could be right. Even so, it seemed like a person would be careful to get their facts straight before giving a statement to a member of law enforcement. "I was curious, so I asked Mariah flat out what she'd been doing the rest of the day."

"What did she say?"

I made air quotes with my fingers. "She puttered around the resort." I also told him what she'd said about Gerri and their relationship. "She referred to her as a 'second mother.'" *There I go with the air quotes again.*

"You think she was being genuine?" he asked.

"For the most part, yes," I said. "But I'm a mother, so I know how we are. Our kids come first and we'll do anything to protect them. Mariah might have liked Gerri and had a good relationship with her, but all of that could have changed once Gerri had control of the trust. If Mariah thought Gerri was standing in the way of her children's happiness, or withholding money she thought could be used to their benefit, she could have turned into a mother bear."

Everyone knew you shouldn't come between a mama bear and her cubs, or she just might eviscerate you. Truth be told, I'd experienced that same surge of primal maternal instinct a time or two myself—once when a bully picked on my son J.J. on his way into school and stole the money I'd given him to spend at the Scholastic Book Fair, and another time when Mitchell was turned down by a girl he'd asked to the prom. *How dare she break my son's heart!* I'd wanted to throttle both the bully and the twit who couldn't see what a great catch my son was. I hadn't actually throttled them, of course. They'd only been kids. But I could see a mother momentarily losing her composure if she was desperate to keep her kids from harm or hurt.

I went on. "Mariah might have taken advantage of the fact that Sterling was playing golf yesterday and Andrea was at a tennis lesson to approach Gerri on her own. She'd know the women were riding the parkway. Reyna has been posting photos and their daily itineraries on their social media accounts. It would have been easy to intercept them along their route." Todd had proven that much.

The deputy's head bobbed as he absorbed the information. "I'll give that theory some thought. By the way, I was able to get a copy of Gerri's will from her lawyer's office. Turns out Mariah is one of Gerri's heirs."

"She is?" The fact that Mariah would inherit Gerri's fortune gave her a clear motive for killing the woman. But had she actually done it?

"Gerri appointed her CPA as trustee to manage Mariah's portion. She set it up for what the attorney called 'staggered distributions.' Five percent of the trust property would be paid out to Mariah each year for twenty years."

In other words, even though Mariah would inherit property from Gerri, she wouldn't get it outright all at once. *"Mariah's portion?"* I repeated. "So, there were other heirs?"

"That's correct," Deputy Gillespie said. "Gerri left only a third of her property to Mariah. She left another third to her brother. She left the remaining third to Reyna."

I supposed it wasn't necessarily unusual for a childless woman to leave her property to a close friend, but the information nonetheless gave me a moment's pause. Reyna had brought the metal skewers for roasting marshmallows, but did she have one with her on Wednesday's ride? Would the lightweight metal skewer have been enough to damage Gerri's helmet even if Reyna had struck her with it? It seemed unlikely. What's more, the scenario seemed impossible given that Reyna had been riding the lead bike and Gerri had taken up the rear.

But could someone else have gotten their hands on a skewer? Maybe kept one after they'd made s'mores Monday night? It would have been difficult to obscure such a long skewer. It was too long to fit fully inside a motorcycle saddle bag. *But it would have been easy to hide in a sidecar . . .*

No, I told myself. *There's no reason for Bessie to have killed Gerri.* At least, no reason I was aware of. "Who's Gerri's executor?"

"Also the CPA," the deputy said. He gave me the accountant's name and phone number so that I could enter them into my cell phone. "Give her a call. You two can make arrangements for Gerri's property that's here at the lodge."

The most logical plan would be to have one of the riders put their bike in Gerri's trailer and drive her SUV back to Raleigh. They could take the personal items I'd collected from her room, too, and turn them over to the accountant. I'd suggest this arrangement to the CPA when I spoke with her.

Deputy Gillespie moved on. "The officer from Seven

Devils found Todd's hiking poles at the trailhead at Grandfather Mountain."

Brynn stepped out of the laundry room down the hall, where she'd apparently been eavesdropping on our conversation, and walked to the lobby to join us. "What do hiking poles have to do with the investigation?"

The deputy looked from Brynn to me. "I guess the cat's out of the bag now. But I suppose it doesn't matter. Brynn's already aware of the damage on Ms. Burnham's back fender anyway." He turned to Brynn and explained the situation, telling her how Gerri's helmet bore evidence of being struck.

"Someone whacked Gerri upside the head?" My assistant put a hand on her belly, as if the thought of someone taking a swing at the woman's head made her sick. *I understand that feeling.* "That's why you were looking for Todd's hiking poles?"

The deputy nodded. "Exactly. We thought he might have used them to hit Gerri."

"And?" I asked, prodding him along.

"His hiking poles aren't new, but they aren't damaged, either."

"Are you sure the poles the officer found are Todd's?" I asked. "Could someone else have left their poles?"

"They're definitely Todd's," the deputy said. "He gave us the color and brand name so we'd know what to look for. The ones the officer found matched his description. He'd even written his initials on the handles in permanent marker."

I mulled this new information over for a moment. "Is it

possible Todd planted the poles to make it look like he took a hike, but that he just left instead and didn't actually go on a hike?"

"I suppose it's possible," the deputy said, a skeptical frown on his face. "But I'd say the odds are low. It would be a risky way of trying to deflect suspicion. After all, someone could have taken the poles and left him without a verifiable alibi."

Looked like I could cross Todd off the list of suspects, tentatively, at least. That still left plenty of others. Erika. Katie or Sadie. Sterling. Andrea. Mariah. The drunk birthday girl.

No sooner than I'd had the thought about the coed, the deputy disavowed me of it. "By the way, I tracked down the drunk girl who took y'all's photo at the overlook."

"You did?"

"She says she didn't do it."

Brynn said, "She could be lying, couldn't she?"

"Doubtful," he replied. "She gave me the names of her three friends who were in the car with her. I've spoken with each of them. They all said nothing happened. They said they didn't even see the women from the motorcycle club after stopping at the Table Rock Outlook. They headed on down the parkway and didn't make any more stops before driving back to Charlotte."

Looked like I could cross the birthday girl and her friends off my list of suspects, too. Shortening the list felt like we'd made some progress, even if we had yet to identify the killer. *Speaking of identification* . . . I circled around the desk, unlocked the drawer, and retrieved the bag containing the television remote. I handed it over the counter to the deputy.

He raised the device to his forehead in an improvised salute. "Thanks. I'll be in touch once the lab has a chance to lift and run the prints." With that, he headed out the door.

Once the door swung closed behind him, Brynn turned to me, her expression curious. "What was in the bag?"

"The remote control from Katie's room. He's going to see if they can positively identify her, see if she's got a criminal record."

"Ooh!" Brynn's auburn brows wagged. "Things are getting juicy."

They certainly were. I'd have been happy if things *weren't* juicy. In fact, as far as I was concerned, things could stay bone dry. *Ugh.* The thought of bones only made me think of Gerri and the crushing blow her helmet had taken. I wondered if her skull had been fractured in the crash. I'd be surprised if it hadn't. Motorcycle helmets were designed to take quite a beating. If the helmet had given way, human bone could likely give way, too. *How horrible.*

Brynn returned to the laundry room and I placed a call to the CPA's office.

After I'd identified myself, the accountant's assistant said she'd been expecting my call. "Mrs. Burnham's lawyers contacted us with the sad news. We were so sorry to hear it." The woman informed me that her boss was unavailable at the moment but would give me a call back, if not this afternoon, then sometime tomorrow. "Extended tax returns are coming due and she can hardly catch her breath."

"No problem." Having worked retail gigs many Christmases, I understood how some jobs were much busier at certain times of the year than others. Though the lodge had been open only a matter of weeks, business had picked up quite a bit with the fall foliage reaching its peak. I knew it would decline for a few weeks once the leaves fell, then pick up again when the ski season began. I bade the woman goodbye and ended the call.

While Brynn vacuumed the lobby and great room, I went out back to sweep dirt, leaves, and twigs off the deck. The wind had already done most of the work for me, so I finished quickly. Over the muted growl of the vacuum, my ears detected the buzz of a single motorcycle engine. I went inside. Through the front windows, I could see Erika securing her motorcycle. I walked over to Brynn, who was bent over, using the hose attachment to suck dust from the baseboards. The woman was nothing if not thorough. She couldn't hear me coming over the sound of the vacuum cleaner, and she didn't appear to have seen me coming, either. I reached down and put a hand on her shoulder to get her attention. She shrieked and dropped the hose.

When she turned to look and realized it was me, she put a hand to her chest and stood up straight. "You nearly scared me to death!"

I realized then that, despite Brynn's calm demeanor, she'd been put on edge by Gerri's murder. "Sorry, Brynn." I cut my eyes to indicate the front door, where Erika was using her keys to come inside.

Brynn nodded in understanding, realizing I'd just wanted to let her know that one of our guests had returned—one who was a prime suspect in the murder investigation.

"Hello, Erika," I said as she came through the door with her helmet in her hand.

In reply, she offered only a flat, "Hey."

"Did you have a nice ride?" She might be a murder suspect, but she was still my guest. I should be cordial, at least until I knew the truth.

"No," she said. "It's no fun to ride alone."

I wasn't sure how to respond, so I didn't. She wouldn't have had to ride alone if she hadn't been so reckless, but pointing out that her loneliness was her own fault didn't seem like a smart idea. I gestured to the registration desk, where her damaged motorcycle fender lay on the counter. "Deputy Gillespie returned your fender."

She turned, spotted the part, and walked over to the desk. She stared down at it for a few beats before glancing my way. "Does this mean I've been cleared?"

My impulse was to feign ignorance, pretend to be staying out of the investigation, but she'd have to know I'd be curious and would have asked the deputy about the status of their case. "Not yet," I told her. "The deputy said the lab needs to analyze things first."

"They'll clear me soon, then."

There was a touch of smugness in her voice, and I wondered whether she knew they'd clear her because she was innocent, or because she'd hit Gerri with something other than her own motorcycle and knew they wouldn't be able to match the paint on her bike to the dent on Gerri's back fender.

"I'm glad to have this back," she added. "My front tire was kicking up loose gravel all day and there was nothing to keep it from hitting me." She set her helmet down on the counter next to the fender, pulled up the leg of her jeans, and showed us her right shin. The skin bore telltale pink welts where she'd been pelted with rocks. Some of the larger spots had already begun to turn into bruises. With the black-and-blue marks on her skin, she resembled a Dalmatian.

"Ouch," Brynn said. "That had to hurt."

"Pain lets you know you're alive." Erika grabbed the fender from the countertop and raised it in the air. Brynn and I both flinched and instinctively threw up our hands to protect our faces. On seeing our reaction, Erika's face fell and she lowered the fender. "I wasn't going to throw this at you. Jeez! I was just going to ask if you had some tools so I can reattach it."

I felt a twinge of guilt that we'd hurt Erika's feelings, but our reaction had been natural. She was suspected in a violent murder, after all. "Rocky will be back soon," I said. "He's got all kinds of tools."

"Cool." With that, she headed down the hall to her room, helmet in one hand, fender in the other.

By then, it was the end of Brynn's workday. She glanced at the clock hanging on the wall behind the registration desk, frowned, and whispered, "I don't want to leave you alone in the lodge with *her*." She cut her eyes down the hall to indicate the room in which Erika was staying.

It was sweet of Brynn to be concerned, but even if Erika had killed Gerri, it seemed unlikely she'd attack me. I'd given her no reason, and chalking up a second victim would only make matters worse for her. Still, the girl was a loose cannon, as Brynn had told the deputy the day before. She seemed to have little impulse control. Who knew what she might do?

Fortunately, the problem was solved when Rocky's truck rolled into the parking lot. "Rocky's back," I said, pointing to the front windows.

Brynn's shoulders relaxed in relief. "Good." She returned the vacuum cleaner to the housekeeping closet and retrieved her purse. She passed Rocky and Molasses coming in as she was on her way out. The two humans exchanged a quick verbal greeting, while the dog wagged his tail to let Brynn know he was happy to see her. She gave him a quick pat on the head and a "Who's a good boy?" before continuing on her way.

Rocky walked over to me. "Any news?"

"Lots." There was much to tell. I wasn't sure where to start but figured I'd just proceed with things in the order they'd happened. "Mariah Burnham stopped by."

"She did? Why?"

I raised my palms. "She said she wanted to speak to Reyna and express her condolences, but she could have been lying. She might have come to fish for information." I told him how she'd contradicted Andrea by saying she had not, in fact, been shopping all day as her mother-in-law said. "She told me she'd only gone to a children's clothing store to pick up a few things for her kids."

Rocky stroked his beard in thought. "Maybe Andrea thought Mariah had been shopping all day and was simply mistaken. Andrea had been at a tennis lesson, right? She might not have been aware of Mariah's whereabouts and just assumed she'd already left to check out the stores."

He could be right. Although Andrea said they were staying in a two-bedroom suite, the resort was a large place. If Mariah had truly been "puttering around" the resort, Andrea might have assumed her daughter-in-law was hitting the nearby stores, especially if she'd expressed an intent to do so at some point in the day.

"There's more," I said. With Brynn having heard about the damage to Gerri's helmet earlier, I was no longer sworn to secrecy on that detail. I told him how Gerri's helmet had been struck on the right side, and filled him in about the officer from Seven Devils finding Todd's hiking poles in the parking lot at Grandfather Mountain. I also told him the tipsy college girls were no longer persons of interest. "The deputy returned Erika's fender. He said the lab took a paint sample to compare to Gerri's fender. He'll let me know when they get results. But that's not the only thing the lab will be looking at. They'll be taking fingerprints from the remote control from Katie's room and running them through the system."

"Why?"

"Because there's a very good chance Katie's not who she says she is. Her motorcycle is registered in the name Sadie Hardin." I told him about my suspicions that she could be connected to the men in the van, that they might all be part of a motorcycle theft ring from Mississippi. "The dog on her keychain looks just like the Mississippi State mascot, and there's a Sadie Hardin around her age and height who has a driver's license issued in that state. It seems much more likely she's Sadie Hardin than Katie Martin. I don't even know what to call her now. Do I stick with

Katie? Go with *Sadie*? *Sadie* seems best. There's no going back. I can't unknow what I know, you know?"

"You could do a mash-up and call her Skatie."

"Now there's a creative solution."

We shared a chuckle.

"There's still more," I said. "I also saw a roll of cash in her backpack." I explained how I'd spotted the zipper gap in the mirror and been able to snap the pic without having to touch her backpack.

Rocky's eyes gleamed with admiration. "You sure are good at finding clues and putting them together."

I beamed with pride. "I suppose I do have a knack for crime solving. But speaking of putting things together, would you mind reattaching Erika's fender to her motorcycle?"

"Be happy to," he said.

We walked down the hall to Erika's room. Through the door, we could hear the sound of the young woman sobbing. Whether she was crying from guilt over causing Gerri's death, loneliness, or grief, we couldn't be sure. Rocky and I exchanged a glance before I raised a hand and knocked. "Rocky's back!" I called. "He can put your fender on for you."

Erika's voice came from inside. "Just a second!" We waited a moment and she opened the door. Her eyes were pink, puffy, and a little wet, but she tried to act like things were normal. She held the fender out to him. "Thanks, man."

Rocky took the fender from her and looked it over. "Want me to try to get the dents out first? I've got a propane torch. It should do the trick."

Erika's face brightened in surprise. "You'd do that for me? Really?"

"Sure," Rocky replied.

"Wow," Erika said. "Thanks!"

I got the sense that she wasn't used to people offering to do nice things for her. Gerri had mentioned to me on Monday that the young woman had "had it hard." Despite the fact that Erika was still a murder suspect, my heart broke a little for her. Everyone should have someone they could count on. I sensed that Erika had no one, at least now that Gerri was gone.

The three of us went outside. Erika and I followed Rocky to the tool shed. He unlocked it and rummaged around until he found a small blue propane tank about a foot long with a brass nozzle on the end. He set up two wooden sawhorses and placed a piece of plywood atop them, forming a make-shift worktable. After donning a pair of tinted goggles and heavy work gloves, he admonished us to stand back. He looked down at his dog. "You too, Mo."

I patted my leg and the dog padded over to me. I reached down and scratched behind his ears, knowing he'd stay put as long as he was getting the attention.

Rocky ignited the torch, and I found myself squinting against the bright flame. Erika raised her arm to block the intense glow. He ran the flame back and forth over the metal, and used pliers and a hammer to bend and shape the fender. The metal creaked as he forced it into shape. A few minutes later, the fender was still missing paint and bore scratches, but at least it was no longer bent and mangled. Rocky extinguished the torch and raised the goggles to examine his handiwork.

Erika stepped up beside him. "Dude!" she cried happily. "That looks a million times better."

Rocky lifted a shoulder, not as impressed with himself as she was. He took his handyman skills for granted. "The fender still needs some touch-up paint, but at least you won't have to replace it." He tugged his gloves off and left them on the improvised workbench. Rounding up a toolbox from the shed, he said, "Let's get it back on your bike."

CHAPTER 20

Misty

Erika cradled her repaired fender to her chest, as if carrying a precious baby. I followed the two of them over to her motorcycle and watched as Rocky reattached the metal piece. Erika surreptitiously wiped a fresh tear from her eye when he finished and thanked him again before going back inside. Did this tough-as-nails biker chick have a soft side, or was this merely an act to deflect suspicion? It was impossible to know for certain.

I helped Rocky dismantle the worktable and return the sawhorses, plywood, and torch to the shed. He locked it up and turned to me. "How about dinner at my place tonight? I've got some fabulous lasagna."

I pointed an accusing finger at him. "You didn't think it was so fabulous when I served it to you."

He fought a grin. I followed him inside and we walked down to his room. After washing up, he removed the leftover lasagna from his fridge, plunked it onto a plate, and slid it into his microwave to warm it up. Once it was heated, he cut it in two, transferred one of the pieces to a second plate, and set them on the table. He pulled two cans of flavored, carbonated water from his fridge and plunked them down on the table, too.

Setting the topic of Gerri's murder aside for now, we chatted about more pleasant topics. His youngest daughter, who attended Appalachian State University in the nearby town of Boone, had earned all A's on her recent exams. His middle daughter, who worked as a hairdresser, had been hired to style hair for a bride and her seven bridesmaids. "The wedding will be held in the Overlook Barn this Saturday evening," Rocky said. "She plans to stop by the lodge after she's done fixing their hair."

The Overlook Barn was a popular event venue in Beech Mountain, encompassing a delightful rustic barn and mountaintop meadow with beautiful views of the Blue Ridge Mountains. It was a perfect place to hold a wedding and reception. I wondered whether I should ask to meet Rocky's daughter while she was in Beech. I was curious about his girls, but had yet to meet them.

He beat me to the punch. "I told her I'd like to introduce her to my new boss."

I felt my face flush. I was flattered he wanted her to meet me. That said something, didn't it? "I'd like to meet her, too." Admittedly, I was a bit nervous. I hoped she'd like me. Her opinion would likely mean something to her father. It would mean something to me, too.

We'd just finished our meal when the club returned to the lodge, the sound of their cycles preceding them. I stood from the table. "I'd better get back to the desk in case they need anything."

"I'll be out in a little bit," Rocky said. "As soon as I'm done washing these dishes."

He set our plates on the floor to let Molasses lick the cheese remnants and tomato sauce from them. I supposed I should have been disgusted, but instead the gesture seemed sweet. The dog clearly considered the samples to be a nice treat.

I was sitting at the desk ten minutes later when Sadie— as I was now officially calling her—walked up. "I can't find the remote control to my TV. I've looked everywhere. Under the bed. In the drawers. Behind the dresser. It seems to have disappeared."

Uh-oh. I'd forgotten to replace the one I'd taken from her room earlier and given to Deputy Gillespie. I made up a lie on the spot. "Sorry! I knocked it off the table when I was cleaning your room and it broke. I meant to replace it, but it slipped my mind. I'll get you a new one." I slid off the stool and opened a drawer below me to retrieve a replacement remote and batteries. After inserting the batteries into the compartment, I slid the plastic cover into place and handed it to her. "Here you go, Sadie."

Oops. My use of the name had been unintentional, subconscious, but it didn't escape the young woman's notice. A dark cloud of alarm passed over her face. *Uh-oh.* I'd tipped my hand, hadn't I?

Fortunately, the cloud passed when I gave her a smile and said, "Do you like maple candy?" Maybe my feigned nonchalance would convince her she'd misheard me and that I'd used her alias instead. I retrieved the box from the countertop and held it up to show her. "This box just arrived today. I plan to put these on everyone's pillows when

I clean the rooms tomorrow." I opened the box and held it out to her. "Try one if you'd like."

She reached in and selected a candy. "Thanks. I've never tried maple candy before, but I like maple syrup."

"You'll love the candy then, too."

She walked back to her room, taking her new remote with her. I stared at her retreating back. *Who are you?*

Traffic at the Greasy Griddle slowed by eight. Patty came over to chat as she often did when her husband, a long-haul trucker, was away on a road trip. She'd brought a fresh carafe of hot cider with her for my guests. The ladies poured themselves mugs of the steaming cider. Daisy pulled a small flask from her boot and spiked her mug. She proceeded to pass the flask around. There were several takers, though some preferred their cider unadulterated.

Though most of the ladies had gathered in the common space, both Erika and Sadie remained in their rooms. Naturally, the group was much more demure tonight than they'd been on Monday and Tuesday. Three of them worked on a puzzle that depicted a herd of wild horses on the Outer Banks. I'd picked up the puzzle years ago in a gift shop on a family trip to the beach. The wild horses were descendants of ponies left behind by Spanish explorers centuries earlier. The horses inhabited a stretch of undeveloped land in the town of Corolla at the northern end of the Outer Banks, sometimes venturing among the oceanfront homes and onto the beach. There was another herd on the island of Ocracoke, which lay farther south. Another group of ladies worked on a puzzle that depicted the Blue Ridge Mountains in summer, when the slopes were covered in the bright pink blooms of the Catawba rhododendrons. Others merely stared into the fire, as if looking among the flames for answers about what had happened to their tail gunner.

Patty, Rocky, and I took seats at a table in the corner and sipped our cider.

"What do you think of this recipe?" Patty asked. "I'm trying to come up with a signature cider. I used Stayman Winesap apples in this batch."

"It's delicious," I said. The taste was more tart than the batches she'd brought before and had a wine-like essence, giving it something extra. "The flavor seems more elegant."

Rocky sipped his cider, savoring it for a moment before swallowing. "This is good," he said, "but I prefer the earlier batch. It was sweeter."

Patty groaned. "You two are no help."

"Check with your husband when he returns from the road," I suggested. "He can place the tiebreaking vote."

She waved a dismissive hand. "Eli won't be any help, either. He tells me all my food is delicious."

"Smart man." Grinning, Rocky raised his mug and took another sip.

Patty went on to tell us that she and her husband had a vacation to Charleston planned for early November, after the leaves fell and the leaf peepers disappeared from the mountains, but before the snow arrived and the skiers descended upon the town. "We'll be celebrating our thirtieth anniversary."

"Congratulations." Though I was happy for my friend, a small twinge of envy tightened my heart. My days of anniversary celebrations were over. I knew ending my marriage had been the right decision, but in a perfect world there would have been no need for Jack and I to divorce.

Rocky eyed me over his mug, seeming to read my mind. After taking a drink, he said, "If you'd let me take you out on a date, you could have some romance, too."

Patty cocked her head and gave me a pointed look. "He's not wrong. I don't know what you're waiting for."

"You know what?" I said, feeling reckless. "I don't know what I'm waiting for, either. Let's do it. Just promise me you won't quit working here if you decide I'm a boring date."

Rocky smiled. "I can't imagine that will be the case, but I agree. I like working here. I like living here, too." He reached down to ruffle his dog's ears. "So does Mo."

"Eli will arrive home Sunday afternoon," Patty said. "Why don't we make it a double date? I wouldn't mind a dinner out, get to eat someone else's cooking for a change."

I looked to Rocky. "Sunday work for you?"

"Let me check my calendar." He leaned back and twiddled his thumbs for a few seconds before sitting up again. "Yep. I'm free."

"Then it's a date." *A date!* A little thrill rocketed through me. It had been forever since I'd had a first date with someone. I was glad Patty had suggested that she and her husband come along. Having another couple there would take some of the pressure off.

When we finished our cider, she stood to go. Rocky and I walked her to the door.

She raised a hand as she walked out and tossed a "See you in the morning!" back over her shoulder.

Once she'd gone, Rocky pointed to the computer at the

registration desk and whispered, "Should we check the camera feeds? See if the guys in the van came by last night?"

"Good idea."

We went around the desk, Molasses padding along behind us. The dog flopped down on the thick, comfy blanket I'd folded and placed on the floor for him to nap on. Rocky pulled his stool up close to mine and took a seat while I accessed the camera feeds. He smelled like a mix of pine-scented soap and WD-40, a manly and enticing scent. I started the feed at the time last night when we'd pulled our cars up around the motorcycles and wrangled the bear into position as a prone sentry. We ran through each of the camera feeds at fast speed, stopping the footage when we spotted movement. All we saw during the night were a few deer wandering by and a bear nosing around the outdoor garbage bin. The big beast pawed in vain at the metal and eventually wandered off, disappointed that he couldn't access an easy meal. It was unfortunate that the bears had learned that refuse cans made an easy place to forage. Besides the trash they tossed all about, which made a messy eyesore, the plastic and paper they inadvertently digested wasn't good for them. Unsecured trash bins also lured them into more populated areas, where they were more likely to be struck by a car. That said, the bears sure were cute as they ambled about.

When we'd watched the feeds all the way through, Rocky said, "Looks like they've moved on."

"Maybe." I wasn't sure what to make of the fact that we didn't see the van or anyone prowling around the lodge last night. I was glad the guys in the van hadn't returned. If they were motorcycle thieves, maybe they realized that the ladies in the club had taken pains to secure their bikes and no longer made good targets. Maybe Sadie had warned them off, believing things had become too risky with law enforcement coming by to investigate Gerri's death. But what if they hadn't moved on? What if they weren't trying to steal the bikes and there'd been some other reason they'd been lurking about two nights ago? What if the guy who'd prowled around the lodge was a bad ex who'd stalked Sadie to the lodge? I supposed I wouldn't feel completely settled until several nights went by without them making an appearance. "Let's check the feeds again in the morning, see if they show their faces tonight."

By then, it was nearly eleven o'clock. Most of the bikers had gone to bed, and I was ready to hit the hay, too.

"Good night, Rocky." I bent over, cupped Molasses's furry jowls in my hands, and gave him a kiss on the snout. "Good night, Mo. Sleep tight."

Rocky returned the sentiment. "See you bright and early for coffee."

I tossed and turned and got twisted up in my sheets that night. Though my body was exhausted, my mind wouldn't stop working. It felt like I'd just fallen asleep when my alarm woke me Friday morning.

Groaning as I slid out of bed, I went through my usual routine in zombie mode. Shower. Dress. Feed my cat and tell her how beautiful she was and how the sun rose just for her, although it had yet to do so today. I did three jumping jacks to get my blood moving, closed my door gently behind me, and crept quietly down the hall. Rocky and Molasses were walking up the east wing. We met in the lobby.

Seemed we'd just bade each other good night and here we were telling each other "Good morning."

Rocky had donned a plaid flannel fleece-lined coat. Seemed the majority of his wardrobe was plaid, much of it in flannel fabric, typical mountain attire like the buffalo plaid I'd adopted as my work uniform. I liked his style. It was masculine yet colorful, and made him look like a lumberjack. The coat told me he planned to take Mo outside for a potty break.

We walked together through the dimly lit lobby. The sun had yet to dawn and the sky was pitch black, but the lights on the exterior of the lodge and from inside the Greasy Griddle cast some soft illumination on the parking lot. When we reached the doors, Rocky stopped in his tracks, staring outside. "What the hell?"

CHAPTER 21

Misty

I looked outside, too. Across the parking lot, Patty was coming out of the diner. She pushed a stainless-steel cart loaded with warming trays for the lodge's breakfast buffet. A carafe of her delicious hot cider sat on top.

In the early morning darkness, she couldn't see the two people who'd flattened themselves against the building on either side of the diner's door, but Rocky and I could. One was tall, the other average-sized. They both wore black balaclavas to hide their faces, and their eyes were obscured by ski goggles strapped over their ski masks. With sleek dark heads and large reflective eye coverings, they looked like some sort of human/bug hybrid from a low-budget horror movie. Their black puffer jackets and padded black ski pants made it difficult to tell their sex for certain, but seeing no obvious curves, I assumed both were men.

I stood, frozen in fright, as the two hidden figures accosted Patty as she stepped out of the diner door. Though they wore ski gloves on their left hands, both had their right hands in their jacket pockets and appeared to be pointing their pockets at Patty. My heart felt as if it were trying to beat its way through my ribcage. "They have guns!"

As Patty raised her hands in the air, Rocky bolted out the door. Molasses followed after him, but at a much slower pace, blocking my way as I unfroze and tried to run. "Move, boy!"

The dog strode outside with me on his heels. Mo stopped in front of the lodge to stare across the lot, his furry, furrowed brow saying that he wondered what was happening. I scooted around him and ran after Rocky, who'd sprinted halfway across the lot by then.

The intruders turned their heads at the sound of our pounding feet. Patty seized on their momentary distraction, taking the opportunity she'd been given. She grabbed the carafe of hot apple cider and unscrewed the top in one swift, smooth motion. With a cry of "Ha!", she tossed the blistering liquid in the face of the taller of the two.

The intruder shrieked in agony when the hot cider soaked the balaclava and scalded his skin. A puff of steam, dangling in the cold morning air before dissipating, rose from his head. He yanked his right hand from his pocket and I noted he wore a glove on that hand, too. He tugged at his ski mask with both hands, yanking and yelping. With the gloves impeding his dexterity and the strap of the goggles holding the mask tightly in place, he couldn't get the balaclava up and over his head.

As the taller guy struggled, the smaller one reached out to try to help him. *Big mistake.* Patty again seized the moment. She shoved her hands into oven mitts, picked up the warming tray of steaming gravy, and poured it over the smaller guy's head as if he were a warm biscuit waiting to be served to a hungry customer. He, too, cried out in agony. "Aaaaaagh!" No doubt he was suffering a third-degree gravy burn.

"Let's get out of here!" yelled one of them. It was impossible to tell which of them had shouted since their faces were still covered with the goggles and balaclavas, and now one of them was dripping with globs of gravy, but the voice had definitely been male. They turned to run in our direction.

Rocky intercepted them just a few feet from where Patty stood with the tray of hot grits in her hands now, ready to treat her attackers to a second helping of southern-style dissuasion. The taller one moved like a linebacker. Rocky's shoulder took a direct hit from the robber as he barreled by. Rocky whirled and wobbled, but managed to stay on his feet. The two masked prowlers darted past me, heading to the trailhead by the lodge. With their heads and faces still covered, I couldn't get a good look at them. I'd never be able to identify them in a lineup. I hoped it wouldn't come to that.

When I finally reached Patty, I cried, "Are you okay?"

"No!" She fisted her oven-mitted hands on her hips. "Those damn fools ruined my breakfast!"

Panting from adrenaline and exertion, I bent over and put my hands on my knees, looking up at her. "You could've been shot!"

"Nah." She flung her mitted hand in a dismissive gesture. "The pointed fingers were an act. A person can't shoot a handgun in ski gloves. Their finger wouldn't fit into the trigger."

Wow. I was impressed she'd been able to have a coherent thought while under such pressure. But, then, I had a coherent thought of my own—*a very clever and cunning coherent thought.* If the would-be robbers thought they were getting away, they just might be mistaken.

I forced myself upright and whipped around to face Rocky. "Patty and I will call the police. You drive down to Perry Park. I bet they left a getaway car waiting there." The park was just down the mountain, at the other end of the relatively short trail. But even though the trail wasn't long, it was uneven, rocky, and bisected with hundreds of exposed tree roots that posed a tripping hazard. Hikers had to be attentive and careful in the best of conditions. The trail would be especially difficult to traverse in the dark. Even if they had a flashlight or used a light app on their phone, it wouldn't be easy. Rocky could drive to the park faster than the attackers could get there on foot. "Use a screwdriver to puncture their tires. But don't stick around. You could get hurt. Let the police handle things."

Rocky gave me a nod and ran for his truck. He passed Molasses, who'd been slowly moseying across the parking lot to the diner. The dog turned his head and looked after Rocky.

"Mo!" I called, patting my leg. "Here boy!"

The dog turned to me and continued walking my way while Rocky gunned his engine and zoomed out of the lot in his truck. His tires sent up a high-pitched shriek not unlike the one Todd had made when turning donuts in front of the lodge a couple of days before. Seconds later, lights turned on in several of the rooms at the lodge, my guests rudely awakened by the screeching sound.

Patty was inside the diner, speaking with emergency dispatch on the phone. A male cook and a female server stood near her, their faces slack and eyes glazed with shock. They must've witnessed the incident from inside the diner. I stepped inside, bringing Mo along with me. It was probably a health code violation to have the dog inside the restaurant, but it wouldn't be safe for him to wait outside in the parking lot. The police might not see the black dog in the dark when they pulled up.

Patty held the phone to her ear, clutching the spiral cord as if holding on for dear life. "Send an officer to Perry Park, too. They headed down the trail on foot. We think they might have left a car there."

With any luck, the officers could nab them, whether they were on foot or on wheels.

Patty had barely hung up the receiver when flashing lights illuminated the parking lot, the beams bouncing off the diner and my lodge. More lights flashed along the road as a second Beech Mountain PD cruiser sped past the diner and lodge, and continued down the curvy road to the park.

The patrol car pulled to a quick stop in front of the diner, and a male officer bounded out. "Everyone okay here?"

Patty nodded, but I noticed she was shaking. She'd been exceptionally brave and ingenuous in fighting off her attackers, but she was definitely *not* okay. I'd merely witnessed the incident and I was quivering, too. It was horrifying to think how much worse things could have been if Patty hadn't disabled the robbers so quickly.

I walked over, draped an arm over her shoulders, and said, "Why don't we sit down?"

She nodded, and we shuffled over to a booth, taking seats side by side as the officer slid into the seat across from us.

He held his radio at the ready and leaned forward across the table. "What happened?"

Patty cleared her throat. "I was heading out the door to take breakfast over to the lodge just like we do every morning, and two people came out of nowhere. They had ski masks on. Tinted goggles, too. I couldn't see their faces at all. They had their hands in their pockets like this." She formed a gun with her hand and slid it up under her apron to demonstrate. "I could see the edge of ski gloves at their wrists, so I knew they didn't actually have guns. The shorter one said, 'Give us all your cash. We know you've got some in the register and some in your safe, so don't try to lie to us.'"

It sounded like the men knew her routine. *Could they be the men from the white van?* The vehicle had been in my lot Tuesday morning as Patty came out of the diner to bring the breakfast over. Maybe they'd spotted her then and realized the situation posed the perfect opportunity to get inside and rob the place. The diner wouldn't open for another half hour, so there would be no customers on site to witness the crime or get in their way. They'd probably thought they could get in and out fast. So, they had the means, but were their motives purely money? Who were these guys? Were they the same guys who'd checked out the motorcycles? I couldn't shake the feeling it was all connected.

Patty said, "I reacted on reflex. I tossed hot cider in the tall one's face and upended the tray of gravy over the short one's head. The cider was straight off the stove and nearly boiling. Same for the gravy. They turned tail and ran toward the trailhead by the lodge." She gestured to me. "Misty sent her handyman down to Perry Park to puncture their tires."

"I thought it would slow them down," I explained.

A male voice came over the officer's radio. "I'm pulling the van over. They didn't get far with those flat tires."

I felt my chest swell with pride. *Looked like my tactic had worked.* But my self-satisfaction was short-lived when the officer's voice came back. "They're bailing! They've headed into the woods! I need backup! Now!"

The officer leaped from the table. "I'll be back!" He ran out to his cruiser and peeled out of the lot, sending up another loud screech.

By this point, several of my guests stood in front of my lodge, no doubt wondering what in the world was going on. I took Patty's hand and gave it a supportive squeeze. "I'd better get over to the lodge before my guests think they've been abandoned."

Patty nodded. "I'll be over with the food as soon as I can."

"No rush," I said. "I'm sure the ladies will understand if you need some time to decompress."

Patty's server and cook stepped over. "We'll round up more cider and gravy, Patty. You just sit and relax for now."

She looked up at them and offered a weak smile. "Thanks, you two."

I rounded up Molasses, and we walked outside. I raised a hand and waved to my guests. "I'm on my way!" I called across the lot.

Mo, as usual, was in no hurry as he trailed me across the lot. The mellow dog was born without a sense of urgency.

We finally reached the women. Daisy was there, along

with her sister Dahlia—sans her ID cane. I supposed she
didn't need it at the moment. In fact, I hadn't seen her with
it since we'd stopped at the lookouts on Wednesday. *Hmm.*
Bessie and Shotgun had come out, too. So had Kris, Graffiti,
and Lexi. Looked like Erika, Reyna, Sadie and the others
had either somehow slept through the sound of the screeching tires or ignored it, assuming it was just some idiot driving too fast as he took a nearby curve. The women were all
dressed in their nightclothes, which ranged from a cute pair
of pink polka-dot pajamas on Lexi to a thick plush bathrobe
over a lacy nightgown on Daisy. Most of them wore slippers,
though Graffiti wore only a pair of ankle socks.

Bessie crossed her arms over her chest to ward off the
early morning chill and stepped toward me. Her terrier
looked up at her as if awaiting instructions and, hearing
none, made his own decision to step forward too. "What's
going on out here?" she asked.

I hiked a thumb over my shoulder to indicate the diner.
"Two people tried to rob the diner when Patty came out to
bring our breakfast over."

The women gasped and murmured amongst themselves.
Lest the escaped thieves return and try to rob my guests
or take hostages, I stretched out my arms and herded the
women together. "Let's get inside and lock the door so we'll
be safe."

Once we were all in the lobby, I locked the front door and
turned on the interior lights.

Kris glanced out the window at the diner, and her eyes
sparked with concern. "Is everyone okay over there?"

"Luckily, yes," I said. "Just shook up. Patty chased the
robbers off with scalding cider and gravy."

Dahlia snickered. "That'll teach them."

Daisy shivered and pulled her robe tighter around herself. "Do they have any idea who the robbers are?"

"The officer didn't mention anyone." Of course, I had my suspicions they were the men in the white van with the chrome bumpers, but innocent until proven guilty, right? Besides, I still had a hunch that the men were somehow in cahoots with Sadie, I just didn't know how, exactly. I didn't want to tip my hand. If I shared my suspicions with any of these ladies, word might get back to Sadie and she might take off. "Hopefully the police will catch them. The robbers ran down the trail to a getaway car. The cop who went down the mountain after them called for backup. He said they'd ditched the vehicle and run into the woods."

The excitement over, at least for now, Bessie yawned and rubbed her eyes with her fists. "I don't know about the rest of you, but I'm not ready to start my day yet. I'm going back to bed."

"Me too," said Kris. "My alarm wasn't set to go off for another hour."

Daisy put a hand on Dahlia's upper arm and the two headed down the hall.

Lexi shrugged. "I'm wide awake. There's no way I can go back to sleep now. Might as well have some coffee."

A cup of coffee sounded pretty good to me too. "I'll get the pot going."

Patty and her server arrived a few minutes later with the breakfast items, and together we set up the buffet. When we finished, I turned to Patty. "I'm so glad you weren't hurt. I wonder if we should consider some new security measures for the breakfast delivery."

She chuckled. "You think I should start packing heat instead of just hot cider and gravy?"

"I'm thinking we should install some motion-sensor lights on the front of the diner. That way, if someone is lurking about, you'll be able to tell because the lights will turn on and warn you. Maybe the light will even scare them off."

She dipped her head in agreement. "That's not a bad idea."

I knew Patty wouldn't see it this way, but I felt partially responsible for the attempted robbery. After all, if she hadn't had to open her door to deliver breakfast to the lodge, the bandits wouldn't have had the chance to try to force their way into her diner to rob the place. "I'll cover the cost and have Rocky install the lights. It's the least I could do."

"I know better than to argue with you," Patty said. "The only way you'd be quiet is if I shoved a biscuit in your mouth."

"Be my guest." Her biscuits were scrumptious, perfectly flaky. I ate at least one of them every morning, sometimes two. Thank goodness my housekeeping duties at the lodge burned a lot of calories. Pushing a vacuum cleaner around, hauling trash bags, and lifting wet sheets and towels out of the washing machines provided a daily workout. I recalled Patty mentioning that her apple press gave her arms a workout, and judging from how toned they looked she must've made many gallons of cider. Good thing, too. It had surely taken some muscle to lift that full tray of thick gravy and pour it over the robber's head.

She stepped forward and I met her in a mutually comforting hug. When she released me and backed away, she said, "I hope the police give me a second go at those creeps. I've got a wooden spoon I'd like to take to them."

A pink hint of sunrise peeked over the peaks when I bade her goodbye at the door of the lodge. "Let me know what you hear!" I called after her. Rocky and the officer who'd come to the diner had yet to return. I could only wonder what was happening on the mountain. Were the robbers in custody? Or was the chase still on?

CHAPTER 22

Yeti

The sun was just starting to rise over the distant ridge when a dog trotted past her window, his nose to the ground. Two men trailed after the dog. Both carried large flashlights to light their way. This dog appeared to be performing some type of work but, as far as Yeti could tell, most dogs were utterly useless. They spent their time shedding fur, chewing things up, barking at squirrels they had no hope of catching, or some other such nonsense. What's more, they did their dirty business outside in the, well, *dirt. So disgusting and uncivilized.* But not every creature could be so fortunate as to be born feline. She supposed she'd have to take pity on the dogs. If nothing else, the big furry one who Misty and Rocky called Molasses provided her with company on occasion. He could even be entertaining, rolling around on his back in the grass outside her window and kicking up his feet like a canine clown.

She watched as the men and dog disappeared down the

trail. They seemed to be tracking something or someone. Might it be the two people who'd run past the lodge not long before?

CHAPTER 23

Misty

Half an hour later, the sun had risen, several of the other women had joined Lexi for coffee and breakfast in the great room, and Rocky had returned to the lodge. I rushed out the door when I saw his truck pull into a spot. It was then I noticed a Watauga County Sheriff's Department vehicle parked at the end of the building by the trailhead. A decal on the sheriff's department patrol car identified it as a K-9 cruiser. I hadn't seen the cruiser pull in, but I'd been tending to the breakfast buffet, wiping up drips and stirring the trays to make sure the food stayed evenly warmed.

I approached Rocky as he climbed out of his truck. His shirt was untucked and disheveled, and a couple of buttons were missing. He sported a wide, raw scrape on his cheek and blood oozed from a gash in his forehead. "Oh, my gosh!" I cried. "Are you okay?"

"I'm fine," he said. "Nothing some disinfectant and a Band-Aid won't take care of."

My gut puckered in guilt at the thought he'd been injured

because I'd sent him down the mountain to disable the robbers' getaway vehicle. "I'm so sorry! I didn't intend for you to get hurt."

"It's not your fault," he said. "Any blame is on me. But it was your idea to begin with, so I'm willing to share the credit." He reached out to chuck my chin affectionately.

"Come inside. I'll fix you up." Having two rambunctious boys, I'd doctored many a cut, abrasion, and bruise over the years. I'd even wrapped a few sprains in elastic bandages. I hustled Rocky inside, grabbed the first aid kit from under the front counter, and removed a gauze pad and disinfectant. After soaking the pad in the acrid liquid, I began to clean his wounds.

He flinched as I dabbed at his cheek. "Ouch!"

I used to tell my sons, *"Be a big boy for mommy,"* but such a statement seemed wildly inappropriate now. Instead, I said, "Fill me in. What happened?"

"When I got to Perry Park, I found a white van with chrome bumpers parked there."

"I knew it! I knew the guys from the van would be involved somehow."

"Yep, you called it," Rocky agreed. "I heard crashing in the woods and could tell they were getting close. I figured I'd only have time to pop one, maybe two tires. Most vans have rear wheel drive because it's better for handling the cargo weight, so I went for the back tires first."

"Quick thinking."

"Quick thinking is all I had time for." He grimaced as I continued to clean the wound. "I wasn't sure I'd have time to get back to my truck and drive off before they reached the park, so I hunkered down behind a boulder where they wouldn't see me. They jumped into their van and floored it. But the two flat tires were all it took to render the van useless. They couldn't control the steering and weaved all over the place."

I finished with his cheek and started on his forehead, feeling a swell of self-satisfaction. "I'm so glad my ploy worked."

"Not exactly," Rocky said. "Your plan had room for improvement."

I brandished the bottle of disinfectant. "Don't make me hurt you."

"You're hurting me now!" Rocky flinched as I dabbed again.

"Point taken," I said. "So, how did you improve on my plan?"

"You told me to use a screwdriver to pop the tires, but I used a scratch awl instead. It was the better tool for the job."

I'd never heard of such a thing. "What's a scratch awl?"

"It's a long, pointy tool used to mark lines or points on a piece of wood so you can tell where to saw through the wood or insert a nail or screw. Basically, it's a skinny spike."

"Ah." I nodded in understanding. "That was indeed a better choice. What happened after they tried to drive off?"

"The cruiser rounded the corner and was on their bumper in seconds. They must have realized they'd never escape in the van. They jumped out and ran into the trees. The driver didn't even turn the van off. It rolled off the road and hit a tree. Anyway, the cop took off after the taller guy, so I went after the smaller one. Tackled him just a few yards off the roadway. For a little guy, he put up quite a fight. We rolled around until the backup officer arrived and took him off my hands. They lost the big one in the woods."

It would be easy to lose a target in the forest, especially in the dim light of dawn. Even when the sun was high in the sky, it couldn't penetrate the thick canopy. The woods were dark and shadowy, with lots of places for someone to hide. "That explains why the K-9 team was called out."

"Yep," Rocky said. "With any luck, that dog will sniff the guy out."

"The robber you caught," I said, "did you see his face?"

"Sure did," Rocky said. "I pulled his mask off after I tackled him. He's got a mug only a mother could love. 'Course, my opinion could have been influenced by the fact that he was greasy and blotchy from the gravy burn."

Circling back to vehicle, I asked, "Did the van have a North Carolina license plate? Or was it Mississippi?"

"North Carolina," Rocky said, "but turns out the plate was stolen. After the officer aborted the search for the tall robber, he ran the license plate through his computer system. They belong on another cargo van, a Ford rather than a Chevy. He ran the van's VIN, too. It showed that it was registered in Mississippi."

"Why'd they swap the license plates?" I mused aloud. "You think law enforcement was already after them? That they're wanted for other crimes?"

"Who knows?" Rocky said. "But they clearly wanted to mislead somebody. Maybe the van is stolen, too. I'm sure the police will sort it all out."

I applied the Band-Aid to the gash on his forehead, fighting my natural instinct to place a kiss next to it, and tossed the packaging in the trash. "Let's go over to the Greasy Griddle and give Patty an update."

We headed across the parking lot. As we drew closer to the bright lights of the diner, I noticed a wet spot on the asphalt where Patty or her staff must have hosed off the spilled cider and gravy. Smart. A bear might have smelled the gravy and thought it would make a yummy breakfast. The bear would've been right, of course, but a big furry beast licking gravy from the pavement might have kept her customers at bay.

The bells on the door jingled as we pushed it open and walked into the diner. Patty had several plates loaded with pancakes, hash browns, and biscuits lined up and down her arms. How she could carry so many dishes at one time was beyond me, especially after what she'd just gone through. Maybe returning to her usual routine brought her comfort. She dropped the plates off at two booths and came over, wiping her hands on her apron. "Did they catch the guys? Please say they did."

"One of them is in custody," Rocky said. "The other fled into the woods. They've got a K-9 on his trail."

"Good," Patty said. "I hope the dog bites him in the butt." She squinted when she noticed the scrape and bandage on Rocky's face. "Did you get hurt?"

"I got into a tussle with the little guy," Rocky said, "but I showed him who was boss." He cocked his eyebrows and looked at me. "Be honest. My bravery turns you on, doesn't it?"

I gave him a coy smile. "A little."

Patty shooed us away with her oven mitts. "Get out of here before you make my customers lose their appetites."

Rocky and I left the diner and aimed for the lodge. As we walked, I ran my gaze over the lineup of motorcycles in front of the lodge. The sun was up by then, and I could see all of the bikes clearly. One was missing—the one with the Indian Motorcycle logo on its cover, the one registered to Sadie Hardin.

I stopped in my tracks. "Sadie's motorcycle is gone."

By the time Rocky stopped, too, he was a few feet ahead of me. "Uh-oh." He turned sideways so he could speak to me but also see the bikes. "You think it was stolen?"

"Maybe." I supposed the guys who'd demanded the diner's cash could have stashed the motorcycle in their van before moving ahead with the robbery attempt. "Or maybe there's another explanation."

"Like what?"

"Like Sadie's the tall robber who ran off into the woods." It certainly seemed like she had some kind of connection to the crime. The escape van was registered in Mississippi, Sadie had a keychain with the Mississippi State bulldog mascot on it, and she'd apparently lied about her identity. Maybe she was working in cahoots with the driver? But if that was the case, who had the driver given the thumbs-up signal to when he'd looked under the cover on Sadie's Ninja in the wee hours of Tuesday night? We hadn't seen any sign of Sadie leaving or coming back into the lodge on the security cameras, and if Sadie had been involved, the prowler would have been able to get inside the lodge instead of just creepily checking the doors. There had to be a third person, didn't there?

I had no answers and frankly, I was tired of being left in the dark. "I'll knock on her door. See if she's here at the lodge." I hadn't heard any noise in her room next door to mine this morning, but I'd been half-dead when my alarm went off, a virtual zombie.

Rocky followed me as I passed the women eating breakfast in the great room and made my way down to Room 3. I raised a hand and rapped on the door. We waited a few seconds, but no one answered. I raised a hand and knocked again, this time adding a "Hello? Anyone in there?" Again, no one answered. Could she be asleep? Maybe wearing ear plugs or ear buds? When my boys had their ear buds in, they couldn't hear a thing, especially me asking them to pick up their rooms or take out the trash.

I motioned for Rocky to follow me next door to my room. There, I picked up the receiver and hit the number three on the dial. Through the wall and adjoining door, we could hear the faint sound of the phone ringing in Katie's room. It rang once . . . twice . . . three times. No one answered.

Venturing back out into the hall, I used my master key to open the door to Room 3. I pushed it open just a few inches and peeked inside. The bed was rumpled and empty. The bathroom door stood open and the light was off. No one was in the room. An eerie feeling invaded my gut as I cut Rocky a look. "She's not here."

"This is odd."

It wasn't just odd. It was extremely suspicious.

Movement in my peripheral vision drew my attention to the lobby up the hall. Deputy Gillespie stood there speaking with Reyna. She must have let him in the door. *Could he have news for us?*

I rushed down to the lobby, Rocky following. After a

quick greeting, he said, "Excuse me" to Reyna and Rocky, and took me aside. "We got a hit on your guest's prints. She's indeed Sadie Hardin." He discreetly pulled his handcuffs from his belt. "I'll be taking her into custody. She's wanted in Mississippi."

"For what?"

"She's a suspect in three restaurant robberies in Starkville."

"She might be up to her old tricks." I gestured to the front windows. "There was an attempted robbery at the Greasy Griddle this morning. Two people confronted the owner and demanded cash. They ran off down the trail after Patty threw cider and gravy on them."

"I'd heard some chatter about that on the radio."

I told him how I'd gotten the idea to disable their vehicle and sent Rocky down the mountain to puncture their tires. I gestured to where he stood, getting himself a fresh cup of coffee from the urn. "Rocky tackled the smaller of the two. That's how his face got injured. As far as we know, the other one's still on the lam. Watauga County sent out a K-9 team to track the person down."

"That explains the cruiser in your lot."

From behind me came the sound of someone rapping on the glass door of the lodge. I turned to see the Beech Mountain police officer who'd been at the diner earlier now standing on the stoop. Beside him was the deputy from the Watauga County Sheriff's Department, along with his dog, a beautiful tan shepherd with black markings. Looked like the manhunt had been called off. I rushed over to unlock the door and let them in.

Deputy Gillespie tipped his hat at his fellow law enforcement officers and chuckled mirthlessly. "This is becoming quite the party."

The three held a quick huddle to share information. I stood just outside their circle shamelessly listening in. Hey, nobody'd told me to buzz off.

The officer from Beech Mountain said, "The guy we've got in custody is Trevor Hoyt. He claims to be the boyfriend of a woman named Sadie Hardin. He says she's been a guest at this lodge for the last few days, and that she was with him this morning when he attempted to rob the diner."

Their exchange confirmed my suspicions. Sadie Hardin had indeed been the taller of the two would-be robbers. That meant the male voice I'd heard must have come from the shorter person, who must be Trevor Hoyt. The two sounded like a modern-day Bonnie and Clyde. My heart sank. Though I'd surmised earlier that the young woman could be up to something, I'd hoped nonetheless that she was innocent, that she was only attempting to avoid a loser ex-boyfriend. I didn't want to believe she could actually be a criminal. But those hopes had apparently been for naught. I sighed, sad to see a young woman throw her life away. *Such a waste.*

Gillespie said, "Miss Hardin is wanted in Mississippi for allegedly robbing three restaurants there. Where's her cohort say she is now?"

The officer raised his palms. "He doesn't know where Sadie went once they bailed on the van. Far as he knows, she's still somewhere in the woods."

The K-9 officer grunted in frustration. "My dog lost the trail along Pond Creek. With the rain we had earlier in the week, the creek's full and moving fast. My guess is she realized a K-9 pursuit might be likely and she walked in the creek to avoid detection. We've got officers searching the area now."

The dousing with hot cider aside, the early autumn morning was quite cold. According to my phone app, it was only forty-three degrees outside. In wet boots and clothing, Sadie could suffer hypothermia. At the very least, she'd be uncomfortable and have a harder time moving with the extra weight of the water in her clothes.

The sound of a motor out front drew all of our heads to the door. To my surprise, Sadie rode up on her green Ninja and stopped. Also, to my surprise, she looked perfectly dry. She glanced over at the law enforcement vehicles without turning off her motorcycle or removing her helmet.

I raised my hand and pointed. "That's her!"

CHAPTER 24

Misty

I've never seen three men and a dog move so fast. There was a scuffling sound as they dashed to the door. The officers bumped into one another as each tried to be the first to get outside and grab the woman. Seeing the men coming for her, Sadie raised her hands in the air. Deputy Gillespie and the officer from Beech Mountain PD each grabbed one of her arms, while the K-9 officer reached over to turn off her motorcycle. The dog sniffed her leg and boot. I wondered what guilt smells like. Sour milk came to mind.

I rushed to watch out the front window as Gillespie reached down and lifted the faceplate on Sadie's helmet. The young woman's bewildered face appeared. Her eyes were wide and her mouth hung agape but, to my surprise, there were no telltale blisters or pink splotches on her face to evidence the cider scalding she'd received not long before. *Maybe the liquid hadn't been as hot as we'd thought.*

Rocky came up to stand beside me at the window,

cradling his coffee mug in his hands. The bikers gathered around, too.

Reyna's brows formed a concerned V as Deputy Gillespie cuffed Sadie's hands. "Why are they arresting Katie?"

"Her real name is Sadie Hardin," I said. "She's wanted for robbery in Mississippi. Multiple robberies, actually."

"What?!" Daisy stepped up close to the window and put her hands on it, her breath fogging the cold glass in front of her. She shook her head slowly. "That can't be right. She seemed like a nice person. A little shy, maybe, and quiet. But nice. She even pet-sit my cats one time. They loved her." She released a loud breath that made an even bigger cloudy spot on the glass. "I just can't believe it."

"Me neither," said Dahlia.

Just because none of us wanted to believe it didn't mean it wasn't true. I continued to fill in the group. "The guy Rocky caught earlier says he knows her. He claims she was involved in the attempted robbery at the Greasy Griddle this morning, too."

Reyna's face was perplexed as she shook her head. "She's never struck me as the criminal type."

Yet Sadie was, evidently, the criminal type. And as for being struck, the jury was still out on whether she had anything to do with Gerri's murder, but the fact that she was accused of being involved in other violent crimes could mean it was more likely she was guilty of that, too. Could Sadie's boyfriend have been attempting to force Gerri off the road to rob her when she crashed? If so, what was he trying to take? Even though Gerri was wealthy, she wasn't likely to have much of value on her when she was on the motorcycle ride. There'd been no jewelry among her belongings. Maybe they'd hoped to steal her debit or credit cards. Or maybe they'd hoped to take her motorcycle and leave her stranded on the side of the road.

The men and the dog escorted Sadie, now in handcuffs, into the lodge. Sadie cried out to the women. "I didn't do anything! I promise! I was set up!"

Deputy Gillespie silenced her with a look before turning to me. "We're going to take a look in Miss Hardin's room."

I gave him a nod. "Sure."

They took the young woman down to her room, where they closed the door behind them. Once they'd disappeared into the room, my guests returned to the lobby to discuss and debate this unexpected turn of events.

Patty had seen things transpire from the diner and scurried over, bursting through the door. "What's happening?"

I motioned for Patty and Rocky to follow me to my room. I quietly opened the door, put a finger to my lips in a shushing gesture, and tiptoed over to the door that adjoined my room and Sadie's. They tiptoed over, too. We bent our heads down and put our ears to the door to listen.

In typical cat fashion, Yeti was curious about our action. She hopped down from the bed, sauntered over, and mewed in question. *Meow?* I was fairly certain the sound would translate to *Why are y'all eavesdropping?* I bent down and picked up my cat to quiet her. Unfortunately, she began purring in my arms, her rumble making it harder for us to hear the conversation taking place in the adjacent room. The men's voices were mostly just low rumbles, too, though Sadie's distraught voice was louder and could easily be heard through the wall and door.

"I didn't go to the diner this morning!" she cried, her voice sounding as panicked as her face had looked when they grabbed her. "I rode up to the Emerald Outback to watch the sunrise."

The Emerald Outback was a set of hiking trails at the pinnacle of the mountain a short drive from the lodge. The trails were popular with both hikers and mountain bikers alike. The name was a callback to the Land of Oz theme park that had operated at the peak from 1970 to 1980. My parents had taken me to the park as a child, and I'd loved skipping down the yellow brick road, visiting Emerald City, and watching the actors perform integral scenes from *The Wizard of Oz*. Though the place was no longer open year-round, various events were held throughout the year at the park, including an annual Autumn at Oz event for three weekends early each September.

Sadie elaborated. "I haven't been able to sleep well since Gerri died."

She was telling the truth about this, at least. I'd heard her making noises in her room in the late hours of the night when I, too, had been tossing and turning. But was her inability to sleep due to grief and concern, or was it due to guilt or fear that she'd be found out?

As one of the men asked her another question, there was a muffled *wah-wah-wah* sound reminiscent of the adult voices in a Peanuts cartoon.

Patty whispered, "What did they say?"

I raised my palms and shrugged. Rocky did the same.

"Trevor is lying!" Sadie cried. "I've never committed any crimes. Not in Mississippi and not here, either!"

There was more deep, unintelligible rumbling before the

young woman said, "A guy that goes by Jinx. I don't know his full name. His last name could be Jenkins, maybe? He and Trevor met playing pickup basketball at the park."

None of us could quite make out what she said next. We eyed one another and put our hands to our ears, shaking our heads in silent sign language.

When the conversation seemed to be wrapping up, we stood. I deposited Yeti on my bed before we scurried out of my room and returned to the reception desk, trying to look nonchalant.

The members of the motorcycle club were now engaged in an argument in the great room. Like the items in the breakfast buffet, their debate was heated. While they'd initially expressed surprise on hearing that Sadie was a wanted robbery suspect, after more time for thought some seemed to have changed their minds.

Bessie said, "We hardly knew her, really. Do you think she had something to do with Gerri's crash, too?"

Lexi said, "She wasn't even on the ride, remember? I was riding her bike."

And wearing her helmet, I recalled.

Bessie said, "Maybe she was in the robber's van." She turned to Dahlia. "You stayed here with her on Wednesday. Did she leave the lodge during the day?"

"I don't know," Dahlia said. "I was in my room and had my headphones on so I could listen to my students' essays on my computer. I was up to my ears in Hemingway and Steinbeck all day."

Reyna frowned. "She didn't come by and ask you to go to lunch with her?"

"No," Dahlia said, "and I would've turned her down if

she had. After that enormous breakfast I ate, I didn't think I'd ever be hungry again."

The Greasy Griddle's food was certainly delicious enough to inspire gluttony. I was guilty of the sin myself. Maybe Sadie had likewise eaten a big breakfast and not felt the need to venture out of the lodge for lunch.

Graffiti said, "Maybe she fell down on purpose at the falls. She could've faked the injury to have an excuse not to ride with us on Wednesday."

Having prepared an ice bag for the injured young woman, I felt the need to chime in. "Sadie might not have been honest about her name, but the goose egg on her wrist was real."

The woman immediately hushed when, back down the hall, the door to Room Three opened and the men brought Sadie out.

When they reached the lobby, Deputy Gillespie addressed me. "We're taking Miss Hardin to the station. We'll continue our interrogation there. Don't touch anything in her room until we get a chance to collect any evidence that might be in there."

I gave him a nod. "Yes, sir."

At the door, Sadie cast a glance back at the other women. Her eyes were wet and her cheeks were tearstained. Though her face was filled with emotion, she said nothing more, seemingly overwhelmed by what had transpired.

As Gillespie and the local police officer took Sadie out and placed her in the Beech Mountain PD cruiser, the K-9 handler from Watauga County turned to me, Rocky, and Patty. "Miss Hardin said she thinks the other person at the diner this morning was a guy her boyfriend hung out with back in Mississippi, where they're all from. In case she's telling the truth, I'm going to take my dog back out in the woods and keep searching."

Patty thanked him for being thorough. "This is all so bewildering! I'll be glad once things are sorted out."

She's not the only one.

Once the door closed behind the man and his dog, the lodge erupted again in debate. Half of the women were convinced that Sadie had always given off an "odd vibe," as Bessie put it. Others came to her defense, including Erika, who appeared to be off the hook with the group now that one of their members had been arrested. "Sadie must've had a reason for changing her name. Don't jump to conclusions until we hear her side."

Reyna said, "We might not get that chance. They may ship her back to Mississippi and we might not ever see her again." Reyna covered her face with her hands, as if it was all too much and she needed to shut it out for a moment. When she removed her hands, she said, "We should all stop guessing and let the professionals figure it out. We came here to ride. So, let's ride."

A ride was something they could all agree on. Reyna, having naturally assumed Gerri's role, debriefed the group on the day's plan. They'd head north on the Blue Ridge Parkway and ride over the famous and oft-photographed Linn Cove Viaduct. After, they'd stop at Julian Price Memorial Park to hike part of the Tanawha Trail. I knew from experience that they were in for some spectacular scenery. I hoped the beautiful views would take their minds off all the strife they'd suffered this week, even if only for a few moments.

CHAPTER 25

Misty

Brynn arrived for work that morning just as the ladies were climbing onto their bikes and heading out. She raised a hand in greeting as she made her way into the lodge.

I gave her a coy look over my coffee mug. "You missed some big fun this morning."

She plunked her purse down at the registration desk and slid out of her jacket. "What are you talking about?"

"Get your coffee and we'll fill you in."

While she fixed her usual morning coffee, Rocky and I gave her all the details on our crazy morning.

Her mouth hung open. "Sheesh! I can't believe so much happened before my shift even started."

It had certainly been a busy couple of hours, time moving at warp speed like when we'd fast-forwarded through the security camera footage. Even so, I found myself wishing time would speed up to the point that Gerri's killer was identified. I wouldn't be able to fully relax until then.

As Brynn started in on the housekeeping, Rocky and I

walked over to the diner so he could take a look at the front door and determine what type of motion-sensor lighting would work best there. Patty came out to discuss the matter with us.

As the three of us were standing there discussing the lights, my ears picked up the sound of a loud motor approaching. Having quickly become accustomed to the sound of my guests' motorcycles, my first thought was that one of the ladies was returning from their ride. Maybe one of them had forgotten her cell phone or wallet and planned to catch up with the others after retrieving the item. But then I realized this sound was not only different from a motorcycle engine, but that it was coming from overhead. *Chup-chup-chup.*

Patty clued in before I did. "Looks like they've called in a chopper."

She pointed to a dark spot over the grayish-blue ridges in the distant sky. Rocky and I turned to look. Sure enough, a helicopter was headed in our direction, moving high above the treetops like a metallic hawk searching for prey to swoop down on.

The population in western North Carolina was relatively low, and the area's law enforcement agencies tended to be small with limited resources. While it wasn't necessarily unusual to see a medical helicopter picking up injured folks in this remote wilderness area, I couldn't recall ever spotting a police helicopter out here. My guess was the agencies couldn't afford them and, regardless, helicopters weren't likely to be of much use in a region with so much forest impeding the view of the ground. The dog was probably a much better tool for hunting down an escaped suspect. Still, it couldn't hurt to have eyes on the roads from above in case the missing robber darted across an open road, or tried to hitch a ride or carjack a tourist. They must've called in the chopper from a larger city like Asheville or Winston-Salem.

The chopper swooped in closer but then slowed to a stop, hovering in the sky over a spot just a short way down the mountain.

My eyes still on the helicopter, I said, "This means Sadie wasn't involved in the robbery." With her already in custody, there'd be no need to call in a chopper. "You think the dog team found the other guy?" Maybe the helicopter was acting as some sort of backup unit, to ensure he didn't escape.

"Could be." Lines formed around Rocky's eyes as he appeared to be forming a mental map of the mountain. "I'd say that whirlybird is right above the Buckeye Recreation Center."

The center was a spacious, relatively new facility operated by the city's parks and recreation department. It featured an outdoor pavilion, both indoor and outdoor tennis courts, a fitness center, a jungle gym, and an indoor playroom for kids. *Had the robber entered the town's rec center? Could children be in danger?* The mere thought made my body feel as if it had gone hollow, but an instant later my feet were moving. I swung my index finger toward Rocky's truck and called, "Let's go find out!"

The three of us piled into Rocky's pickup. On the drive down the mountain, I texted Brynn to let her know I'd left the lodge but would be back soon.

Patty called the Greasy Griddle from her cell phone. "We're going to see what that chopper's all about."

We pulled into the rec center parking lot to see a group

of people gathered on the far end of the grounds, shielding their eyes from the autumn sun as they stared up at the helicopter. Even the people playing tennis had interrupted their game to gather at the net and look up at the chopper, which had begun to slowly circle low in the sky. Several law enforcement vehicles were parked in the lot, though we didn't see an officer anywhere.

The muted *chup-chup-chup* grew much louder as we parked and climbed out of Rocky's truck. Seeing no activity on the immediate grounds, Rocky said, "Let's check the boat launch."

The rec center sat on a rise. Just below it sat Buckeye Lake, a small body of water surrounded by thick woods and hiking trails, and stocked with trout for those who like to fish. The lake was too small for motorized boats, but the rec center loaned out canoes, which were stored in a locker at the boat ramp. We turned down the narrow road that led to the dock and boat launch. The Watauga County deputy and his dog stood on the ramp a foot or so back from the water's edge, looking out over the lake. Across the water on the opposite shore stood a Beech Mountain police officer. Another had positioned himself along the bank forty yards or so to the left. In the center of the lake floated an aluminum canoe, and inside that canoe sat a tall guy wearing the same black ski jacket the robber had been wearing when he'd attempted to rob the diner with his buddy earlier that morning. So, the tall person who'd attacked Patty hadn't been Sadie after all. She was telling the truth about that, at least. As the chopper blades *chup-chup-chupped* overhead, they created a chop on the water, small whitecaps forming across the normally placid surface.

Patty threw her hands in the air. "Hooray!" she cried over the din of the helicopter. "You caught him!"

The K-9 handler reached down to ruffle his dog's ears, then cupped the hand next to his mouth to amplify his voice. "You can thank Schnitzel for finding him. The guy was clever. He climbed into a bear-proof garbage bin at a house on Arrowhead Road and turned an empty trash can over on himself so he couldn't be seen. I would've gone right past the bin if not for my dog." He went on to tell us that, when the guy heard Schnitzel sniffing his way toward the bin, he'd bolted. They'd trailed him here. "He grabbed that canoe from a couple who were coming in to dock. He could use the oars as weapons, so I didn't dare send Schnitzel into the water after him. The guy only made it halfway across the lake before my backup arrived."

The guy wasn't just clever, he was stubborn, too. Law enforcement clearly had the guy trapped, yet still he refused to surrender. Instead, he sat in the canoe, floating aimlessly. A couple of times he used the oar to make a mad rowing dash for one of the banks, but each time the officers shifted position on shore so that they'd be ready to nab him the instant he emerged onto dry land. All the lawbreaker managed to do was upset a flock of ducks, who took to the air, scolding him with quacks that were barely audible over the helicopter noise. They flew to the other side of the lake, skimming to a stop and turning to keep an eye on the jerk in the boat.

As we stood there, gazing out at the lake, a second helicopter swooped in. This one drifted well above the police chopper. The logo on the side identified it as a news helicopter. No doubt this manhunt would be the top story on tonight's regional news.

Things seemed to stay in a holding pattern for several minutes. The robber floated in the canoe in the middle of the lake. The officers remained on the banks. The helicopters circled slowly and loudly above us. I was curious about the procedures in a situation such as this. Surely, the officers were growing tired of this idiot's games, and their services were likely needed elsewhere. *Is there nothing they could do?* "Do you just have to wait him out?" I asked the K-9 officer in a near shout.

The officer raised a palm. "That's the plan for now. We're hoping he'll come to his senses."

Patty shook her head. "If that man had any sense, he wouldn't have been sticking up my diner."

As a mother of two rambunctious boys, I'd been forced to become a resourceful problem solver. An idea came to mind now, too. "Could you shoot a hole in the canoe and let it sink? Catch him when he swims to shore?" I formed a gun with my thumb and index finger, just like the robbers had done this morning at Patty's diner. I raised my hand and pretended to shoot the boat. "Pew-pew!"

Rocky leaned over to ensure I could hear him. "*Pew-pew* sounds more like a laser than a bullet. Don't you mean *bang-bang*?"

I turned my finger-gun on him. "You really gonna correct me when I'm holding a lethal weapon? You're lucky I'm not trigger happy." I blew on the end of my index finder and slid my imaginary gun into the imaginary holster on my hip. After the events of the morning, I was feeling a little slap happy.

"That's a clever solution," the officer called, "but unless

the guy pulls a weapon I can't shoot at him. There's a risk the bullet could ricochet and hurt him or someone else."

Just because we'd offered no useful suggestions thus far didn't mean we were done trying.

Rocky stroked his beard thoughtfully. "When I can't get something off my roof or out from under my deck or shed, I use my power washer. The force of the water moves things along."

"Yeah?" The officer cocked his head, brows raised. He whipped his radio from his belt to contact dispatch. "Tell the fire department to send their pumper truck."

It wasn't long before a group of men from the volunteer fire department arrived in yellow jackets, red hardhats, and a shiny red fire truck. The helicopter backed off, circling higher, probably so as not to interfere with communications on the ground. Patty, Rocky, and I stepped back to the edge of the woods where we'd be out of their way. While two of the men worked controls on the truck, a third stepped to the boat ramp and aimed the hose in the direction of the canoe.

The robber was truly a sitting duck now. He raised his middle finger at the firefighters just as the water burst out of the end of the hose. A split second later, the stream hit the guy square in the face. The force was so great it rocked him backward and the canoe capsized. He disappeared under the surface for a moment before coming up sputtering and spewing both lake water and obscenities.

The guy holding the hose offered a remorseless, "Oops. Guess my aim was a little off. I normally have a bigger target."

The robber righted the canoe but, as soon as he did, the firefighter held the stream of water on the boat and ripped it out of the guy's hands. He used the forceful jet to push the canoe out of the robber's reach, then used the torrent to force the robber to swim to the bank, herding him along with the stream. Each time the guy tried to swim off to the left, right, or backward, he found himself up against a barrage of water. Lest he take another blast to the face, he had no choice but to head to the shore. Rocky's suggestion had gotten the scum off the lake, that was for sure.

The criminal flopped onto the muddy bank on all fours. The two officers who'd been standing sentry on the shoreline immediately closed in. One yanked the guy's hands out from under him, and he fell face-first into the muck. The other handed the first officer a pair of cuffs, and in seconds the robber's hands were secured behind his back. The cops hauled the guy to his feet. With mud all over his face, he looked like he'd gotten a spa treatment. The officers started to escort him down the path that led to the parking lot. Despite being soaked and shackled, he was still unwilling to surrender without a fight. He kicked out at one of the officer's ankles. The cops had no option but to throw him to the ground. His final act of rebellion earned him a skid across the rocky path and a pair of shackles around his legs, as well. Normally, I wouldn't want to see anyone being manhandled but, in this case, he'd asked for it. He could've broken the officer's ankle with that kick.

The K-9 officer signaled the helicopter pilot with a salute and a wave. The chopper veered off to return to its home base.

As we turned to go, the cop raised a hand in goodbye to us, too. "Thanks for the suggestion!"

"Any time!" Rocky called back.

Rocky's insider trick had put a quick end to the standoff. I slid him a sideways glance. "How does it feel to be a hero?"

He slid me a smile in return. "Darn good!"

The three of us returned to the rec center and climbed into his truck. As we waited to turn onto the road to head back to the lodge, the K-9 cruiser rolled by. The happy dog hung his head out of the open back window and wagged his tail. They were followed by a second cruiser. This car also had an occupant in the back seat, though this one was human rather than canine and didn't look happy at all. The young man scowled out the window, his puckered face made all the more unattractive by muddy hair, ruddy skin, and several days of stubble. When he turned our way, we could see dark pink spots on his forehead and cheekbones, blisters from the scalding cider no doubt made worse by the impact of the fire hose.

We arrived back at the diner a few minutes later and somehow managed to finish discussing the lighting. Slowly, the day took on its regular patterns. Patty went inside to set about her diner duties, Rocky climbed into his truck to drive down the mountain to the building supply store, and I returned to the lodge.

I found Brynn cleaning Bessie and Shotgun's room. She'd put both a piece of maple candy and a dog biscuit on the pillow. *Thoughtful.* As she replaced the towels in the bath, I gave her an update on the manhunt, how the robber had been blown out of his boat.

She chuckled. "Wish I could've seen that."

I felt guilty now for leaving my assistant behind, but with all those people on the bluff filming the incident with their cell phone cameras, there'd be footage on YouTube soon enough. "Next time something exciting happens, I'll take you along."

Though my sentiment was sincere, I hoped there'd be no more excitement for a long time. Boring days were underrated.

CHAPTER 26

Yeti

The biggest hawk Yeti had ever seen had been circling just down the mountain. Often, when one of the large birds began to circle, others joined in. Such proved to be the case today, when a second bird arrived and flew slow loops over the first. These birds weren't just big, either. They were noisy, too. She'd heard the faint *thwup-thwup-thwup* of wings before, when a hawk took off from the ground or came in for a landing in a nearby tree. But the wings of these birds made a constant deafening *chup-chup-chup* sound. *So irritating.* The only saving grace was that whatever prey they were focusing in on, it wasn't her. She sat in the window, watching, wondering what poor fool was about to become lunch for the huge raptors.

CHAPTER 27

Misty

A couple of hours later, Rocky was installing the motion-sensor lights on the exterior of the diner and I was at the front desk of the lodge, eating yet another meal of leftover lasagna for lunch, when Deputy Gillespie drove up and came into the lodge.

He removed his hat and dipped his head in greeting. "Miss Hardin gave us lots of information. Now that his co-hort has been captured, Trevor has opened up, too. I finally have some answers for you."

"Thank goodness," I said. "My head's been spinning all morning." The dryers had been spinning, too. A lodge full of ladies used an unbelievable number of towels.

Rocky and Patty came in the door. They must have seen the deputy's car drive up and come over to get those answers he mentioned.

Brynn should hear this, too. As an employee of the lodge, she had a right to know what was going on with our guests, and I didn't want her to feel left out again. I walked to the entrance to the east wing. Brynn's housekeeping cart stood in front of the open door two rooms down. "Brynn!" I called. "The deputy's here with some news."

She popped her head out. "Don't let him start without me!" She plunked her feather duster into the holder on the cart and hustled our way.

Once we were all gathered, the deputy filled in the missing blanks of Sadie's story, as told to him by Sadie and Trevor. The other culprit, whom they'd identified as Axel Jenkins, had exercised his right to remain silent, though he'd accepted the offer of a dry jumpsuit to replace his wet clothing. "Sadie says she and this Trevor fella dated for a while, starting a couple of years back. After a few months, he moved into her apartment. She was a full-time college student at Mississippi State at the time, living in Starkville, and waitressed on the weekends. Trevor was a part-time student. He worked as a freelance subcontractor cleaning floors in commercial buildings. Restaurants, mostly. That's how they met. The restaurants generally requested that he clean the floors in the early morning, before they opened for the day. Trevor hung out sometimes with Axel Jenkins."

Gillespie went on to say that Sadie had never learned Jinx's real name and that she never liked the guy. He partied hard, had no direction, and repeatedly borrowed money from Trevor that he never paid back. He also goaded Trevor into doing stupid, childish things, like dropping water balloons onto cars from an overpass.

"Ooh." Patty grimaced. "That could be dangerous."

"Tell me about it," Gillespie said with a frown. "Stunts like that have caused serious wrecks. At any rate, Sadie told

Trevor she didn't like him spending time with Jinx, and gave him an ultimatum—Jinx or her."

Sounded like Jinx was both a bad influence and a dead-beat. Sadie was right not to want him in their lives.

The deputy rocked back on his heels. "Rather than ditch his buddy, Trevor made up lies so Sadie wouldn't know he was still hanging out with Jinx."

Patty's lips pursed. "Trevor sounds like a real peach."

"Don't he, though?" The deputy issued a derisive snort before moving on. "While Trevor was cleaning floors at various restaurants, he noticed the managers often removed the cash from their safes and took it to the bank for deposit right after the banks opened for the day."

Patty's head bobbed in agreement. "It's standard procedure to make deposits in the mornings. Banks aren't open late in the evenings, and it's dangerous to make a cash deposit at an ATM after dark."

In Patty's case, she or her staff would drive down to the nearby town of Banner Elk to make a deposit. While there were automatic teller machines in Beech, there weren't any bricks-and-mortar branch banks.

The deputy continued. "Trevor said he made the mistake of mentioning the cash to Jinx. Jinx concocted a plan whereby he'd show up and rob the restaurants while Trevor was taking his equipment inside. The door would be un-locked then, and he could force his way in." Their plan, as the deputy described it, was actually quite clever. Trevor would pretend to be as shocked and scared as the restaurant staff when Jinx showed up in a hoodie and ski mask. Jinx would hand the staff a note demanding their cash with threats of violence if they didn't comply.

"Initially, Trevor and Jinx agreed to a sixty-forty split. Jinx would keep sixty for doing most of the dirty work, and Trevor would get forty percent for giving Jinx the lead on the restaurants. But with each robbery, Jinx demanded a greater share until Trevor was getting only a ten-percent cut. Trevor no longer felt the risk was worth the reward."

Patty's face soured. "If you're expecting me to feel sorry for the boy, it's not gonna happen."

The deputy chuckled. "I don't blame you. I'm not trying to excuse any of his actions. I'm just relaying what he told me." He went on to say that when Trevor complained to Jinx and tried to back out of the arrangement, Jinx beat him within an inch of his life. Sadie confirmed that Trevor had been brutally attacked, but at the time Trevor told her he'd been jumped by two strangers in a parking lot and couldn't identify them. "Needless to say, Trevor was terrified of Jinx after that."

The deputy noted that the two got away with their scheme several times before a detective investigating the robberies noticed a pattern and began to suspect it was more than coincidence that the freelance flooring cleaner had been on site each time. He figured Trevor had to be involved. "When the detective questioned Trevor, he claimed innocence. He said his girlfriend was the only one who knew his work schedule. He mentioned that she waitressed and knew firsthand how restaurants operated, so she'd know they made cash deposits at the bank first thing in the morning. He also mentioned that she was nearly six feet tall and wasn't a curvy girl, so she could pass for a man if her face was covered and she wore loose clothing."

It was true. Sadie had a relatively flat chest and little in the way of hips, a boyish figure. I felt my ire rise. "Trevor threw Sadie under the bus."

"Exactly," Gillespie agreed. "He thought if he protected Jinx, he'd be protecting himself."

Brynn chimed in. "Did the detective question Sadie about the robberies?"

"Sure did. About four months ago. She said she had no idea the thefts had taken place, and that she wasn't aware of Trevor suddenly coming into large amounts of unexpected cash. But she mentioned that if Trevor was involved, she suspected Jinx was too. She sensed that Trevor was afraid of the guy and might be playing along for his own safety."

Rocky asked, "Did the detective ever identify Jinx?"

"No. At that point, it looked like Jinx was someone Sadie made up, and that Sadie was Trevor's actual partner in crime. Sadie didn't know Jinx's real name, had never seen him in a vehicle she could link to him, and had no idea where he lived or worked. Trevor pretended not to know anyone by the name or description Sadie provided. Trevor wasn't on social media and had no pics on his phone with anyone the police could identify as Jinx. There were calls to and from a prepaid burner phone in Trevor's call history, but he claimed the phone belonged to a girl he'd met at a bar and been flirting with. He said he'd been considering breaking up with Sadie."

I shook my head. If Trevor was smart enough to concoct that story, you'd think he'd have been smart enough to stay away from lawbreakers.

Gillespie wrapped things ups. "Trevor told Sadie he wasn't involved in the robberies and that she'd made a huge mistake implicating Jinx. Trevor seemed very worried, like he thought Jinx might hurt her. Naturally, Trevor and Sadie ended up at odds. Shortly thereafter, she was followed by someone late one evening when she was walking out to her motorcycle in the university's parking lot. He attacked from behind so she didn't get a good look at him. Luckily for her, some other students drove onto the lot and her attacker ran off before he could hurt her too badly. She was pretty sure it had been Jinx, but she thought that if the police hadn't been able to identify him before, they wouldn't be able to track him down then, either. She believed her life was at risk, so she rode home to grab her things and run."

My heart squeezed at the thought of the young woman having to flee her home in terror, to be forced to drop out of school. No wonder she'd hung on to her bulldog keychain. It was a reminder of her past, of who she really was.

"When Sadie was tossing some things in her suitcase, she noticed the finial on her brass headboard was crooked. She hadn't even realized the finial was removable until then. She unscrewed it and found thousands of dollars in cash rolled up, rubber-banded, and stuffed down inside the brass post. She knew for certain then that Trevor had lied to her. She'd been getting by on student loans and waitressing on the weekends, and had no savings to speak of, so she took the money and fled. She has a distant cousin in Raleigh, so she figured it would be as good a place to go as any."

I wondered aloud. "Where are her parents? Why didn't they help her?"

"Her father was never in the picture," Gillespie said. "Her

mom bounces between boyfriends, so there's not really a home for Sadie to go to. Even if there had been, she wouldn't have gone there. She didn't want to be found."

Brynn asked, "How did Trevor and Jinx find her, then?"

"Sadie used to ride with a women's motorcycle club back in Mississippi. Trevor figured she'd join a club wherever she landed. They've been scouring social media to see if her picture would show up in a club's account."

Suddenly, her dark-hair disguise and her reluctance to have her photo taken made sense. "I assume she was blonde when she lived in Mississippi?"

"She was," the deputy said. "Trevor and Jinx figured she might change her appearance, so they looked all the photos over carefully. Trevor says Jinx saw the tip of Sadie's neon-green outfit in the photo posted on the Curve's Facebook page early Monday evening. They were pretty sure it was her. Trevor called the lodge. When you said there was no Sadie Hardin staying here, they figured she might be using an alias. They drove here from Mississippi and took a look at the bikes parked out front during the night. When they saw her Ninja, they knew she was here."

Rocky and I exchanged a glance. That's what we'd seen Trevor doing on the video, looking for Sadie's Ninja. Once he'd spotted her bike under the Indian Motorcycles cover, he'd given the thumbs-up signal to Jinx to confirm they'd found her. We'd assumed the likelier scenario, that the two had been looking for motorcycles to steal.

Gillespie said, "A big part of the stolen money Sadie took from the bedpost was Jinx's share. In case things turned south, he didn't want to be found with the money. He'd swing by when Sadie was at work or class to grab some cash

when he needed it. According to Trevor, Jinx became enraged when he realized Sadie had taken the money, and he
was intent on hunting her down."

My lips pursed. "And Trevor went along with it."

"Yup," the deputy said. "The guy's a sniveling weasel.
Sadie says she didn't know she'd been charged with the
robberies after she fled. She registered her motorcycle and
got a new driver's license right away when she arrived in
Raleigh. The DMV didn't find the criminal charge in the
records since it hadn't been processed yet in Mississippi.
For her license and registration, Sadie used the address
of a short-term rental where she was staying at the time,
the same address she gave you. She's since moved into a
sublet where she hoped she'd be untraceable if Trevor or
Jinx somehow got access to the motor vehicle records. She
trashed her old cell phone and got a new untraceable prepaid phone when she moved to North Carolina. She's been
using an alias socially to avoid being outed and found."

The deputy told us that, since Jinx and Trevor had arrived in North Carolina on Tuesday, they'd been looking
for an opportunity to move in on Sadie so Jinx could recoup
his stolen cash. "Trevor is trying to play the hero, says he
only went along in the hopes of protecting Sadie, but I'm
not buying it. They followed her on Wednesday's ride after
switching the license plates on Trevor's van so she wouldn't
know it was them if she spotted it."

I sucked air through my teeth. "Lexi was on Sadie's bike
Wednesday. If they'd gone after the Ninja, they'd have attacked the wrong person." I wondered if they would have
realized their mistake in time. Lexi was at least six inches
shorter than Sadie, but the difference in stature might have

been hard to tell with the rider leaning forward over the motorcycle.

"Fortunately," Gillespie said, "they couldn't get to her. Trevor said there were too many people around."

One of those people had been Gerri. "You think they accidentally caused Gerri's crash trying to get to Sadie? Or that they purposely tried to get Gerri out of the way and swung at her with something they had in the van?"

The deputy exhaled sharply. "I haven't ruled out either of those scenarios. After Trevor admitted they'd followed the women, I asked him point blank if he had anything to do with Gerri Burnham's crash. He claims he knew nothing about it. He was only aware of that tree that came down and closed the road for a bit. He said he hadn't realized one of the riders had died."

Rocky's eyes narrowed. "You believe him?"

"He looked shocked when I told him," the deputy said, "but he could've been faking. Hard to say. If he did have something to do with Gerri's crash, I might have expected him to lie about being on the parkway. Then again, maybe he figured his van was spotted, or that we could get camera footage proving they were near the scene, and that he was better off coming clean at least about being on the road. Trevor says they didn't get close enough to the riders to cause any trouble, but that could be hogwash. Admitting to robbing a restaurant when you're caught red-handed is one thing, but confessing to a murder that can't otherwise be pinned on you is another thing entirely."

"I suppose so," I said sourly.

The deputy rested a hand on his tool belt. "All of this said, there's plenty of floor-cleaning equipment in his van that could have been used to strike Gerri. Metal hose attachments, scrubbers with metal poles, and whatnot. We plan to take a close look at all of it." He turned to Patty. "By the way, Trevor said he and Jinx have eaten at the diner separately this week so that they could keep an eye on the lodge to watch for Sadie."

"Got photos of them?" Patty asked. "I don't know what Trevor looks like and I only saw Jinx from afar when he was out on the lake and rode by in the back seat of the cruiser."

Gillespie pulled up the mug shots they'd taken less than an hour ago and showed them to us.

Patty eyed the photos and scoffed. "I remember both of those boys. They used ungodly amounts of ketchup. They were lousy tippers, too."

Rocky chimed in. "What happens now?"

"We'll keep Trevor and Axel in custody, keep working on them to see if either of them might break and admit to causing Gerri's accident. Trevor has said he's got more information on Jinx, but he won't talk unless he's given some sort of plea deal in this morning's robbery. It's not clear if the information he's withholding relates to crimes carried out in Mississippi or here in North Carolina. If necessary, we'll expand our search along the Blue Ridge Parkway, see if we can find the item used to strike Gerri. We'll hang on to Sadie for the time being, too. The DA back in Starkville might want to have her extradited, or he might drop the charges. It's also possible he might decide to reduce her charge to a lesser crime. After all, she did take money she believed to be stolen. Again, it's hard to say at this point. There's a lot to sort through."

It was already Friday and the Curves were scheduled to

check out on Sunday. It was unclear whether Sadie Hardin would be cleared and released by then. "What should I do with Sadie's motorcycle and the personal property in her room?"

"Any chance you can hang on to them for a bit?" Deputy Gillespie asked. "If she's released, she'll need her bike to ride back to Raleigh. Otherwise, she'll have to arrange for someone else to pick up her things."

Rocky said, "There's plenty of room to store her bike in my tool shed. It should be safe in there."

Though I still couldn't be certain whether Sadie had been telling the truth about everything that had unfolded, I'd feel awful if she was being honest and I made things harder on her. "I suppose it can't hurt to hang on to her things for a bit."

"Thanks," Deputy Gillespie said. "I'll be in touch." With a tip of his hat, he headed out the door.

CHAPTER 28

Misty

I spent the afternoon pondering the evidence. I felt fairly certain that Trevor and Jinx were responsible for Gerri's death. After all, they'd been driving on the Blue Ridge Parkway, following after Lexi. Jinx had a history of both threatening violence and of committing acts of violence against others. They'd had no qualms attempting to rob the Greasy Griddle this morning. Trevor had admitted that he knew more than he'd shared so far, but was unwilling to spill all of the beans without some sort of concession. The guy must be smarter than he'd looked in his mug shot. Heck, I'd convict him of third-degree stupidity on that photo alone.

Still, I couldn't help but wonder. *What if it hadn't been Trevor and Jinx who'd caused Gerri's death?* Other than a random stranger, the only remaining viable suspect seemed to be Mariah Burnham. Mariah stood to inherit one-third of Gerri's estate. I had no idea what the dollar value of that share would be, but it would clearly be substantial. Of course, Reyna stood to inherit the same amount, but her relationship with Gerri seemed totally congenial, at least from what I'd seen, and I still couldn't see how Reyna would have had the opportunity to strike Gerri and run her off the road. On the other hand, while Mariah's relationship with Gerri had purportedly been friendly, Mariah's husband and mother-in-law had been openly at odds with Gerri. Maybe Mariah's friendliness had been a ruse, her own method of trying to get her hands on the trust funds. After all, you catch more flies with honey. Her alibi was flimsy at best, too. *"Puttering around the resort"* was suspiciously vague. *Hmm . . .*

Just before five, I received a return phone call from the CPA Gerri had appointed as both the executor of her estate and the alternate trustee of the Burnham children's trust in the event of her death. As executor, the CPA would be responsible for safekeeping and liquidating the property in Gerri's estate. When I'd called the accountant's office yesterday, I'd intended to ask whether it would be okay for me to turn Gerri's belongings over to Reyna to be transported back to Raleigh for distribution. But now, another scheme occurred to me.

After exchanging quick pleasantries with the accountant, I said, "It's my understanding Mariah Burnham, Gerri's stepdaughter-in-law, is one of Gerri's heirs. Mariah happens to be in the area on vacation. She came by my lodge earlier in the week to see Gerri. Would it be all right if I handed Gerri's property over to Mariah? She could then turn it over to you on her return to Raleigh." I gave her a quick rundown of the items currently here at the lodge, which consisted of Gerri's personal effects, SUV, and motorcycle trailer. Although the motorcycle she'd brought to the mountains had probably been totaled in the crash, I supposed the estate would also have an insurance claim for its value.

The CPA sounded relieved that I'd taken a task off her to-do list. "That's a good idea. Should I give Mariah a call to make the arrangements?"

"No need," I said. "I know how to get hold of her."

We bade each other goodbye. Though I could call the resort in Blowing Rock where Mariah was staying, I had no intention of giving the woman prior notice that I planned to pay her a visit. Nope, when Brynn and I showed up at her room tomorrow morning, I wanted it to be a total surprise.

The ladies returned from their ride at half past five. Brynn had already left for the day, and Rocky had taken Molasses out for a long walk down the trail. I sat at the desk with Yeti lounging on the counter in front of me. I'd sprung her from our room to let her have some social time under my watchful eye.

As the women came inside, I greeted them with a soft smile. "How was your ride?"

Reyna raised her hands and face to the heavens. "Breathtaking!"

Daisy said, "I only wish Gerri could have been with us. The scenery was amazing!"

Erika said, "What happened after we left? Did they find out any more about Katie?"

Dahlia corrected her fellow rider. "You mean *Sadie*, remember?"

Erika rolled her eyes. "Whatever."

I gave them a quick rundown of the craziness that had ensued after they'd headed out for their ride. Police helicopter.

Suspect in canoe at Buckeye Lake. Firefighters turning the hose on the escapee to force him to surrender. "The suspect Rocky caught admitted that he and Jinx were on the parkway Wednesday."

The women bristled on hearing the news.

Reyna's face turned purple with fury. "They had to be the ones who caused Gerri to crash."

Graffiti said, "Sadie put the whole club at risk by not telling us about her past. She should've been honest with us."

Bessie said, "It wouldn't have changed anything. Even if we knew her history, we would've welcomed her into the group. That's who we are."

"True," Daisy said, "but we would have taken precautions."

This debate could only lead to discord, so I changed the subject for them. "Where are you all going on your last ride tomorrow?"

"Blowing Rock," said Reyna. "We'll take Schull's Mill Road. It's got lots of fun curves. Then we're going zip-lining."

I'd be heading to Blowing Rock in the morning, too, but for an entirely different purpose. To confront Mariah Burnham. I didn't mention my plan to the ladies. After all, Mariah could be innocent and I didn't want to wrongfully accuse her. I didn't, however, want to leave any stone unturned. I also wanted to make sure the ladies could manage their luggage without Gerri's SUV if I took it to Mariah. "Gerri's property has to be turned over to the CPA who's managing her estate. That includes her SUV and trailer. Can you all manage your luggage without it?"

Reyna said it would be no problem. Though they'd loaded their bags in Gerri's SUV for the drive up the mountain, it had merely been for convenience. "Everyone packed light, other than Gerri, anyway. We've got straps and bungee cords for our bags. We can take our stuff home on our bikes."

The ladies dispersed to local restaurants for dinner. Meanwhile, Rocky, Molasses, Yeti, and I relaxed by the fireside in the great room. Rocky and I read mystery novels, while the animals lay on the rug. Yeti played a version of Whac-A-Mole with the dog's wagging tail. Mo didn't seem to mind.

The ladies returned, and Rocky and I surrendered the great room to the guests. While a few of them hung out and engaged in quiet conversation, most chose to call it an early night, exhausted from a day of riding, hiking, and emotions. Before I knew it, I was lying in my bed with Yeti curled up on the pillow beside me. I fell asleep wondering how things would go in the morning when I confronted Mariah Burnham.

Saturday dawned bright, the sun making promises I hoped the day would keep. I asked Rocky over coffee if he'd be willing to cover the lodge for a few hours while Brynn and I took Gerri's things to Mariah Burnham in Blowing Rock.

He agreed, though he admonished me to be careful. "If they think you're snooping or asking too many questions, they could get upset. People don't like it when someone goes throwing accusations around."

I rolled my eyes. "We're smarter than that. Give us some credit."

"I know you're smart," he said, "but I also know you're determined. I just don't want one thing to get in the way of

the other." He reached out and chucked my chin affectionately. "Don't forget my daughter's stopping by later."

How could I forget? I'd been both eager and anxious
to meet her since he'd mentioned she'd be coming up the
mountain today to style hair for a bride and her bridesmaids.
I wanted to make a good impression, hoped she'd like me.
His daughter could be an influence on him, after all, and
her opinion was important to me. "I'm looking forward to
meeting her."

When Brynn arrived at nine o'clock, I intercepted her
at the door. "Want to go with me to Blowing Rock?" I held
up the keys to Gerri's SUV, glanced into the great room to
make sure none of the ladies could overhear me, and whispered, "I'm delivering Gerri's car to Mariah Burnham."

Brynn's head tilted and a curious gleam shined in her
eyes. "And snooping?"

"Let's call it sleuthing," I said. "Sounds less objection-
able."

"Count me in!"

Rocky loaded Gerri's suitcase into the back of her SUV.
After a quick discussion, we decided that Brynn would drive
the SUV and I'd follow in my Subaru so we'd have a car for
the return ride to the lodge.

We headed out. Just under an hour later, we pulled into
the parking lot at the resort where the Burnhams were staying. Brynn took up tandem spots with the SUV and trailer.
I parked my car in the spot next to the SUV. We climbed
out and glanced around.

"Wow," I said on a breath. While I loved the look of my
casual log-cabin-style lodge and unmanicured grounds, I
had to admit this upscale resort was beautiful. It was made

of gray stone with white mortar, adorned here and there with climbing ivy, and accented by dogwood trees decked out in their bright red autumn leaves. Clusters of colorful pumpkins were stacked at the base of the trees on either side of the double front doors. The resort sat on the edge of the ridge, providing guests with beautiful views of the valley below. Off to the left we could see one of the golf course greens. Three men stood about while another swung his club, a flag flapping in the wind in the distance to mark his target. From off to the right came the *thwock* sound of someone hitting a tennis ball.

Brynn looked to me. "What's the plan?"

Deputy Gillespie had verified both Andrea's and Sterling's alibis, but I figured it couldn't hurt to see if anyone could verify whether they'd seen Mariah "puttering around the resort" as she'd claimed. As far as I knew, Mariah didn't play golf, and she hadn't mentioned taking a dip in the heated outdoor pool I'd seen on the resort's website. I gestured to the tennis courts. "Let's talk to the tennis pro who gave Andrea her lesson. Maybe they can tell us whether Mariah was around."

We walked down to the tennis area and into the small pro shop. Fortunately, we were the only people there other than the clerk sitting behind the counter. I gave the woman at the counter a broad smile. "Hi," I said. "My friend Andrea Burnham mentioned that she had a great lesson here on Wednesday, but she couldn't remember the pro's name. I was wondering if you could tell me who her lesson was with. I'd love to book a lesson too, but I have some questions for the pro before I sign up."

The woman ran her eyes over my buffalo plaid shirt,

jeans, and hiking boots. I might look outdoorsy, but my outfit was definitely not athletic. "Diego's handled all the private lessons this week." She pointed out the window to a young Latino on the first court. A machine on the other side of the net served a ball to him, and he hit it back. *Thwock*. "He's just practicing. He won't mind if you go out there and talk to him."

"Thanks."

CHAPTER 29

Misty

Brynn and I left the pro shop, went to the tall fence that surrounded the tennis courts, and peered through it at Diego. The pro was attractive, with thick dark hair and a trim physique. He appeared to be around twenty-five, old enough to have perfected his game but young enough to still have lots of energy to exert on the court.

"Diego?" I called. "Got a minute?"

He lifted his chin to acknowledge me, returned the ball the machine spit out, then rushed the net, hopping over it to turn off the device. Racket in hand, he jogged over to the fence. "What can I do for you?"

"A friend told me she took a lesson from you earlier in the week. Andrea Burnham?"

A cloud seemed to pass over Diego's face on hearing her name, perhaps because he'd already been questioned by Deputy Gillespie about the woman. "That's right," he said tentatively. "I gave her a lesson Wednesday, right before lunch."

"Um . . . how'd it go?" *What a lame question.* I probably should have come up with some questions in advance, but I'd hoped to sound casual, play it by ear. Heck, I didn't even really know what information I was trying to glean from him. I was just fishing, really.

"The lesson went fine," he said.

Sheesh. He's just as verbose as my boys. "She said you really helped her improve her game. I was wondering if her daughter-in-law came by during her lesson. Did you happen to see her? Her name's Mariah."

"I don't remember anyone else coming around." He frowned. "Why are you asking?"

I shrugged and tried to appear casual. "Mariah mentioned she'd puttered around the resort on Wednesday. I thought she might have stopped by to cheer Andrea on. The two of them are close, two peas in a pod. They look almost like twins. It's so cute."

Diego just stared at me. I supposed nothing I'd just said warranted a verbal response. His fingers drummed impatiently on the end of his racket, as if he wanted this conversation to either go somewhere or end, so that he could get back to his practice.

Fortunately, Brynn realized I was floundering and stepped in. "What kind of drills do you normally run with your clients?"

He lifted one shoulder. "Depends on what they want to work on, what their weaknesses are."

Ugh. I was in over my head here. I knew next to nothing about tennis. As far as I knew, Brynn didn't either. Her silence now confirmed it. I ventured a guess. "I believe Andrea mentioned that you worked on her serve?"

"No," he said. "She felt good about her serve."

Uh-oh. Much more meandering and he'd get suspicious of my motives—if he wasn't already. "Maybe it was her backhand?" I hoped I'd gotten it right this time. Otherwise, I'd have exhausted the short list of tennis terms I knew.

He gave a quick nod. "Yeah, we worked on her backhand. Her two-handed backhand, anyway."

There's more than one type of backhand? Having played tennis only rarely in my life, I hadn't really ever thought about it. But I supposed if there was two-handed backhand, there also had to be one-handed, right? "She didn't need help with her single-handed backhand?"

"It didn't seem like a good idea to work on her one-handed backhand, not with that brace on her elbow. It would cause too much strain."

That brace on her elbow . . . Mariah had been the one wearing the brace on her elbow when they'd come to the lodge on Tuesday evening, not Andrea! My heart rate ramped up and I felt myself heat up in response. "You're sure she was wearing a brace?"

"Yes," he said. "I asked her about it so that I could de-sign the lesson accordingly. I didn't want to make her in-jury worse."

Had Mariah taken the lesson instead of Andrea? "You're sure it was Andrea who took the lesson and not Mariah? I haven't seen Andrea wear a brace."

He shrugged. "Andrea Burnham was the name on my list. She didn't correct me, but that could be because we don't use first names unless specifically instructed by the guest. Resort policy is to refer to guests by their last name, so I would've called her Ms. Burnham. But I usually only use names at the start, anyway, when I introduce myself. We shook hands over the net and got right into the lesson."

"How old did Andrea look to you?"

He barked a laugh. "That's a loaded question."

Brynn pulled at the skin under her chin. "Did she have the start of a turkey neck? Or kninkles?"

Now the guy just looked confused. "What's a kninkle?"

I pointed down at my leg. "Wrinkles around the knee. When women get to middle age, the skin around their knees loosens a little."

He raised both hands in a defensive gesture, his racket rising along with them. "I don't know about any of this. I just shook her hand and gave her the lesson. I spent nearly all of the lesson on the opposite side of the net. I didn't get a good look at her. Now is there something specific I can do for you or can I get back to my practice?" He pointed at the ball machine, as if it were waiting for him.

I gave him a smile and waved him off. "Get back to your practice. And thanks."

He looked confused again. "For what?"

For giving me the clue that might have solved the murder case. "For everything!" I called as we backed off.

His face became even more confused, but he shrugged it off and went to turn on the ball machine.

Brynn and I walked to the front of the resort and put our heads together.

I shared my thoughts. "I came here thinking Mariah might have hit Gerri with one of Sterling's golf clubs, but now I'm wondering if it was Andrea. I'm also wondering if Gerri might have been hit with a tennis racket instead. I want to get into their room and look around." If I called their room from the lobby, it would give them a chance to hide any evidence. I wanted to pop up at the door to their suite unexpected. But how could we determine their room number? There was no way the staff would provide it to us.

Fortunately, Brynn had an idea. "Go to the front desk," she said. "Engage the clerk in conversation. I'll call the resort from my cell phone and ask for the Burnhams' room. See what numbers they push when I'm transferred. I'll hang up before the phone rings. Text me when you're ready for me to make the call."

While she waited outside by my car, I walked into the resort and over to the registration desk. With it being mid-morning, things were slow. The guests who needed to depart early were already gone, and those who planned to leave at the last minute had another hour to go.

I sent Brynn a quick text simply reading *GO* as I stepped up to the desk. "Hi," I told the female clerk. "I was wondering about those beautiful trees outside. I've never seen such red leaves! Do you know what kind of trees they are? I'd love to get one for my yard back home."

Before she could answer my question, the phone rang. She raised a finger in a *hold-on-just-a-second* gesture. She picked up the receiver, stated the name of the resort, and asked, "How may I direct your call?" She listened for few seconds, angled her head to hold the phone with her shoulder, and used her hands to type on her computer. Having located the screen that provided the Burnhams' room number, she reached down to type it into the phone. One, one, eight. *The Burnhams are in Room 118.* She returned the receiver to the cradle and turned her attention back to me. "Sorry for the interruption. The trees are dogwoods. Pink ones. They're just as pretty when they bloom in the spring, too."

"Pink dogwoods," I said. "Thanks!"

I stepped aside and sent Brynn a text. *Meet me at Room 118 with Gerri's suitcase.* I consulted the signage and headed down the hall, squeezing past a housekeeping cart. Another cart stood farther down the hall at an open door. I reached Room 118 and waited. Brynn walked up shortly thereafter rolling Gerri's suitcase along with her.

We engaged in a quick, whispered debate. I asked, "What if she sees me through the peephole and doesn't answer the door?"

Brynn cast a glance at the door to the Burnhams' suite and turned back to me. "Do we even know for sure that anyone is in there?"

"No," I said.

She motioned me over, rapped three times on the door, and called out, "Housekeeping!"

Thinking Mariah and Andrea would be more likely to recognize me than they would Brynn, I did what the two robbers had done the previous morning at the Greasy Griddle. I flattened myself against the wall next to the door. A few seconds later, it opened to reveal Mariah. She was dressed in a nylon track suit again today, though this one was maroon rather than black.

I didn't waste a beat. With a false smile on my face, I turned, grabbed the handle of the suitcase, and rolled it into the suite, forcing her to step aside to let me past. "I was told to bring this to you. It's Gerri's stuff from the lodge."

Mariah looked puzzled as Brynn followed me in without

having been invited. We stood in a living room furnished with a couch, loveseat, and armchair surrounding a square coffee table. A tall, pub-style dinette sat along one wall. On either side of the living space were doors leading to bedrooms. Both doors were ajar, revealing king-sized beds with thick, luxurious coverings. In the room to the left, a large box fan sat on the dresser, the airflow aimed at the bed. My gaze roamed the living room until it landed on the French doors that led out to a covered patio. Andrea sprawled on a chaise lounge outside, her back to us, just the top of her head and her hand visible as she reached for the mimosa on the table next to her. With the doors closed, she must not have heard us come into the room.

I turned back to Mariah and held up the keys to Gerri's SUV. "These are the keys to the Yukon. It's in the parking lot."

She cocked her head, perplexed. "Am I supposed to do something with Gerri's things?"

"Sorry," I said. "I need to explain, don't I? The executor who's handling the estate told me it would be okay to hand everything over to you since you're one of Gerri's heirs."

"I am?" Her brows rose in surprise, but her hand went to her heart, as if the news had warmed it.

"You didn't know?" I asked.

"No." She stared down at the suitcase. "I guess I never thought about it. Gerri was so healthy and active." She looked up now, her gaze moving between me and Brynn. Her eyes blinked back tears and her voice was soft when she added, "It seemed like she had a lot of time left."

Rather than beat around the bush and risk Andrea

coming inside and throwing me and Brynn out of the suite, I got right down to business. "Mariah, I know it was you who went to Andrea's tennis lesson on Wednesday, not her."

An anxious look skittered across Mariah's face and she glanced out the back doors. She sputtered like a faucet with air in the pipes. "How did . . . why . . . who . . ."

"The pro said the 'Ms. Burnham' he gave a lesson to wears an elbow brace. You're the one with tennis elbow, not Andrea."

Mariah bit her lip.

I said, "Why did you lie to the police?"

"I didn't lie!" she cried. When she spoke again, her voice was as weak as her argument. "They never asked me about it."

I gave her a pointed look. "You knew Andrea had told them she'd been at the lesson on Wednesday. I mentioned it to you when you came by the lodge the next day."

She bit her lip even harder and cast another glance outside before returning her gaze to me. "I asked Andrea about it, and she said the deputy must have misunderstood her. She said it didn't really matter because she'd been at the resort all day and that I knew it."

Brynn asked, "Is that true?"

"Well, yes." Mariah gulped. "At least I think so."

I pressed for clarification. "You *think* so? Either you know something to be a fact or you don't."

She hesitated a moment. "Andrea told me Wednesday morning that she was having hot flashes and didn't feel up to going to the lesson she'd already paid for. She said she'd rather stay in her room with the fan on and take a nap, and that I could use the lesson. So, I did. Later that day, I walked over to the outlets, like I told you."

We needed to nail her down. I asked, "Andrea stayed in her bedroom with the fan on all day? You can verify for certain she was in there?"

"Well, not exactly," Mariah said. "I went for a walk before the lesson to warm up. When I came back to get my racket, the door to her bedroom was closed but I could hear the fan running. It was the same when I got back from the lesson. I knocked softly once but didn't get an answer. I figured she was asleep. I watched TV for a little while, then decided to go the outlets. I knew Andrea wouldn't be interested in shopping there, so I didn't bother knocking again. When I got back, she was sitting here in the living room."

"Did she seem agitated?" I asked. If she'd just caused a deadly crash, you'd think she might be worked up, even if the act had been premeditated.

"Not really," Mariah said. "She was drinking white wine and watching an old Sandra Bullock movie."

I glanced around, noting a tennis racket in a zippered cover in the bedroom without the fan, which must be Mariah and Sterling's room. "Is that your racket?" I asked, heading into the bedroom without asking permission.

"Yes," Mariah answered.

I picked up the racket and unzipped the cover to find a Wilson brand racket. It was mostly black, with a green band over the top and silver along the curves on the side. I took a close look at it. The word "Blade" appeared in all caps a couple of inches above the handle. The racket appeared to be in good shape. Remembering how Andrea and Mariah had been dressed as virtual twins when they'd come to the lodge with Sterling, I said, "Where's Andrea's racket?" If Andrea had the same racket, she might have used it to strike Gerri. The silver part along the rim could have left the silver paint on Gerri's helmet.

Mariah said, "I guess it's in her room."

I stalked out of Mariah and Sterling's bedroom and into Andrea's. Her racket lay in its cover atop her dresser. I grabbed it, unzipped the cover, and removed the racket. It appeared to be the same racket as Mariah's, green and black with silver along the side of the rim. It was undamaged and in near-pristine condition, not a single scratch along the rim. *So much for my theory that Andrea had whacked Gerri with her tennis racket.*

Mariah stepped over, craning her neck to get a good look at the racket. "Let me see that."

I handed the racket to her. She turned it on its side and stared down at the writing inscribed there for a long beat. When she looked back up at me and Brynn, her face bore an expression of absolute horror. Her voice cracked when she spoke. "This is a different racket than the one she brought out here from Raleigh."

"It is?" I asked. "How do you know?" It looked just like Mariah's racket to me.

Mariah pointed to some numbers and letters appearing between the word "Blade" and the handle. "This one says SW102. The SW stands for Serena Williams. It's the same racket Serena uses now." She looked up again. "Mine's an SW104. It's slightly larger. It's the model Serena used up until a couple of years ago."

Brynn sucked in air. "Andrea replaced her racket."

Only one reason why came to mind: because she'd used her original racket to strike Gerri and it had been damaged in the process.

Movement in the living room caught our attention. We looked up to see Andrea standing there, champagne flute in hand, only an ounce of two of her mimosa remaining. "What are you doing in my bedroom?!" she shrieked. Her head snapped to Mariah. "Why did you let them in here?"

Mariah ignored Andrea's questions, her chest heaving with emotion. "When did you get this racket?"

Andrea scoffed, but while she sounded indignant, she looked terrified. "That's the same one I've had for years."

"No!" Mariah hissed. "It's not. I bought the exact same one you had because, if I hadn't, you'd have told me I'd made the wrong choice." Her voice rose in volume and pitch. "It's the same reason I dress like you and wear my hair like you. So you'll approve and stop insulting me!" Mariah straightened up, seeming to grow several inches as she stood up to her mother-in-law for what I surmised was likely the first time. "Gerri liked me the way I was. She never criticized and insulted me. And now you've killed her! With your tennis racket! And you bought a replacement to hide your guilt!"

Andrea froze for a split second, her mouth slightly open as if she was about to speak, but then she turned and bolted toward their suite's exit door. Brynn, Mariah, and I left the bedroom and went after her. As Andrea whipped the door open, Mariah hurled the tennis racket at her. It spun through the air until it whacked Andrea in the back but, in her desperation to escape, it hardly seemed to register. She ran out into the hall and turned right, toward the lobby.

In the room, Mariah fell to her knees and burst into sobs. Brynn and I exchanged glances. It would be up to the two of us to catch Andrea.

We darted into the hall after Gerri's killer. Andrea sprinted down the corridor, heading to the lobby. I ran after her with Brynn right behind me. Having played tennis regularly, Andrea was in much better shape than Brynn or me, and quickly got a lead on us. But as she approached a housekeeping cart, she was forced to slow down so she could ease past. I gained on her, sucked in my gut as I turned sideways to squeeze past the cart, and seized the moment to reach out and grab her pony tail. Once I had it in my right hand, I reached my left one up to grab it, too. I slowed to a stop, digging in my heels, simultaneously yanking on her hair and dropping to the floor. Her head pulled back at a sharp angle, throwing her off kilter. Shrieking, she whirled on me, clawing at my face. I dropped her ponytail and threw up my hands to protect my eyes. The quick, cockeyed turn caused her to lose her footing. She stumbled past where I now sat on the floor, but momentum carried her forward and sideways. She crashed into the opposite wall—*bam!*— but it served to keep her upright, and she pushed herself off it to stay on her feet.

Andrea staggered back in the direction we'd come from, once again passing the housekeeping cart. I used the wall to lever myself to a stand and grabbed the handle of the cart. Brynn was on the other side of Andrea. She turned and ran to the second cart down the hall.

With a battle cry, I pushed the cart forward in a zigzag pattern to prevent Andrea from getting past me should she try. Following my lead, Brynn did the same, using her cart as both a shield and a battering ram, too. In seconds, we had Andrea hopelessly trapped between the two housekeeping carts. Hurling expletives, she reached over the carts to try to slap at us, but her attempts were unsuccessful. Up and down the hall, doors opened and guests poked their heads out to see what the ruckus was all about.

A voice came from behind me. "What's going on?" shouted a woman, presumably the clerk from the reception desk, though I couldn't take my eyes off Andrea to turn and find out.

Brynn had the benefit of facing in the direction of the lobby. She yelled past me. "Call the police! This woman's a killer!"

Pinned between the carts, Andrea did the only thing she could. She grabbed handfuls of miniature plastic shampoo bottles and pelted us in the face at point-blank range. While her efforts caused no real injuries, we were forced to close our eyes and turn our heads lest we end up with a scratched cornea. When Andrea ran out of shampoo bottles to hurl at us, she performed a wild dance between the carts, half hula, half belly dance, banging her hips against them to force them apart. She managed to broaden the space just enough that she could lift her right leg and climb atop Brynn's cart. She went headfirst over the other side, performed a flip, and somehow managed to land on her feet. I'd have been impressed if I hadn't been so enraged. She took off running down the hall away from the lobby now.

I circled around my cart and Brynn's, and the two of us ran after the woman. Andrea shoved aside a man who'd been peeking out of a doorway and entered his room. I followed a few seconds behind her with Brynn on my heels.

The man stood gaping in his living room as Andrea ran to the French doors and jerked the right one open to escape onto his patio. She climbed over the railing, one leg at a time. I knew I could move faster if I launched myself from the chaise. I leaped up onto it, swung my arms, and dived over the railing after Andrea, tackling her to the ground. We rolled around for a few seconds like feral cats fighting in an alley, only we had a magnificent mountain view behind us rather than stinky garbage dumpsters. Brynn swung her legs over the railing to come help me.

While Brynn and I weren't able to restrain Andrea, we did manage to occupy her long enough for the resort's security team to reach us and pull us apart. Brynn and I stood, panting, and brushed ourselves off. Realizing the jig was up, Andrea keeled over onto her side, curled up in a fetal position, and wailed. It wasn't long before her wail was joined by another—the wail of police sirens from an approaching cruiser.

CHAPTER 30

Misty

Two hours later, Andrea had been taken into custody and her original mangled tennis racket was found wrapped in one of the resort's bath towels and tossed in a trash bin behind the courts. Mariah had called Sterling in from the golf course to inform him that his mother was a killer. As her stunned husband spoke with the police outside the resort, Mariah confided in me and Brynn. It seemed nothing Mariah did had ever been good enough for Andrea—other than Mariah's decision to choose Andrea's son to marry.

Mariah sniffled and dabbed at her eyes with tissue from their suite. "Andrea told me I wasn't doing enough for my children by not pushing Gerri to release more funds from the trust, but I wanted Sterling and me to stand on our own two feet and set a good example for our kids. It's been a point of contention between me and the two of them. Sterling has been trying harder the last few months, though. He's really made an effort to pull himself together. We hadn't told anyone yet, but he's been attending sales training classes. He'd planned to ask Gerri for his sales job back at the RV dealership, on a commission-only basis so that he'd actually be earning his paychecks. He felt like he'd let his father down before, and he wanted to make up for it."

I had no idea who would be taking over the dealership now that Gerri was gone, and I supposed only time would tell if Sterling was given a second chance and allowed to return. But if he was truly making an effort, I hoped it would work out for him. It was never too late to be the person you wanted to be.

After leaving the resort, Brynn and I intercepted the Curves at the zip-line course to inform them that Gerri's killer had been caught. They were relieved and overjoyed that we'd managed to solve the crime. They'd return home without their beloved ride or die, but at least they'd go home knowing her killer would be brought to justice. Erika whooped and raised a fist as she sailed off down the wire. "Woo-hoo!"

The good news delivered, my assistant and I returned to the lodge.

I sat on my stool at the front desk while Rocky tended to *my* injuries this time, our roles reversed from the previous morning. I grimaced as he dabbed disinfectant on the scratches on my face.

A grin claimed his mouth. "Be a brave girl for daddy."

I couldn't help but laugh. I'd had a similar thought when cleaning his wounds. *Old habits die hard.*

He affixed a bandage over the gash I'd received on my

chin courtesy of a pointy rock on the ledge where I'd tack-led Andrea. "There," he said. "You'll be as good as new in no time."

At fifty, I was hardly as good as new anymore. My warranty had long since expired but, for the most part, I was at least still running smoothly.

Brynn had just ended her shift and left the lodge when Rocky's daughter Carissa arrived late that afternoon. Like her father, she had bluish-gray eyes in the same hue as the blue mountain ridges that had earned this range their name. She also had his same sandy hair, though hers hung halfway down her back in beautiful, loose curls. The three of us went to an early dinner at the Greasy Griddle, conversing easily and amiably over our meal.

Her eyes went wide and her mouth hung open when Rocky explained why he had a bandage on his forehead and I had one on my chin. "You two are superheroes!"

"Nah," Rocky said. "Mere mortals. But we do like to see justice done."

After finishing our meal, we ordered mugs of Patty's hot cider to go and enjoyed them by the fire pit behind the lodge while my guests went out for the final dinner of their trip. Molasses was thrilled to see Carissa, and the enormous dog insisted on climbing up into her lap as she sat in one of the Adirondack chairs.

I couldn't help but laugh. "Can you even feel your legs?"

"Not at all!" she said, laughing along with me. "But who can say no to this adorable face?" She cupped the dog's big face in her hands and placed a kiss on his snout.

Before she left the lodge, I introduced her to Yeti. She ran her hand over my cat's back, and Yeti lifted her heinie in the air to maximize the impact.

"What a sweet cat," Carissa said. "Her fur is gorgeous!"

Yeti could be sweet when she wanted to be, but she'd long-since learned she didn't have to go to much effort where I was concerned. I'd love her regardless.

Rocky and I walked his daughter out to her car and bade her goodbye, but not until she promised to return soon and bring her sisters, brother-in-law, and niece with her.

No sooner had she pulled out of the lot, than Deputy Gillespie pulled in with Sadie Hardin in the back of his cruiser. He parked and released her from the back seat. She looked exhausted, but relieved.

"Sadie's off the hook for everything," the deputy said. "She might have to go back to Mississippi to testify against Trevor and Jinx but, under the circumstances, the district attorney isn't interested in prosecuting her. He realizes she was in a desperate situation and did what she had to do. She's been cleared of any involvement in the diner robbery here."

"That's wonderful!"

The girl managed a feeble smile. She looked as if she could use a hug, so I stepped forward and gave her one. When I released her, I said, "Your friends are inside. They'll be happy to see you."

I knew it was true. Even the ones who'd expressed doubts would be glad to know they'd been wrong and that their newest club member was innocent.

The deputy raised a hand in goodbye and climbed back into his cruiser.

Rocky and I followed Sadie inside, where she shared the good news with the group. Every one of them expressed delight she'd been released.

Reyna said, "We knew all along you were innocent." While her statement wasn't exactly true, it was clear everyone wanted to put all of the doubts and ugliness behind them—and not just where Sadie was concerned, but Erika, too. Reyna turned to Erika, "We took a vote earlier. You're welcome back into the club, so long as you agree to stay in line."

Erika's eyes filled with tears as she offered a grateful smile to the group. "Thanks. I promise I'll always ride safe from now on."

"Bring it in, girls." Reyna raised her arms and flapped her hands in a come-here motion.

The group came together in an enormous, cathartic group hug, holding each other tight for a minute or more before Shotgun's bark came from somewhere in the middle. *Rrrruff!* The poor dog must have felt trapped by all the love and legs surrounding him.

Laughing, the ladies stepped back, many turning to one another now for individual hugs.

With Gerri's murder solved, we could all finally relax. That night, I slept soundly and peacefully for the first time in days.

Late Sunday morning, Rocky, Brynn, Patty, and I stood in front of the lodge, waving as the motorcycle club took to their bikes and rode off in single file, Erika staying well in line this time. Reyna had promised to bring the ladies back again this time next year when they'd take a memorial ride for Gerri. Although their stay had been marred by Gerri's murder, Reyna said the conflict between Gerri and Andrea had been simmering for years and threatening to boil over, and what happened, though horrifying, seemed in some sense inevitable. Reyna could at least be glad Andrea hadn't gotten away with it.

Once the sound of their motorcycle engines faded away, Rocky said, "It's going to seem very quiet around here with those ladies gone."

It certainly would. I'd enjoyed having them in my lodge. Their grab-life-by-the-horns outlook was fun and infectious. Though I looked forward to hosting more so-called leaf peepers in the coming weeks, I doubted any would be quite as spirited as these ladies had been.

That evening, Rocky and I picked Patty and her husband Eli up at the Greasy Griddle. Eli drove a semitruck for a living, and had just returned from making a big delivery in Memphis.

On the drive down to an Italian restaurant in Banner Elk, he shared stories from the road, including his favorite road-side attractions. Alexandria, Indiana, featured the world's biggest ball of paint, while a six-story-tall elephant-shaped building could be found in Margate City, New Jersey. "The creepiest place is Doll's Head Trail in Atlanta." He told us that the trail was on the site of an abandoned brick company. People had dumped all sorts of refuse on the property. When it was reclaimed for a park, a local carpenter had rounded up the discarded things to incorporate into works of art. Evidently, there was an inordinate number of doll's heads among the trash. Of course, North Carolina had its own silly roadside attraction, the world's largest chest of drawers in the city of High Point, which was a hub for the furniture industry.

The four of us enjoyed a wonderful dinner together, talking and laughing. The night was exactly what I needed after the stressful week, a time to relax and just have fun. As far as first dates go, it was one of the best I'd ever had.

When it was over, Rocky and I dropped Patty and Eli back at the diner and returned to the lodge, where I relieved Brynn. She'd graciously agreed to cover the lodge for me while Rocky and I went on our date. She gave me a knowing smile as she rounded up her purse to go. "Good night, you two!"

We had only a handful of guests tonight, and all seemed to be in their rooms or out of the lodge entirely. It was often quieter when the guests weren't all part of one large group. Rocky and I had the fireside to ourselves. He poured us each a glass of wine and we took seats side by side in the comfy chairs.

I turned to him. "I've been meaning to ask, how's your son-in-law's job hunt going?"

Rocky cocked his head. "You trying to get rid of me?"

"Not at all," I admitted. "I just know he and your daughter will be less stressed once he finds work."

Rocky raised his glass, as if in toast. "He got an offer today, as a matter of fact."

"He did? That's great news." For them, anyway. It was bad news for me. I'd have to look for a new handyman once they got on their feet and Rocky moved back into his house in Boone, a forty-five-minute drive down the mountain. I wondered, too, what that would mean for our romantic relationship. While I wasn't yet ready to jump into anything serious, it was nice to have a dependable, interesting man around, especially one as handsome as Rocky and who could fix anything. Nevertheless, I clinked my glass against Rocky's in celebration.

Rocky eyed me as he stroked his beard with one hand. "You know, they've enjoyed having a whole house to themselves. They were in a tiny apartment before they moved in with me."

I had a sense this conversation was leading somewhere and, if it was going in the direction I hoped, maybe I wouldn't have to look for another maintenance man, after all. "Babies might be small, but their stuff sure takes up a lot of space." I remembered when my boys were infants. Their swing, playpen, toy box, and high chair had made our little place feel cramped, too.

"I'm thinking of selling them the house," Rocky said. "Affordable homes are hard to come by these days, and I don't need all that space anymore. It would give them a leg up financially. Besides, Carissa has her own apartment and my youngest will be in the dorm through May." Rocky's youngest daughter was a sophomore at Appalachian State University, which was also located in Boone. "She's already talking about getting an apartment with a couple of friends for the next school year. I figure she could stay with me up here on her school breaks. She loves snowboarding and hiking."

He'd been talking around the subject, but I laid it on the

line. "Are you asking to make our room-for-pay arrangement permanent?"

"I am," he said with a dip of his head. "If you'll have me."

I didn't have to think twice. Heck, I barely had to think about the matter at all. I'd performed the math. Having a reliable repairman on site was well worth the foregone income from his room. What's more, with other repairmen reluctant to drive up the mountain for jobs, Rocky could stay busy full time performing handyman work right here in Beech Mountain, so it benefited him as well. Relocating to the mountain meant he could spend less time on the road and more time in our beautiful town. "Done."

A grin played about his mouth. "You know what this means, right?"

"What?"

"You and I are officially living together. People might start to talk."

In light of the fact that we had yet to even share a kiss, there wasn't much to talk about and, with the latest census showing that only 614 people lived in Beech Mountain full time, there weren't many people up here to talk about us, anyway. The tourists would have much better things to do than gossip about an innkeeper and her live-in repairman. Despite all of this, I smiled. "Maybe we should really give them something to talk about."

He sat up straight. "Are you saying you'll let me kiss you good night?"

"I am." If Gerri Burnham's death had taught me anything, it was that life was short and it was best to seize it.

Rocky leaned over his chair and I leaned over mine. Our

lips met to share a warm and wonderful kiss. Winter and ski season was just around the corner, and I hoped I'd have lots more of these kisses to keep me warm. While no one could predict how much snow we'd get here in the coming weeks, I knew one thing for certain. Moving up to the mountains and running this lodge had been one of the best decisions I'd ever made.